DANCING TOWARD STARDUST

DANCING TOWARD STARDUST

by

Julia Underwood

2024

DANCING TOWARD STARDUST
© 2024 By Julia Underwood. All Rights Reserved.

ISBN 13: 978-1-63679-588-1

This Trade Paperback Original Is Published By
Bold Strokes Books, Inc.
P.O. Box 249
Valley Falls, NY 12185

First Edition: March 2024

CREDITS
Editor: Ruth Sternglantz
Production Design: Stacia Seaman
Cover Design by Tammy Seidick

Acknowledgments

First, a huge thank you to Rad and the rest of the BSB family for taking a chance on me—Sandy Lowe for always being there with help and advice; Ruth Sternglantz with her editing and personal insight, patience, instruction, and humor in helping shape this book to a best effort; and so many people behind the scenes who helped bring this endeavor to fruition with clear and timely publication guidance, cover choices, deadlines, print planning—I know the list is long.

Additional thanks go to my friends, P, L, and C, who read the manuscript as I wrote it and offered invaluable suggestions. Without all of the amazing authors who dedicate their time and skills to writing inspiring sapphic romance novels, I would never have been motivated to write my own.

I offer my deep gratitude to those willing to read this book—I hope your expectations are rewarded. For those taking the journey of two hearts…happy ending, always.

For Jake, my canine co-author who was right there next to me
for every single word until submission of the initial manuscript…
I'll always miss you.

CHAPTER ONE

Cate leaned back into her office chair. Her Wednesday morning pen tapping was inconsequential. It was simply an irrelevant metronome marking time as Cate stared at the yellow legal pad in front of her. Computers were a godsend, but sometimes she just needed to scribble some notes. This morning she had questions, but no answers. What the hell had Robert been up to? And how was this going to impact his widow, Meg? Cate pondered these questions as she turned her head and took in the cityscape through her office window before letting her gaze drift back over her shoulder to the Berkeley Law credentials with *Catherine Colson* visible beneath the glass, and a large, mesmerizing watercolor of a fog-teased Golden Gate Bridge spanning the bay. After all, this was San Francisco.

Listening to the quiet, she could barely hear the occasional horn-blare of traffic on the streets of the Financial District three stories below. Cate was the only one here. She hadn't heard Piper come in yet. There would be no missing her arrival—the opening of the door with a whirlwind whoosh, the loud clomp of boots, and the hum of greetings that Piper always offered her plants each morning. Cate's paralegal made an entry unlike any client. And Cate had no law partners. That was because she didn't want any permanent partners—of any kind. Been there. Done that.

Cate refocused on the task in front of her. She'd had no problem with the main list of queries, asking her to clarify a few routine audit concerns for Mullins Investments regarding legal exposure. But the one item still stood out. It seemed that Robert's past actions were just catching a closer look. This particular issue from the firm's auditors was unusual—it personally reflected on Robert Mullins.

He was no longer running Mullins Investments, but after considering all she knew about the company, talking to the current CEO, and obtaining permission to pursue the probe as she saw fit, Cate had decided to make a few discreet inquiries while not disclosing the specific Robert-related issue. The result was an unsettled feeling that maybe she needed to broaden her scope a bit to make a final judgment that this audit item carried no legal exposure for the firm.

Hearing Piper's flamboyant arrival, Cate gave her a few minutes to settle in. Then she exited her inner office sanctum to enter the reception area where Piper, though her paralegal, now sat working at the desk because keeping an adequate receptionist was an ongoing challenge. Piper had recently turned thirty, and some days, the dozen years between their ages felt like so many more. Piper had scattered the area with greenery—succulents, ferns, a renegade vine heading across a side table from its pot. It was *so* Piper. Cate just shook her head at the foliage furnishings—except for maybe the cactus in the corner. Cate was a bit partial to that prickly plant.

"No luck with a receptionist yet?" Cate asked.

Piper smiled at Cate. Cate suspected Piper would say that she considered her boss to be a hard-ass. Demanding and independent. But she knew that, for some reason, her paralegal wanted to consider her a friend too. Cate Colson didn't do friends, except for maybe Pete, who wouldn't let Cate destroy the bond they'd formed in college when they were both coming out. No, Cate didn't do friends in the sweet, confiding, emotional-bonding way that Piper probably defined friends. But because Cate had on rare occasion let her guard down in front of Piper, dropped her usual carefully managed boss demeanor, and exposed her concealed compassionate side, Piper had worked hard to bond with Cate on a more personal level. She tolerated Piper's gregarious outreach because she didn't want to lose a good paralegal. At least, that's what Cate liked to tell herself.

"No, boss. But it's not a problem. Things are running smoothly," Piper assured Cate.

"Well, let me know if there's an issue, and we'll at least get a temp in here. I have no clue why we can't get good help." Cate shook her head in frustration.

"No clue," Piper mumbled as she gave Cate the side-eye.

"I perceive that you think you might have a clue." Cate crossed her arms over her chest. "Care to share?"

"Nope, Not going there, Cate." Piper pressed her lips together, indicating that she wasn't going to touch the topic. Piper only used *Cate* instead of *boss* when things drifted to the personal. It was evident to Cate that Piper thought she played a role in the difficulty the office was having in retaining good help.

"I have standards. High standards," Cate asserted.

Piper grinned at her boss. "I know you do. Some of the highest standards I've ever seen." Piper rolled her eyes up at the ceiling, offering a hint at the height of those standards.

Reflecting on the commitment to excellence she'd maintained to get where she was professionally, Cate frowned. Piper didn't know all that she had sacrificed over the years, the battles she had fought to become the respected attorney that she was. They'd only worked together for a few years now. That was decades short of the time Cate had devoted to becoming exemplary at her profession. Catherine Colson was proud of the reputation she had built over the years for being an attorney who successfully got the job done.

Cate did legal work for a number of businesses and Mullins Investments was one of them. Robert Mullins, the founder and former CEO, had built the firm from the ground up. Her legal services had been retained, even after the firm's management had undergone a change.

"Do you need something?" Piper changed the subject.

"I need you to call Robert Mullins's widow. To set up a time for her to come in to talk with me, if she's willing." Cate turned to head back into her office—thinking more about Meg Mullins.

She'd met Meg numerous times at the social functions sponsored by Robert's firm for employees and their spouses, as well as for associated businesses including Cate's law practice. Cate had always found Meg, like her husband, to be impeccably attired and articulate. Cate had also found her to be warm and down-to-earth, not the least pretentious—unlike Robert. Yes, Meg Mullins was both charming and attractive.

Cate brought her thoughts back to the issue in front of her. She needed information. Answers. She took a deep breath. Meg had been married for decades to Robert, the deceased past client whose actions

Cate was clarifying for his former investment firm. Cate had a job to do. And that meant she needed to meet with Meg Mullins in a professional capacity. To ask questions she did not want to ask.

❖

On Thursday morning, when her cell phone began to ring, Meg was brutalizing a banana, some kale, a few sections of orange, and a handful of almonds into a smoothie puree that looked nothing like the original ingredients—and mentally planning her trip to San Francisco. Before answering the phone call, she turned off the blender and quickly poured this breakfast into her favorite cocktail glass.

There had been a stylish, cut crystal, two-glass wedding gift, but Meg had never been much of a cocktail drinker, only occasionally partaking of wine or beer. So, while Robert had utilized one tumbler every evening for his splash of Jack, she'd resolved that she'd use her half of the crystal set too. Robert had dubbed her morning drink Margarita's Virgin Sunrise Kale Cocktail, no matter what she put into her breakfast beverage. *Almost as good as a glass of Sex on the Beach*, she'd told him when their marriage was young and she was giving it her best effort. *And who's been hanging out at the beach with you?* he'd shot back. *Because if it had been me, it couldn't possibly be close.* He'd smirked. *Dream on, Shark Boy*, she'd replied with a chuckle as she'd raised her drink and toasted. *Hail to kale.*

That was before the mileage of marriage, the mileage of life had revealed some of the truths about both of them—but not all the truths. That was before her husband, Robert, was gone. Before her children were grown. Before she began contemplating what she didn't mind leaving behind, what she still needed, what she wanted from life now.

Meg leaned over to check the cell phone screen on the warm beige marbled quartz countertop. It read *Jessie*, so she answered the morning call.

"Hi, Mom. Did you swim this morning?" Jessie greeted her.

"I did. Is this my half-age child?" she teased, picturing her azure-eyed, curly-topped adult offspring on the other end of the conversation. Jessie, with eyes and hair the color of her own.

"Did you just call me your half-wit child?"

"Never," Meg clarified. "You're now twenty-five, and I'm the big five-oh, so you are half my age."

"Way to make me feel old," Jessie said.

"So, two times old must be *really* old?"

"You know I was never the mathematician in the family."

"Good dodge." Meg laughed. "Maybe I'll keep you in the will after all." Jessie would know what getting old felt like in a few decades. "How's Luc?" she asked.

"They're great. They're loving the EMT training program—a great balance of science and adrenaline. Just what they love."

Jessie was the middle of Meg's three children and was nonbinary, as was their partner, Luc. Jessie had swerved their fine arts degree into the successful career of a tattoo artist not long before Robert passed, much to Robert's displeasure after sending them to the California Institute of the Arts with its private school fees. Jessie was happy—so Meg was happy. Meg had not been surprised when Jessie and Luc came out publicly. Sometimes she blew it on their pronouns, but she was working hard to show her acceptance and respect for the amazing people they both were. She wanted to get it right for Jessie and Luc. Robert had struggled more. Mostly with how it had reflected on him.

"So, anything I can help with this morning, babe?" Meg picked up her cocktail glass and took a sip of her smoothie.

"We were just wondering if we could borrow the camp stove in your garage because Luc and I are going camping with some friends at Big Sur at the end of the month. Ours isn't working."

"That's fine. And you can keep it. I'm not going camping at this *really* advanced age."

"Great. I'll come see you late Saturday afternoon to pick it up, if that's okay."

"Sure. I'll enjoy the visit." Meg smiled to herself as she thought of her artistic middle child. Of the crayon-holding, chubby appendages that had grown into long, slender fingers holding a Faber-Castell Pitt artist pen, sketching out tattoo designs on smooth, white notepads. Creating everything from appealing nature themes to complex geometric forms.

"Will you have time to go out and get something to eat?" Jessie asked. Meg knew that Jessie was aware that while she had grown tired of all the kitchen chores when everyone had been living at home, now she spent too many meals alone.

"I'd love that," Meg replied.

"See you then, Mom. Gotta go. Love you."

"Love you too." Meg ended the call, then finished her smoothie and a cup of coffee.

❖

Before the call, Meg had been for a morning swim at the community pool, taken a shower, made a pot of coffee and the smoothie. It was time to get on with whatever the day presented. That included finalizing next week's San Francisco trip.

"Got plans for the day?" she asked Oscar, looking down at the fourteen-year-old ochre cat who had wandered into the kitchen from his napping bed on the couch in the family room. Someone else was thinking breakfast—Oscar gave her the brush-off as he beelined for his food bowl.

"Of course you have plans for the day—a little chicken entrée, a nap, a bit of windowsill bird watching, another nap." Oscar looked up at her from his breakfast. "You're such a handsome ol' boy."

Oscar's life was about as exciting as hers. While Oscar wanted to be an integral part of a household, his independence was evident. Oscar didn't seem to mind eating alone, sleeping alone…She did. Not that she'd ever admit it to anyone except herself.

Life had certainly taken a turn for the worse. First the diagnosis of diabetes for Robert, then cardiovascular disease and renal issues. Comorbidities could be hell, especially when a person did not take care of themselves, and as self-focused as Robert had become as he'd aged, he had not made his health a priority. Comorbidities took Robert two years ago, after twenty-eight years of a marriage that Meg had worked at from the time she was twenty. Three kids before she was twenty-eight: Natalie not long after the wedding, Jessie five years later, and then Ben two years after that—it was her children that Meg focused on and treasured. And now a widow. As the world moved on, Meg was working at moving on too.

Meg had to acknowledge that she was torn. There were some things she missed in a relationship, and there were things she absolutely didn't miss. She often told herself that there were worse things than living by herself. Besides, she had Oscar. Meg had even been to a few online dating encounters at the relentless urging of her best friend, Grace—disastrous dinner dates. Finally, she'd let Grace set her up with a man Grace knew, so that Grace could relax about her empty dance card—specifically, dating Stan, which she'd been doing for the past three months. It was her concession to Grace's caring concern, that she would attempt to get back in the saddle, but none of the dating Meg had done had led her to want more.

But Meg was pleased to be more actively reviving the personal pursuits she'd subdued for family life—and Robert. And she was working to find herself, to figure out some things she'd never addressed.

Meg had loved art and writing since she was a child. She'd spent hours painting alongside her grandmother, who had been a well-known watercolorist. She had also kept a journal as a teenager. Meg had coveted dreams of becoming a professional artist, maybe even a collected one, although Robert had always insisted he could support them and had called her Mona Lisa Meg when he found her sketching, painting, or working on a mixed-media collage.

After high school, she had been trying to define who she was, and where she was headed both personally and professionally. She'd taken a few art courses along with other general education courses, including biology, at the community college in the year after high school—when her plan had been to transfer to a four-year school for an art degree. She'd found the biology fascinating, and a course that she'd hoped would help with her art. And while she'd felt a strong, confusing attraction to fellow high school swimmer Lizzy Brown that would have appalled her parents, she'd done no serious dating before college when she'd met Robert, a self-confident young man, at a party. Four months later, with a positive pregnancy test, her world had been turned upside down. They'd married and lived in couples' student housing until Robert graduated from Stanford and launched his career. He had founded Mullins Investments, and she had abandoned her dreams.

Robert had always been busy and inattentive, and more so as their marriage progressed, both emotionally and physically. Meg had resigned herself to the fact that both she and Robert had their individual issues and then she had done her best to make the marriage work for her children. Meg became the dedication, the sacrifice, the love that held her family together.

Once the kids were old enough to attend school, Meg had started dabbling in art again, craving the opportunity to build on the skills her grandmother and the community college courses had given her—it had been a struggle. Through the years, Meg continued to pursue her art, if only during stolen hours in the back office. It offered a piece of passion she'd almost lost when she'd married. Art had been the one thing that was hers through the chaos of anchoring a family, and a godsend in the hard times after Robert had died. His career in investment and asset management had left Meg without financial worries, but she needed productivity in her life.

Six months after Robert's death, Meg had secretly pursued her interest in writing as well, establishing a blog, *Slouching Toward Stardust*. She hadn't shared it with her family or friends. It was a place where she felt free to write and post what she was feeling, free to run with any idea that appealed to her and be herself. It was not only liberating to be her anonymous self—it was another source of sanity for Meg. And to her surprise, she was continually picking up additional readers.

SLOUCHING TOWARD STARDUST WITH MEG THE UNMUZZLED

"Elusive Ingredients"

There should be some beauty in cooking. Some art. Some sacred bliss. How could there not be with the holy matrimony of cuisine and the Krebs cycle? There used to be. Before one husband, three children, and an incessant frenetic stream of fueling family and drop-ins frayed the pleasure of the culinary experience. Before the perpetual acquisition of provisions, the ceaseless plating of fodder, the endless scouring of kitchenware became a drudgery. An assumed act of obligation that became weary convention, even after the nest was empty—even now, alone. *Or maybe that* alone *is the issue. My current cuisine lacks some elusive ingredients: celebration, comradery, gratitude. I want them back.*

In the grocery store parking lot, there is often a man with a small brown dog. An unassailable covenant between canine and human. The man plays a polka on a well-worn squeeze-box, swaying side to side as the notes course from his essence to the instrument. A small accordion similar to the one my mother-in-law played around the nighttime campfire decades ago for her grandchildren—joyous wild things silhouetted by flames as they performed their forest frolic to a serenade for the generations. On the asphalt, the small mutt sits quietly, waiting for the occasional passerby to deposit a donation into the open case on the ground, then offers an appreciative howl in the key of F when the deed is done. The pup's thanks is accompanied by a dignified nod of the head from the maestro. Best bang for the buck I'll ever receive.

I have witnessed the man pocket his earnings, case his instrument, and soldier across the pavement past large SUVs, compact Beemers, state-of-the-art Teslas, his gait uneven as he sports a limp. Not leaving his companion in order to go inside the restaurant, he instead slips behind a car and edges forward on foot in the drive-thru lane with his disciple at his heels. At the window he places his order, collects his fare,

*and then moves to sit on a nearby grassy strip where he carefully plates
the burger and french fry acquisitions on a rumpled handkerchief.*

*The man closes his eyes in pause, and so does his partner. Not
some rote declaration to a deity, but a dedicated transition to shared
sustenance. Then the little pooch performs a pirouette, and they begin
to partake of their bounty. Two thankful souls appreciating the beauty
of a fast-food sandwich. The art of french fries. The sacred bliss of
sharing a meal.*

CHAPTER TWO

Today Meg needed to finalize her plans for next week's two-night visit to San Francisco. She would make the trip across the bay late Monday morning from her home in Trinity Hills—a home Robert had selected.

He had commuted to San Francisco in his silver Porsche, conducting business the entire drive in his state-of-the-art car. Some nights he'd stayed over when he needed to work long hours, sleeping in a spare room at the residence of one of his firm's investment advisors. In fact, he'd spent a lot more nights away those last several years of their marriage, the trade-off for business success. Meg had worked hard to be supportive of Robert and understood that running a successful investment firm was demanding. That was why she had learned to handle almost everything else in their lives. She had been committed to making her family life work, and for that she'd needed to make her marriage work—that had been her focus.

Meg had been to San Francisco for business a time or two as a widow—quick trips to finalize the necessary aspects of Robert's side of their life, although that had mostly been accomplished online, in a local bank branch, or in a local legal or title office—but she hadn't been to San Francisco for enjoyment in the last two years. Meg hoped that this getaway would give her a chance to do some thinking, experience a change of scenery. She could use a change of scenery.

First, she would talk to Grace, to verify that Grace was still planning on taking Oscar while she was away. The cat was happiest when he was embedded in a busy household while maintaining his independence—

loving Meg, but only on feline terms. Grace's household offered him that on the occasions that Meg could not. And Oscar had his people, approving of Grace as well as Meg. He'd never cared for Robert. Grace was always willing to have him over and give the elderly feline his pills—for hyperthyroidism, for his kidneys, for acid reflux. Nothing like old age to bring on the pillbox, she and Grace had joked.

She'd met Grace at the elementary school years ago when their kids were just starting school, and time had solidified their relationship. Grace and her husband, John, had two kids close to the same ages as Meg's. Grace worked part-time at a real estate agency and volunteered foster care for a local animal rescue—that was how Oscar had joined Meg's family twelve years ago. From kindergarten to empty nesters, Meg and Grace had shared the years. Shared their lives. Grace had been a safe harbor when Jessie and Luc had declared their nonbinary status and Robert had not been supportive. Grace had been a rock of support after Robert's death.

❖

"Hey, it's me," Meg stated into her phone when Grace picked up.

"No kidding. Because everybody else is taken," Grace replied.

"All right, smart-ass. I've heard that one before. And I didn't call for your wit—or wisdom. I'm calling to make sure you can watch Oscar next week from Monday late morning until Wednesday late afternoon or evening while I'm in San Francisco." Meg sat on a kitchen stool and waited for Grace's response.

"I've got my date with Oscar on the calendar. I can let myself in and grab him on Monday about noon, bring him here. I only have one old cat-friendly foster dog right now, so he'll fill a void. Oscar's my party boy—he's always up for some pillow kneading, anchovy pizza, a snooze in the hammock, maybe a little midnight pole dancing. John will enjoy his visit too."

"I'm so jealous," Meg said. "Oscar never midnight pole dances with me. And I'd take a partner like John who loves my cat, my kids, my eccentricities."

"Are you suggesting that I'm eccentric?" Meg could hear the humor in Grace's voice.

"Not merely a suggestion," Meg countered. "It's why I love you."

She enjoyed bantering with Grace, the comfortable relationship they had.

"Love aside, what's the trip?" Grace asked.

"It's a way for me to get back into San Francisco for some personal fun," Meg admitted. "I'm planning to meet up and talk a little art with a journalist doing an online piece about my grandmother's art."

Meg had agreed to talk to Carol, who wrote for the online human-interest magazine *Bay Area Heartbeat*, over coffee on Tuesday morning. The journalist was interested in writing an article about her grandmother. She'd heard that Meg dabbled in art—inspired by her grandmother.

"If they're interviewing you, it will be a great piece," Grace told her.

"Thanks. I hope so. And I had a call yesterday. I agreed to meet with the lawyer who represents Robert's old investment firm, Catherine Colson, on Tuesday afternoon—whatever that's about. I'm a little nervous." Meg visualized Catherine Colson. She was a striking professional woman who had always caught Meg's notice on the occasions they'd met. "And in between, by staying over I'll have time to organize my notes for *Bay Area Heartbeat*, visit some bookstores, and maybe eat something special in San Francisco."

"It sounds like a much-needed trip. Except for maybe the lawyer—I hope there are no legal issues related to Robert. And changing the subject—how are you and Stan doing?" Grace questioned. Grace had sold a house to Stan.

"I'm dating," Meg responded. "Maybe it's just me and a lack of hormones because the sparks just aren't flying." Meg felt no romantic feelings for Stan, but she was trying to please Grace. She was beginning to realize she needed to please herself.

"And here I thought it was just me and my hormones these days," Grace said. "Nothing like maturing, huh?"

"Maybe it's not just hormones. He insists on calling me *Margaret* instead of *Meg*. Only my grandmother called me *Margaret*, and she said it with a lot more respect. I have images of him picturing me in Margaret the Naughty Maid attire."

Grace guffawed. "That's just *so* you, Meg."

"Hey, I'm not a total prude. But not the Naughty Maid either." Definitely not with Stan.

Grace continued to chuckle.

"I don't want to be just another notch on someone's bedpost, so I'm keeping it out of the bedroom," Meg confided.

"I hear you," Grace said, her tone consoling. "You just do what's best for you, sweetie."

"I should probably let Stan know I'm out of town next week because he's gone on a golfing trip this weekend, and I'm not planning on seeing him before I go. Not that it's his business. But when he wants to get together, he keeps calling and calling. I sometimes feel like it's really the chase that interests him." Meg frowned at the idea of being sought after by Stan.

"Maybe a few days in San Francisco will give you time to figure it out," Grace suggested.

"Maybe." Meg was realizing she did need to figure it out, but she wasn't sure she was ready to acknowledge what she might discover. Feelings she had kept buried for thirty years. But now she was coming to the realization that it was time to admit that she had buried those feelings, the physical stirrings, where she wouldn't need to examine them too closely these past three decades. Her family had always been her most important consideration—and now that had changed. She was a widow, and her kids were grown. Maybe it was time to examine whether there might be more to her measure of some women.

"Well, safe trip if I don't talk to you this weekend. And don't worry, Oscar's in good hands. I'll make sure he gets his meds."

"My only worry is getting that feline to like old boring me after a trip to your place," Meg said. "And if I haven't said it lately, I couldn't ask for a better friend."

"Same here. See you next Wednesday with your cat."

Meg picked up Oscar and scratched his ears. He leaned into her and purred. "You ready for a little pole dancing, ol' buddy?" she asked him as she gazed back into his amber-eyed assessment of her. He rubbed his head against her chest and purred some more. She was happy he'd be in good hands, that he probably wouldn't even miss her.

Meg confirmed the interview with Carol from *Bay Area Heartbeat* for Tuesday morning at a Philz Coffee in the Financial District. Catherine Colson's office had called yesterday and set the Tuesday afternoon appointment at two o'clock, so that was taken care of too.

Finally, she focused on Stan. If she didn't let him know that she'd be out of town next week, he would likely call her repeatedly. Stan was in and out of her life depending on his schedule, yet he seemed to constantly need assurances that she wasn't seeing anyone else—as if just seeing him wasn't challenging enough. Meg didn't want the anxiety of this complicated relationship. Oh hell, this was exactly why she didn't want to date.

She took a deep breath and made a decision. Picking up her phone, Meg called Stan. She told him that she appreciated the time he'd spent with her, but that after some consideration she had come to the conclusion that their dating wasn't working for her right now in her life. True to form, he seemed most concerned that she might be seeing someone else. She assured him that she wasn't.

"Plenty of women would be thrilled to go out with me, you know," Stan responded, his tone smug.

"That's good then. I'm glad to know there are no hard feelings." Meg wished him the best and thanked him again, then ended the call. She exhaled a huge sigh of relief.

Slouching Toward Stardust with Meg the unMuzzled

"Measure of a Woman"

I can admit that I have felt the magnetism of some women through the years, and not just an aesthetic appreciation. I've always attributed my attraction to the artist in me. A love of art my grandmother fostered—a way of looking at the world she passed to me, through an artist's lens. I've seen myself as a sketcher, a painter who is drawn to my many subjects because of something defined as character. That is the word my grandmother used when she explained the pull she felt for a subject she painted—it had touched her heart, embedded in her soul.

An old wooden barn—glazed and striated in mixed hues of the siennas (red-tinged burnt sienna and yellow-tinged raw sienna), sepia, Payne's gray, ultramarine and phthalo blues, dioxazine purple, yellow ochre, maybe a touch of alizarin—exuding years of weathered existence. A dried sunflower with faded petals, shrunken and curled into the marvelous remains of botanical debris, with soft-edged and hard-edged undulating shadows. The similarities and differences of human hands—the shapes, the shades, the textures.

And so, I have taken the measure of many of the women I have encountered. I am not immune to classic beauty, but there has been so much more to my gauge of a woman. The life in an eye—did it twinkle, tease, convey what the mind was thinking? The color—was it a cerulean blue, smokey gray, brown stippled with suggestions of gold, or a soft gentle green? A flat hue or the matching hue, but saturated with a fervor for living? And the mouth—did laugh lines journal a positive outlook, a downturn express difficult times, a lip-pursing relay internal contemplation? The angle of a woman's body—not the physical curves, but the attitude of form. Was she at ease with herself, constrained, theatrical, vibrant—did it change with circumstance? Did the subject connect with my artistic soul? Those were the things I have told myself attracted me to some women. Because I appreciated their characteristics like I appreciated the complexities of my art subjects.

But perhaps…possibly…probably…there is more to that attraction. Something I need to explore. Something I need to finally define.

CHAPTER THREE

The drive across the bay was uneventful on Monday, and Meg had checked into her hotel room by midafternoon, her Honda CRV safely deposited in the nearby garage. Robert might have wanted a silver Porsche, but Meg had always needed a practical car when they were raising the kids—before everyone left home. She'd agreed to updates but felt no need to change from a utilitarian vehicle. Enough had changed.

Meg headed out and visited a few stores in the Ferry Building, wandering the bookshelves in Book Passage before stopping at a restaurant to purchase two fish tacos for outdoor dining. The wandering crowds of tourists, the sounds of traffic out on the Embarcadero, the mixed aroma of bay water, boats, and food all added to Meg's enjoyment of the change in her environment. She relaxed and absorbed the ambience of big city life until it was early evening and time to return to her lodgings.

Back at the hotel, Meg settled down to review her notes for her art interview in the morning. Grace texted her a cat emoji followed by a thumbs-up, so she knew Oscar was doing fine. She retired early but didn't sleep well in the strange bed. While she wasn't concerned about the *Bay Area Heartbeat* meeting, she did worry what the legal meeting was about.

A woman with a short gray pixie cut waved at Meg from across the room when she walked into Philz Coffee at ten o'clock the next morning.

Meg waved back and approached the woman. "Carol?" A nod and

a smile. "Meg Mullins. Thank you for your interest in my grandmother's work."

"I should be thanking you. Let me get you a coffee. What would you like?"

"A soy latte would hit the spot," Meg responded. "Thanks."

"Sounds good to me too. And it's the least I can do after you agreed to the interview."

Meg studied Carol as she retrieved the two lattes. She had looked up the *Bay Area Heartbeat* and had seen that Carol researched and wrote articles regularly for the online magazine. Carol was probably in her late sixties with a petite frame and an observant demeanor.

"Is outside at a table okay with you?" Carol asked.

"That's perfect." Meg followed Carol outside with her drink and they sat down in the morning sunshine.

"So, I know quite a bit about your grandmother and her art." Carol shared her perspectives on the approach she hoped to take in writing the article. "I just need to finalize some things for that part of my article. And learn more about how she had you painting with her when you were a child. I'd like to include the aspect of generational art in the story, if that's okay."

Meg was thrilled with this idea. "I'd love that—as a legacy to my grandmother. Not that her paintings aren't legacy enough."

They spent almost three hours drinking coffee, getting acquainted, and discussing art—her grandmother's history, how her grandmother fostered Meg's love of art, her own amateur pursuit as she'd raised her kids, and the therapy role it had played when Meg was widowed. She also explained how much she enjoyed the volunteer art class she taught to the seniors at a local assisted-living facility, coming back full circle to a generation that reminded Meg of her grandmother in her later years.

"Before you go, I'd love to see some of your work if that's okay," Carol asked Meg. "It would be wonderful to include a few photos of pieces to make this a true multigenerational article."

Meg was rather shy about sharing her amateur efforts but realized they might make the article about her grandmother's legacy more interesting. Meg wanted the story to be a success—to honor her grandmother. Meg kept to herself the fact that she'd once had a dream of becoming a professional artist, a collected artist like her grandmother. That was in her past. Buried.

"I have some photos on my phone. My grandmother taught me how to set up the lighting and take pictures, and they're very good resolution. I could forward them if you'd like. Let me show you." Meg showed Carol some photos of her work.

"Your work is fantastic, Meg. Amazing. You certainly have your grandmother's talent. They'll be perfect for the article. Thank you."

❖

After the meeting with Carol, Meg decided that she didn't have time to head back to her hotel room to drop off the notes she'd brought for the *Bay Area Heartbeat* interview before her two o'clock appointment at the lawyer's office, so she grabbed a turkey Fogbuster sandwich at Miss Tomato. The law office was not that many blocks away, and Meg knew the area because Mullins Investments was also nearby. Meg had been sitting most of the morning, so she was happy to walk.

When she came out of the elevator on the third floor of the professional building, Meg saw the door with the plaque inscribed *Catherine Colson—Attorney at Law*. She drew a deep breath and ran a hand through her short, wavy hair before opening the door and heading into a reception area filled with beautiful plants.

"Hi, you must be Margaret Mullins." The attractive young woman sitting at the desk sported a mop of unruly red hair that pushed her cute looks into the impish realm. "Thanks for coming in. I'm Piper. I'll let Cate know that you're here."

"Thanks, and please call me Meg."

"Okay, Meg. Have a seat and I'll be right back." Piper headed to a partially closed door behind the reception area and knocked lightly as she opened it enough to stick her head in. "Meg's here," Piper reported into the room.

As Piper backed out of the office, a woman Meg recognized as Cate Colson walked past her and into the reception area. "Hello, Meg— it's good to see you again. I appreciate you coming in." Meg noticed Cate's almost imperceptible perusal of the outfit she'd so carefully selected. She hoped that her black dress slacks with a fitted pale pink blouse underneath a charcoal blazer were appropriate for whatever this meeting was about. Meg wondered what Cate saw and if Cate thought she passed muster.

Cate was as stunning as Meg remembered. Meg looked back into her contemplative scrutiny. Seductive umber eyes infused with a salting of smoldering burnt sienna. The artist in Meg loved eyes. Cate wore her mahogany-hued hair pulled into a loose low bun, and the light brown undertones of her smooth complexion only perfected the rest of her features. She was attired in a fitted navy business suit with an above-the-knee skirt, offset by a white silk blouse beneath the jacket, with navy heels that completed the professional look. Cate. Always in a flattering, impeccable ensemble.

Meg subtly expelled a nervous puff of air, then offered a smile. "It's good to see you again too, Catherine. As you know, the investment firm's executive oversight was restructured after Robert's death, and I have nothing to do with it. So, although I'm not sure why I'm here, I'm happy to help you however I can."

"You know you can call me Cate. Come on into my office, and I'll explain."

Meg couldn't help but notice her compelling presentation as she followed Cate to her office—the confidence in her carriage, the movement of her hips, the firmness of her calves, the defiant strands of hair adorning her long slender neck. As they entered, Cate turned and asked Meg if she wanted Piper to fetch her a drink.

"Thanks, but I just came from an all-morning coffee meeting, and I'd float away if I drank another drop." Meg waved the folder of notes she still carried from the morning meeting with Carol.

"It's nice you've been able to accomplish more than just this meeting here in San Francisco," Cate said.

"It's been a good trip. A chance to spend a few days in the city, treat myself to a bit of bookstore browsing, good food, and this morning's meeting with a journalist from *Bay Area Heartbeat* who is doing an article on my grandmother."

"Here—have a seat. I take it your grandmother was someone of importance. Tell me a bit about her?" Cate asked while maintaining her demeanor in a genial but professional mode.

Meg considered Cate. She'd bet she was a good lawyer, establishing a rapport before she got down to the business at hand, whatever that was. Meg decided she had nothing to lose and so went on to tell Cate about her paternal grandmother as a watercolorist. She also explained that while her grandmother was a collected artist, her favorite memories of her grandmother were painting with her as a child. Cate slowly relaxed back into her office chair as Meg talked.

"So, you were Margaret Burke as a kid, and you painted alongside the famous Josie Burke. Now I'm impressed," Cate offered. "Did you manage to contribute any paint to her works of art? Maybe you should have signed them too." Cate teased her with a mischievous twitch of her lips, then seemed to catch herself. Meg watched Cate straighten a bit and struggle to morph back into her serious lawyer persona.

"It sounds like you know who my grandmother was," Meg replied in surprise. Meg had actually been enjoying herself. She'd only seen Cate in full-blown business mode, and she found the one-on-one, almost congenial Cate rather intriguing. Friendship-level intriguing, Meg mused. That was all she was willing to seriously contemplate while sitting across from Cate, summoned to her office for some legal reason.

Cate turned and looked up toward the wall behind her. Meg followed her gaze and studied the gorgeous watercolor of the Golden Gate Bridge, then looked back at her.

"You have one of her paintings," Meg exclaimed, not trying to suppress her delight. "I was with her when she did the groundwork for painting that one—plein air. She brought me out to the beach for the day. And then I sat next to her in the studio as she finished it up. I painted a big orange blob."

"I bet it was a beautiful orange blob," Cate stated, amusement in her tone.

"The beauty of it was that I thought so," Meg admitted. "I took my art very seriously, even at age five. Another lesson from my grandmother."

"So, have you painted any orange blobs lately?" Cate fell back into teasing her.

"Not orange blobs," Meg assured her with a chuckle.

"Okay. I'm going to have to drag this out of you. Do you still paint?"

"Nothing like my grandmother. It took a back seat to family life, but I still love to pick up a pencil or paintbrush, or do a bit of mixed media. Just for myself. Draw, watercolor, create a collage." Meg was enjoying herself, wanted to share her love of art with Cate.

"For yourself," Cate repeated. "I bet you're a gifted artist," Cate softly murmured as she studied Meg for a moment longer.

Meg felt herself blush. "For myself," she confirmed.

❖

Cate blinked a few times as she considered the appealing woman sitting across from her. She'd already noted that Meg was impeccably attired, and as always, her short honey-blond head of hair was perfect, casual but classy with its expert cut.

Cate locked her appraisal directly into Meg's waiting blue eyes. She needed to interview Meg regarding Robert and a matter for a client. Meg was Robert's widow, and Cate was going to reveal things that would undoubtedly cause her pain. Cate straightened in her chair, vanquishing the rare relaxed posture that had snuck into their exchange about art and the revelation that she had a painting by Meg's grandmother, hanging on her wall. As she considered Meg, Cate felt a strong pang of regret at having to shift into professional mode and hoped that her professional mask was in place.

"My client is Mullins Investments—with the new management," Cate explained. "They've agreed that I can talk to you about this… related to Robert. It came up in the latest audit, and I don't perceive it to be a legal issue at this time, but they want it clarified. You don't have to talk to me, Meg. And I also need to make clear that we don't have an attorney-client relationship. I'm just trying to nail down some facts for the firm, so I can advise them and they can move on."

Meg's iridescent blue eyes widened a fraction. Cate gazed into them. That magnetic azure innocence—until she told her the rest. Meg remained composed. Waiting.

Cate chewed her lower lip as she glanced down at the paperwork on her desk. Then she looked back up at Meg and gave a sigh. "It seems Robert used an apartment here in San Francisco, hidden in the firm's finances and uncovered in this last audit. As far as I can tell, there was nothing illegal. All monetary expenses and fees seem to have been covered through a special company account, but it raised some questions. Do you know anything about it?"

Cate saw Meg's manner shift to high alert. Disbelief. Agony. Grief. A succession of emotions traversed Meg's beautiful face. Cate could imagine them hitting her in the center of her chest like a physical blow—watched her concentrate on each breath, trying to maintain a calm rhythm of respiration. Inhale. Exhale.

"What the hell is going on? What the hell has Robert done?" Meg stared at Cate and fell silent.

"Do you know what Robert used it for?" Cate reworded her question. Damn. It had been ages since she'd hated this job.

"I have nothing to hide. He stayed in San Francisco some nights. To avoid the commute because he had so much business to conduct. But he told me he was staying in the spare room of one of the employees in the firm." Meg's eyes brimmed with moisture. "The cheating bastard." Meg's final declaration was spoken in a whisper.

"I don't know for sure what he used the apartment for," Cate offered. "What employee?" Cate struggled to maintain her professional demeanor. She had just rocked Meg's world to its core. But she couldn't let her sympathy for Meg interfere with the job she needed to do. Meg would need answers too.

"Robert said it was Joe Gideon. An associate investment advisor in Robert's firm."

"Did you ever have occasion to talk to this Joe Gideon about the spare room?" Cate asked.

"No. I haven't seen Joe in years. The only place I would have encountered him was at the occasional firm function, and while he was likely there, he didn't cross my path," Meg explained. "Maybe even avoided me if he was in on it."

"Okay. Don't jump to conclusions. I'll track down Joe Gideon and see what he has to say. If it turns out there's a chance of financial liability for you, I can contact the personal accountant that Robert used, with your permission, to see if I can clarify that for you." Cate believed that Meg deserved the facts, now that she'd informed her of the apartment's existence.

"Come on, Cate." Meg cleared her throat. "You don't get to our age without knowing damn well that Robert was up to no good." Meg stood up. "I'm so fucking gullible."

Meg began to cry, and Cate came around the desk and handed her a tissue. She needed to offer the woman what comfort she could while maintaining a professional distance. Her questions had just caused Meg's distress.

"Our personal accountant is Ned Baily. Robert dealt with all the finances. I'll make sure he knows you can contact him if you need to clarify anything." Meg's voice was unsteady. "I know you don't have to do that for me. If you do, I'm happy to pay."

Cate waved her hand, dismissing the offer. As they reached the office door, Cate stopped her as Meg opened it. Cate spoke in a gentle tone. "I'm so sorry. You don't deserve this. You don't deserve any of this. And I hate that I'm the one to cause your pain."

"Thanks. I don't blame you. This is on Robert. Just please let me know once you have all the facts."

Cate followed Meg out to Piper's area, assuring her that she'd get back to her. She owed Meg the truth. She just hated to be the one to deliver it. She'd already broken Meg's heart. And Cate knew what that felt like.

"Let Piper call you a ride," Cate suggested as she locked eyes with Piper, who was standing off to the side in the reception area.

Piper cocked an eyebrow at Cate. Cate knew this wasn't the image Piper usually saw at the law office—this was a glimpse of her more compassionate side. The one that she kept buried beneath the professional attorney presentation she worked so hard to maintain in her legal world. The exposed caring that probably made Piper want to consider her as *Cate* sometimes, and not just the boss. In fact, Piper had probably overheard her sounding unusually personable with Meg at the beginning of their meeting, when they'd engaged in the discussion about Josie Burke's art. When she'd let down her guard to the charisma that was Meg Mullins.

"I'm good. But thanks." Meg managed a response as Cate watched her leave, knowing that she'd just shaken Meg's world.

❖

There wasn't always that moment, but for Meg there was. The split second after which everything changed. She knew her marriage had not been perfect, but this was a seismic shift in how she perceived it. And the aftershocks were bound to be devastating. She couldn't tell the kids—they didn't deserve that baggage regarding their father. She'd need to deal with her feelings in a very discreet way. That was going to take some effort.

Meg would remember this tectonic moment for the rest of her life. The instant Robert had finally, fully broken her heart. The recognition that she was irrevocably ready to relinquish her fidelity to a marriage that had ended two years ago—or maybe longer ago than that. Ready to leave Robert behind. She'd made choices. She'd always ignored her attraction to Cate after meeting her at several Mullins Investments social functions. And Meg knew that she would remember the chemistry she'd felt during the art discussion today, as well as the kindness and empathy Catherine Colson had just offered her. She'd felt a connection.

Meg rode the elevator down to the lobby where she'd had a different perception of her past just over an hour ago. To a ground floor that now existed in a different world. Meg pushed open the door to the street and headed out to the rest of her life. One where she loved her children but wished Robert had never existed. And then Meg squared her shoulders and moved out into the afternoon chill.

Meg wandered aimlessly for some time and was still several blocks from her hotel. It was approaching half past four when Meg decided to walk the rest of the way to her lodging. She resolved that she wasn't ready to give up her day in San Francisco tomorrow and head home early. She wasn't going to let Robert do that to her—he'd done enough. She'd reserved the room. She'd stay the night.

On the walk back to her hotel, Meg acknowledged that there was a world of pain to unpack, but it would take time. She needed to separate who she had been as a wife from the woman she wanted to be now. To explore the person she had left behind at age twenty. The feelings she had suppressed. But not tonight.

As she arrived at her hotel, Meg realized that she was emotionally exhausted. Once in her room, she decided that she wanted to remember her pleasurable morning meeting with Carol from *Bay Area Heartbeat*. The art they had discussed. And after that, the initial, unexpected discussion with Cate about her grandmother and art—the enjoyment that she'd extracted from both conversations. Meg needed to focus on the best parts of her day before she contemplated the worst part. To put all the anguish that Robert was causing her aside for the moment and lose herself for an hour in a blog about her pleasure in creating one of her recent watercolors—a painting of one of the Bay Area's great blue herons, a bird she had photographed in the large Grove Park near her home. Because her art gave her back so much more than what she put into the pieces she created. And right now, she desperately needed to remember the enjoyment it brought her.

SLOUCHING TOWARD STARDUST WITH MEG THE UNMUZZLED

"Painting the Great Blue Heron"

I once had a watercolor teacher who often told the class, "Art is my religion." I've come to appreciate what she meant. Over the years, my art has not only been a link to the love I shared with my grandmother, but it's been a solace, a devotion, a blessing in my life.

❖

Things never come out the way you plan. After you create the regal resemblance with a stick of graphite (eraser essential) on deckle-edged plane, you bury this profile of the beast of beautiful quills beneath masking fluid. You wet and dry the background with undersea green over Venetian red, then you repeat the glaze, day into night and night into day. Perfection is elusive: blemishes own the immaculate image that dwells in your head. And so, you give that image up, pulling the plumage, exposing the heron shape as it emerges from its shell of silhouette-saving substance. When the feathers are free and the creature is taking your measure, you must first paint the eyes, the ones that radiate soul from mere pigment suspended in water. Because without soul, you have nothing.

After that act is done, you use the brush to dress this attenuated avian in elegant hues of bronze and blue until he has all but a leg to stand on. You pause to acknowledge the joke on your species— worshippers of thin ankles, shapely calves, firm thighs. For you have come to comprehend that the real worth is in the function. Knobby knees on bony branches, the supporting undercarriage—these are magnificent marvels of the mission at hand. When the limbs are done, you step back, comparing the piddling paint on the page to the stunning grace of the cosmos. You know that your rendering is a flawed study of a miracle. Or maybe simply a prayer of reverence. And you know that the attempt is joy enough. For it's not what flows from you to the paper, but what flows from the paper to you.

CHAPTER FOUR

After finishing the new blog entry, it was approaching seven o'clock and Meg realized she shouldn't just sit in her room and dwell on how her perception of the memories of her marriage had shifted. She headed out from the hotel in search of dinner. She rarely had more than a glass of wine, but after considering what she'd learned today, she decided she'd like to find a place where she could have a real drink.

Meg roamed a few blocks, taking in the sounds of evening traffic—car horns and brakes—drifting in from Market Street. There was a shroud of fog floating in through the city canyons, ghosting the pinnacles of the taller structures. Meg found a bar and ended up sitting on a barstool next to a much older woman who could have been her mother—she shared a perspective that made Meg smile after a day that drove her to alcohol. She offered Meg some advice and their conversation settled Meg a bit. After a third drink toasting her future, Meg collected herself. It was after nine o'clock when Meg finally made her way back to her hotel, hoping to get a decent night's sleep before facing another day. Before facing tomorrow.

As she arrived back at the room, her phone rang with an unknown number displayed. At least it wasn't Grace or one of the kids with more bad news, Meg considered through her alcohol-therapy buzz.

❖

"Hello…?" Meg's voice was hesitant when she answered the call.
"Hi, Meg. It's Catherine Colson. Cate."

Meg repeated the name, sounding surprised. "Cate, I didn't know you had my number."

Cate suspected that Meg had been drinking. Who could blame her? Meg's diction hinted at the amount of therapy she'd consumed.

"Piper had it." Cate paused for a moment as she remembered the look her paralegal had given her as she'd found Meg's number for Cate before heading home for the evening. *The Meg Effect*, Piper had offered, barely suppressing her mirth. The perceptive Piper had sensed that she was drawn to Meg. *Go home. Before I fire you*, Cate had admonished her with an effort to put some steel in her voice. Piper had chuckled. *No respect*, Cate had grumbled as she acknowledged that Piper was one of the few people she couldn't intimidate, no matter what tone she took. Maybe that was why she still had a paralegal.

"What can I do to help you?" Meg asked.

"I called for two reasons," Cate continued. "Are you still in San Francisco?"

"Yup. A little bit tipsy and a whole lot pissed," Meg told her with a hint of slur to her words.

"That's my girl," Cate drawled before she realized how intimate she sounded. Crap, what was it with this woman? Cate chastised herself. She'd convinced herself that she was just calling to follow up from their meeting earlier in the day.

"Well, at least I'm somebody's girl." Meg hiccupped. "But we haven't even had a first real date yet."

Cate couldn't help but laugh. Hmm…this was interesting. "First real date?" Even when she wasn't sober, Meg was engaging. But now Cate was concerned about whether she was okay for the night.

"That came out wrong," Meg said. "Must be the liquor." She changed course. "Two things?"

"Yes. I needed to let you know that you left your folder in my office from your *Bay Area Heartbeat* interview."

"Oh, thanks," Meg responded. "I'd completely forgotten about that part of my day. As you know, it only got worse. A hell of a lot worse."

"I'm sorry." Cate didn't want to think about Meg. But here she was, calling her on the phone. Worrying about her.

"It's not your fault. And what's number two? At least I'm sober enough to still be able to count," Meg congratulated herself.

"Um…two. I wanted to make sure you're all right." Oh hell, she didn't do caring. But Meg had been drinking because of a terrible day. Because of information she'd shared with Meg.

"Fifty years old. Just found out I was cheated on by my deceased husband. Yeah, me—I'm doing just great…"

Pursing her lips, Cate exhaled. She interrupted before Meg could continue. "Can I come by your hotel and bring you your folder?" Cate cleared her throat, then decided to plow ahead. "And I just happen to be picking up some takeout." Cate paused. "I could share it with you. I bet you haven't had dinner." Holy crap, now she was friggin' Mother Teresa.

"I'd like that," Meg answered. "I could use some company…uh, if you don't mind that I'm tipsier than I've been in years."

Meg told Cate where her hotel room was, and Cate assured Meg that she'd be there in about half an hour.

"That will give me just enough time to go and drown my sorrows in the shower. Maybe sober up a bit."

"That sounds like a plan," Cate murmured as she struggled not to think of Meg in the shower.

❖

Cate knocked, and the door to Room 205 opened to reveal a barefoot Meg in tight black spandex leggings and an oversized ivory sweatshirt—short, damp, honey-blond hair and those mesmerizing blue eyes only escalating her appeal. Meg gave her a welcoming smile. Cate ignored her emotions and moved on into the room. She'd given herself a lecture on the way over that this was simply a professional welfare check. Even though she knew that was bullshit. She was attracted to the woman. She'd found Meg alluring whenever she'd encountered her at Mullins Investments' social functions. Not just physical attraction. She'd always liked Meg, and she thought Meg liked her. As bad as today had been with the news she'd had to share with Meg, Cate had felt a bond along with the chemistry of attraction. She'd thoroughly enjoyed their art discussion, and she'd had an overwhelming desire to comfort Meg, to be there for her after the news she'd disclosed about Robert.

Cate acknowledged that a part of her wanted to know Meg better, but she knew that would only end badly. She had a job to finish. She didn't have time for friends, except maybe Pete, and that was professional too. She didn't do intimate in the same way she was sure Meg did intimate. Intimate was no-strings-attached for Cate. Since Laurel. And then there was the fact that from everything she knew, Meg was straight—she'd been married to Robert for decades. She took a deep breath and promised herself that she could balance her professional role with a little time spent looking out for the inebriated Meg. After all, she'd certainly helped cause Meg's intoxicated state.

Cate set the food bag on the table in the corner of Meg's room. Two chairs made it a suitable dining space. She unloaded a box with pot stickers, two chicken salads, and two bottles of water. She also pulled a packet with two ibuprofen tablets out of her suit jacket pocket. Cate took the jacket off and placed it on the back of one of the chairs after setting the hangover relief on the table next to the food.

"Preventive medicine," Cate declared as she nodded at the packet.

"You're such a considerate person," Meg said. "Thanks to you, maybe I won't feel like hell tomorrow."

"No woman has ever accused me of being considerate. A few other choice words, but not that." A memory flashed across Cate's mind of Laurel's words before her ex finally gave up on her and left: *Cate, you're an insensitive, work-obsessed jackass.* And she had been, as she'd put in the long hours necessary to build a successful legal practice and not offered Laurel the companionship she craved. She'd lost Laurel because of her own failures.

Cate struggled to refocus while trying to keep Meg's praise in perspective. It was well-marinated praise.

"You might be a lawyer, Cate, but you don't want to litigate this with me. I've got thirty years of courtroom-level debate experience with some extremely skilled offspring. You'll lose. There's a very decent, good heart underneath that legal persona you hide behind. You're guilty."

Cate bit her cheek. Damn, she even liked tipsy Meg. "Now sit down here, and let's get some food into you. Then you need to get some sleep."

❖

As they sat together before diving into the food, they talked. Meg told Cate about her three children when Cate wanted to know more about her offspring.

"Natalie is my oldest at thirty. Nat's an architect. Lives down in LA with her husband. She became an evangelical when she married him four years ago—never religious before that, so it's been interesting. Especially since Jessie, my middle child and twenty-five-year-old, is nonbinary. As is their partner, Luc. Jessie is a tattoo artist, and Luc is training to become an EMT. In Santa Clara."

"How does that work at family functions?" Cate wondered. "The LGBTQIA+ and the religion?"

"Not a topic for discussion as Natalie hasn't been around for family functions much since she married—she doesn't know that Jessie came out. Only a brief appearance for Robert's funeral," Meg said. "They rarely see each other as Natalie mostly stays in LA. We talk on the phone but don't see each other much, and I'm not going to have the discussion on the phone." Meg paused. "I love them both."

"It sounds complicated," Cate told her. It didn't seem like Meg's family had fully dealt with it yet. Cate knew all about the clash of some religious individuals with coming out. Firsthand. Her mother had been sure she was going to hell. But other religious family members had been wonderful—understanding that you didn't try to rob people of being themselves. That you appreciated and loved people for who they were—that had been her dad.

"I loved her first," Meg stated, a touch of sadness evident in her voice. "From the moment I knew she was growing inside me. Even more at first seeing her. All the joy and love through the years."

"Before?" Cate questioned.

"Before Jesus." Meg sighed. "Although I don't believe Jesus would have wanted it the way it's turned out—so judgmental for so many people. But Nat seems happy. That's what I always wanted for my kids. That they're happy."

Cate's intent had not been to make Meg more despondent, so she shifted the conversation.

"So, you have two children," Cate concluded.

"No, three." Meg smiled. "There's also Ben, age twenty-three. Ben just started teaching high school mathematics in Sacramento. He has a girlfriend, Sarah, who teaches too."

"You had your hands full," Cate said. "And now what do you do?"

"I have several friends through book club, a little art as a hobby, volunteer work. My best friend, Grace, and I go to lunch, movies, and just visit. And of course, I've got Oscar, my cat, to keep me on the straight and narrow," Meg joked. "He gets me up at dawn, and I head to the pool for a little lap swimming every morning."

"No wonder you're in such great shape," Cate couldn't help but comment. Meg was lean and well-toned, and even without makeup, so naturally attractive.

"So are you," Meg noted, taking her time to study Cate more closely. "What do you do to maintain your fetching physique?" Meg cocked an eyebrow with an upward twitch of her lips, making a nonverbal connection with Cate.

"Well…" Cate swallowed under Meg's appraising eye, suddenly wondering if Meg was really straight. It must be the alcohol, she concluded. "My law practice keeps me fairly busy, so I'm not sitting around eating bonbons. I watch my diet, and although I enjoy swimming, with my schedule I use a treadmill at my place here in San Francisco, and another that I just bought for my dad's house in Trinity Hills. I also like to bike when I get the time, which is not often."

"Your dad's in Trinity Hills?" Meg inquired.

"We just moved him into assisted living. I'm an only child, and my mom died from breast cancer, so it's just been Dad and me for almost seven years. We didn't sell his house, as he wasn't emotionally ready for that—but he's eighty-four and needs a lot more help. The social aspects of assisted living have been good for him too. And I like getting out of San Francisco on weekends when I can—so I stay at the house, take him to lunch, bring him over for dinner. It's where I grew up. Before I left for Berkeley."

"I'm in the Sycamore Village development in Trinity Hills," Meg disclosed. "Where's your dad's place?"

It was a small world, Cate thought. "My dad's house is not far from your place. An older development just east of Sycamore Village."

"I offer free art lessons to the seniors at The Terraces. Where is your dad living?" Meg asked.

"The Terraces." The gods were conspiring, Cate mused.

"Small world," they said in unison.

"And your parents?" Cate asked.

"They both passed away at a fairly young age a decade ago. And I was an only child, so no extended family on my side."

"Well, it sounds like you have great kids. And I'm sure you're a wonderful mother."

"I try." Meg smiled as she eyed the food.

They settled in to share the pot stickers, and each ate a salad. Meg had sobered up considerably by the time they finished talking and eating—by the time it was approaching midnight and Cate needed to leave.

Cate bagged the trash to throw in a can on the way out. She put her jacket back on.

"Thank you, Cate." Meg beamed her appreciation. "You've been a lifesaver. I loved your company tonight. Sharing a meal with you."

"No problem," Cate offered, trying to sound a bit less pleased than she felt. "Take the ibuprofen and get some sleep. You've had a hell of a day." Cate reminded herself that she didn't do relationships anymore. She didn't have time for them. And she was no good at them. But this woman intrigued Cate—she connected with that buried spot in Cate's heart and created a physical desire at her core that had nothing to do with her heart. It was time to get out of there.

Meg walked Cate to the door. She held Cate in a prolonged hug and then brushed her lips lightly across Cate's cheek, just catching the corner of Cate's mouth.

Cate closed her eyes and took in the tantalizing smell of Meg. Then she whispered, "Good night, Margaret Mullins."

"Until next time, Catherine Colson, Attorney at Law."

Until next time. Oh hell, The Meg Effect was going to be lethal.

SLOUCHING TOWARD STARDUST WITH MEG THE UNMUZZLED

"The Bar"

Last night I arrived on a barstool by following the Google map on my phone. The one that showed red teardrops at all the locations where people drink away their pain on the grid of streets in this town. Teardrops—how appropriate.

I landed in that fine establishment after crashing into some heart-crushing truths. The specific red teardrop location didn't matter. My destination was a vodka martini, or maybe whiskey on the rocks. Or two, or three. Maybe even more, and I rarely drink.

As I contemplated how I had been duped for some portion of my marriage, someone slipped onto the seat next to me. Not what I wanted, but then not much had been going my way. I dared a glance to the side. A nicely dressed woman, my mother's age—if Mom had still been alive. I relaxed. I missed my mom.

"Bad night for you?" she asked.

"Understatement," I offered.

"Cheating bastard?" she responded.

"Unfortunately, yes," I said as I looked more closely at the perceptive older woman.

"Well, my advice is to drink one stiff one to the good riddance of the SOB and then move on."

"I was contemplating a few more than that," I admitted.

"After number one, dedicate 'em to tomorrow," my companion suggested. "Tomorrow will be a better day. Your life is now one bastard lighter." She sounded just like my mom.

I smiled for the first time that evening.

CHAPTER FIVE

C ate hadn't crawled into bed until after one o'clock. When she arrived at work Wednesday morning, it was almost half past nine. She was always there before eight o'clock.

"I was about to send the police looking for you," Piper said in greeting.

This was not the professional image Cate had struggled to maintain in her practice. "I had business to attend to." Cate scowled at her paralegal.

"Late-night business?" Piper suggested with a sly grin. After all, she'd been the one to give Meg's phone number to Cate before she'd gone home last evening.

Cate ignored her and headed for her office, pausing just before she entered with a stern look back over her shoulder.

"Should I be advising you to plead the Fifth?" Piper continued undeterred.

"Are you trying to practice law without a license?" Cate asked. "I'd advise you to get me the number of a Joe Gideon at Mullins Investments. I've got work to do. So do you."

"On it, boss." Piper laughed as Cate disappeared from the reception area.

❖

Once in her office, Cate reflected on her office meeting with Meg yesterday. And then her evening in the hotel room, looking after an intoxicated Meg. She needed to make this call and update Pete. Cate shook her head, pulled out her phone, and selected a number.

"Hello, Cate. Have you been avoiding me? I feel neglected, cutie pie." Cate could hear Pete's amusement as he emphasized the *cutie pie*. She knew he used the endearment to trigger a response because he loved her like a sister—including teasing her like they were siblings.

"Needy doesn't suit you, Pete. I just talked to you yesterday morning," Cate retorted, her tone edged in the best chill she could deliver. "And that's Counselor Cutie Pie to you."

Pete was the only person besides her father who could get away with calling her by endearments. She and Pete had bonded at UC Berkeley decades ago when they were both undergraduates struggling with coming out. He now had a husband, Matt. Pete was a rare friend who refused to dump her, no matter how hard she had tried to isolate herself after her breakup with Laurel five years ago. And Pete had been tapped as the new CEO of Mullins Investments after it had been restructured after Robert's death.

"To what do I owe the pleasure of today's call?" Pete asked.

"Just passing on an update. I met with Meg Mullins yesterday afternoon." Cate got down to the reason for the call. "I made sure she knew I was working for you and she had no attorney-client relationship with me. That I represent the firm, like we discussed. And this is not a legal issue unless something unsuspected turns up. Just a further clarification of the apartment matter, so the auditors can put it to rest."

"Okay." Pete continued to listen.

"There wasn't anything in the apartment to identify who had been using it?" Cate asked.

"It had been thoroughly cleaned. But Robert likely would have had that done when he found out about his health issues."

"Well, that's no help then," Cate answered. "And if the apartment is what we think it is, I told Meg that with her permission, I'd check with their own accountant to make sure Robert didn't owe any personal taxes on the added fringe benefit of this apartment that could hurt Meg further." The idea of this fringe benefit riled her, considering what it was doing to Meg.

"So, what did Meg say when you told her about the apartment?" Pete asked.

"Meg didn't know much. She did tell me that Robert told her that he was staying in a spare room at a Joe Gideon's place in San Francisco when he stayed over. She said Joe Gideon is an associate investment advisor at Mullins, and that she had never spoken to Gideon about it."

"Okay, I know who Joe Gideon is. I'd like you to talk to him and get his statement, if you would…um, put this to bed." Pete was obviously enjoying himself. Put this to bed. She could hear the humor in his voice.

"I'm waiting on the callback from Gideon. But you need to know Meg isn't stupid about what Robert was probably using it for. I broke her heart yesterday afternoon."

"Oh, shit. I'm a jerk. I've always liked Meg. A lot."

"There's more." Cate cleared her throat. "In the spirit of full disclosure." She wasn't going to tell him how enticing she found Meg.

"You didn't sleep with her, did you?" Pete wisecracked.

Damn, Pete just couldn't help himself when it came to her love life. And it wasn't like she didn't keep imagining sating this fucking attraction. "Shut up, Pete," Cate warned him. "The answer is no. She left a notebook in my office after our meeting, and I did track her down last evening at her hotel and returned it to her." She could almost hear him thinking—he knew her so damn well.

"And?" Pete coaxed.

"And she'd been drinking, so when I returned the notebook, I took her some dinner and some ibuprofen. Talked to her for a while."

"Holy smokes. What happened to hard-ass Cate?" Pete was having too much fun with this. "I'm proud of you."

"Knock it off. I just want you to know that I spent some time with her outside of the audit clarification." Cate paused. "Welfare check."

"Welfare check, huh? So, I guess you're trying to tell me you like her." Pete teased her some more, but Cate didn't deny it. And she'd known he'd be a pain in the ass about it. Instead, he surprised her. "Let me talk to Joe Gideon and clarify what he knows. Or doesn't know. Then I can call Meg, so you're not balancing your lawyer role with ah…anything personal."

"I'm not walking away from clarifying for the auditors that this has no legal aspect," Cate said. "I have a job to do. I'll just steer clear of anything personal with Meg."

Of course Pete had focused on her love life, and Cate knew it was because he cared about her. "Personal," Pete drawled. "I like the sound of that from you, Cate. I'd given up on hearing that word out of your mouth."

"Get serious for a minute here," Cate countered. "Why would you think that Meg isn't straight? She's certainly lived an exclusively straight life from everything I know. She just discovered her deceased husband most likely cheated on her...probably cheated a lot. She has three grown kids. She has no interest in me."

"Your call. But don't sell yourself short. You're not half bad when you're not in ice queen mode. Ice queen mode—beautiful, but heartless."

"I am heartless. A bona fide heartless bitch. I've got a reputation to uphold. A legal career to maintain. So just try me," Cate shot back.

"No, Cate. You might have walled it off, but there's a heart in there," Pete gently told her. "It's just a little damaged. But it's had five years to heal. Finish this up yourself, if you insist. Then see where things go. Meg might at least make a good friend."

"I've got work to do. Calls to make." Cate changed the subject. First Meg. Then Pete. Telling her she had a heart. A heart she'd spent five years working to protect.

"Keep me informed," Pete implored. "And let's have lunch one of these days. You're my very favorite bona fide heartless bitch." Pete laughed as he hung up.

❖

It was midafternoon when Meg pulled into Grace's driveway after spending her morning in a coffee shop writing and then doing a little shopping in San Francisco. The front door opened and out came a short, sturdy woman with a huge smile and silver streaks striating her chin-length brunette bob. Grace waved, and Meg headed into the house. Oscar came over and rubbed against her legs. Meg leaned down and scooped her old ochre boy up.

"How did he do?" Meg asked, happy to have Oscar in her arms. She was ready to take him home.

"A perfect gentleman," Grace responded. "He's welcome here anytime."

Meg buried her lips into the fur on top of Oscar's head.

"You look tired, lady. Rough trip?"

"Terrible," Meg answered, thinking of Robert. "And good. Very good." That part would be Cate. "Can I tell you about it later? I'm absolutely beat."

"Sure, sweetie," Grace offered. "Let me help you get all of the feline paraphernalia into your car. This cat of yours needs a valet."

Meg smiled at Grace. "You know you're the best. Get together tomorrow?"

"It's a plan," Grace agreed. "Until tomorrow, then."

❖

Meg took Oscar into the house before unloading the car and unpacking. She went through the mail and then decided to feed Oscar and make herself a salad before crawling into bed and escaping into Quebec and Three Pines with her new Louise Penny book purchase—right now, she could certainly appreciate a duck who said *fuck, fuck, fuck*, instead of *quack, quack, quack*. Meg wasn't ready to process all that had happened in the last three days—her world had shifted too much. Reading was a good diversion. Tomorrow would be soon enough to deal with her emotions.

But she didn't make it to the second chapter before she started nodding off. Meg turned out the light, and the next thing she knew, Oscar was up on the bed telling her it was Thursday morning—time to get up. She made sure Oscar had food, suited up, and headed to the pool.

After her swim and coffee, Meg decided she was hungry, and rather than her usual smoothie, she'd appreciate a bowl of oatmeal with some fruit this morning. But first, she needed to talk with Grace, so she called Grace and reached her at the real estate office.

Grace greeted her with, "I hope you had a decent night's sleep."

"Like a rock, until my devil cat woke me up with a slap to the forehead."

"And yet you still love that boy."

"I do. And then he head-butted me on the cheek with five minutes of purring feline adoration...or hunger." Meg smiled, focusing on the joy the darn cat gave her.

"Can't knock that. I'm working until almost four o'clock today. I could probably abandon John and do an early dinner," Grace advised.

"If you want to come here. I don't want to tell you what happened in a public place. I'd like a little privacy."

"That doesn't sound good, sweetie."

"It was the trip from hell. With some really pleasant surprises. Life-changing," Meg admitted to her best friend.

"Holy smokes, I hope you're okay. I'll pick us up something to eat and bring it over if that works for you. Do you want salad or primavera pizza?" Grace asked.

"I could use something more substantial than salad. Pizza sounds perfect."

"Good. I'll see you then." Grace hung up, and Meg headed out to her backyard to gather some strawberries for her oatmeal. She loved spending a little time in her garden in the mornings, and after the last few days, not only had she missed her garden, but she knew it would help her feel better. After that, she caught up on the laundry, then did some reading and blog writing.

❖

Grace arrived at Meg's place a little after four o'clock with the promised vegetarian pizza in tow. She put the pizza on the granite countertop before giving Meg a hug. Oscar had been napping in his bed in the family room but pranced into the kitchen with his tail held high as soon as he heard Grace's voice.

"Hello, you two." Grace greeted both Meg and Oscar. "Two of my favorite critters."

Meg smiled. Grace always lifted her spirits. "I'm not speaking for Oscar, but I'll confess to feeling like a critter. Maybe one the cat dragged in."

Grace studied Oscar. "He says he didn't do it."

"He'd never confess, but this time he's innocent." Oscar looked up at Meg, aware that they were talking about him. He'd received all the attention he wanted, so he headed back to the family room.

"Shall we dish the food and talk?" Grace asked.

"I made a salad too," Meg offered.

"That sounds delicious." Grace opened the pizza box on the countertop and admired the salad. They loaded their plates and sat down at the table in the kitchen.

"So, do you want to tell me about it?" Grace asked, assessing Meg.

"I might as well. I need to tell someone, and I'm not going to tell the kids."

"That bad, huh?" Grace frowned.

"Probably worse. Enough to get me drunk," Meg admitted.

"Holy shit, Meg. And you barely even drink. I take that it's related to the meeting with the lawyer."

"That's the first piece of it," Meg informed her. Meg swallowed her bite of pizza and looked at Grace. "The lawyer's name is Cate Colson. She told me Robert had an apartment hidden in the company's financials. I could only conclude that he probably used it for cheating on me when he stayed over."

"That fucking bastard." Grace didn't hold back. "Good thing he's deceased or I'd kill him myself."

Meg had to laugh. That was why she loved Grace. "Not before I killed him first." Meg wiped away the liquid welling in her eyes.

"Oh, sweetie. What a mess. Are there legal complications?" Grace looked at Meg with compassion.

"Cate doesn't think so for the firm—it was set up so the company paid all the expenses. And if it's what it seems, she'll clarify there's no personal liability for me. She's still verifying that he actually wasn't staying where he told me he stayed—in the spare room of a colleague. I'm not stupid, though, he was cheating. Not stupid—just gullible."

"That fucking bastard." Grace repeated her declaration.

"My feelings exactly," Meg agreed with a sniff. "But there's something else I need to let you know." Meg rubbed the back of her neck.

"What else could there be?" Grace shrugged her shoulders in obvious bafflement.

"Before I left, I called and talked to Stan—broke things off with him." Meg studied Grace for her reaction.

"So, you made a decision. Do you feel better?" Grace asked.

"Aside from everything else, I have to admit that was a huge relief."

Grace shook her head. "I'm sorry it didn't work out. That it caused you stress. Pushing you into Stan was my doing."

"I knew it wasn't working…and it's not on you. You were only trying to help me. But you have to make me a promise. You'll let me handle my own love life from now on." Meg studied Grace, waiting for her reply.

"You've got it," Grace promised. "I only wanted to help."

"I know, Grace. And I love you for it. But I need to figure out that aspect of my future for myself."

Grace nodded her understanding. "So, is that everything?" Grace asked, her tone suggesting that she thought that was enough.

"There's more. Cate called me at the hotel room after I crashed there on my drunken derriere, brought me dinner and ibuprofen, and then stayed and talked to me while I sobered up."

"She sounds like such a good person," Grace noted.

Meg chuckled. "Don't say that to her. I've heard over the years that she's worked hard to create a strictly professional lawyer reputation—unapproachable in terms of personal relationships except for maybe an old college friendship with the firm's new CEO. The kind of reputation likely needed in the legal environment she travels in. Although before she gave me the news about Robert, we had a great conversation about my grandmother and art. She has one of my grandmother's paintings in her office. I think she let her guard down."

"It sounds like the charming Meg Mullins worked her magic."

"Her barriers seem very important to her. Like she's walled herself off." Meg stopped in deep thought, then decided to speak again. "It's more complicated than that. At least that's what I'm feeling. We had a real connection. I hugged her before she left at about midnight—in my still mildly intoxicated state. Kissed her cheek—brushed the side of her mouth. And I know she felt something. Wanted more."

Grace raised her eyebrows.

Meg swallowed. Looked at Grace. "And I did too."

Grace studied her for a long moment. "Do you think it was the alcohol?" Grace's tone indicated surprise and maybe a touch of hurt. "I only want you to be happy—whatever makes you happy. But we've been friends for a long, long time, and we've never discussed anything close to this."

"I've never talked to anyone." Meg pinched the bridge of her nose and sighed before deciding how to respond to Grace. "I was married. Had a family with kids who needed me and who I loved. I was young and clueless, contemplating all of my sexual feelings, although I hadn't acted on any of them. I got pregnant the first time I slept with Robert. I've made decisions that I've never regretted. Choosing my marriage and building a family. I love my family."

As Meg paused, Grace nodded. They remained silent until Meg decided to finish.

"I tried my best. Robert and I had some good times. It worked until it didn't. There were so many layers. Robert changed. I changed. For whatever reasons, it certainly didn't work by the end."

"I know that," Grace agreed. "And I understand. You're a good person, Meg. I value our friendship."

Meg nodded and smiled at Grace. "If I'm being honest—and I'm trying to be—I've noticed women, but it was not a path I could explore. We married at twenty when I found out I was pregnant with Nat. We both changed. My feelings for Robert shifted over time, but that can happen over the course of any marriage."

"And Cate?" Grace asked.

"I'm attracted to her. And I like her." Meg realized she was ready to make the verbal admission to Grace. "I can't speak for her, but for me, the other night was my twenty-year-old self telling this fifty-year-old woman that it's finally time to figure herself out." Meg knew she'd always been drawn to Cate at social functions—but she'd made a commitment to her marriage and family. Now she was at a different place in her life. Maybe it was time to consider what that attraction might mean.

❖

Cate had left a message for Joe Gideon the day before when he didn't answer his phone, but he hadn't called back. It wasn't until almost five o'clock that Piper knocked on her door and told her that Gideon was returning her call. Cate picked up the phone.

"This is Joe Gideon. Sorry for the delay in getting back to you. I had some major dental work done and missed some work—I had to do some catching up today."

"Hello, Joe. Thanks for returning the call. I'm a lawyer retained by your firm, and I have a question related to something that came up during the latest audit that I'm hoping you can answer."

"Sure, Cate. I know who you are. What can I help you with?"

"I'm not at liberty to offer you all of the background details, but I need to inquire if you have a spare room in your home and if anyone from the firm has stayed there in the past."

Joe didn't answer right away, so Cate waited him out. Then he said, "I don't have any idea what this is about, but I guess I should ask if I need a lawyer?"

"I don't think so. But you're certainly welcome to get one."

"Oh heck. I can just answer. Nobody from the firm has ever used my spare room. It's my wife's office space. She mostly works from home—a freelance website designer. I think only my mother and my wife's cousin have ever stayed with us. There's a pretty uncomfortable foldout couch in there. Does that help?"

Cate knew it wouldn't help Meg, but it sounded like an honest response. "That answers my question, Joe. I appreciate your time." Cate hung up. So Joe had confirmed it—Robert had lied to Meg. Cate sighed. This was going where she was afraid it was going.

Cate had clarified that Robert had set it up so there were no outstanding financial obligations for the company, but now she had a clearer picture of what the apartment had been used for. She had another call to make.

Meg had told her she would authorize their personal accountant to discuss this whole fiasco with Cate, so Cate had Piper get Ned Baily, the accountant, on the phone. He double-checked the retrieved tax filings and assured her that everything was in order. There was no outstanding liability hanging over Meg for the fringe benefit of a company-paid apartment. Cate hated what Robert had done to Meg, but she remained professional and thanked the accountant. At least Meg didn't have that additional issue to deal with.

Cate contemplated calling Meg because she had promised that she would let her know what she discovered, but it was getting late in the afternoon, and this was a call she was extremely torn about making. She'd love to hear Meg's voice, but she knew she'd only be confirming Meg's justification for feeling crushed about the apartment. She wrote up her legal opinion for the auditors, advising them that there was no obvious legal exposure she could discern for the company. She emailed a copy to Pete too.

Then Cate sat back in her chair and decided she would talk with Meg tomorrow. That should finalize her contact with Meg. She had been unsettled since she'd left the hotel. Cate needed to move past this consuming feeling that she wanted to spend time with Meg. Get to know her better. Hell, she wanted to sleep with the woman, and she barely knew her. That might work for a no-strings-attached encounter, but besides the fact that Meg was likely straight, she'd definitely perceived that Meg was far deeper than a no-strings-attached relationship—the only kind Cate was willing to consider. She leaned back and rubbed the corner of her mouth where Meg's lips had brushed it. Fuck.

SLOUCHING TOWARD STARDUST WITH MEG THE UNMUZZLED

"Garden Box Number 3"

There are some mornings when I need a little garden time. The cool caress of fresh air. The warm kiss of the sun. I was having one of those days. And so, I headed outdoors, thinking strawberries. Petite ruby jewels hiding in the green leafery of my second backyard garden box—fresh, sweet oatmeal toppers.

But then I pivoted my focus to the third box. Mom and Dad's legacy box, reaching into my world from theirs. On this day when I needed it most, a scattering of hand-height youngsters, descendants of those estate sunflower seeds carried home from my parents' front yard a decade ago.

Sunflowers. My favorite botanical. Every summer, stretching and reaching eight, ten feet to touch the sky—basking in a bright solar embrace on their journey up. The flower buds and young blossoms tracking the sun. Like the mythological water nymph, Clytie—deeply in love with the sun god, Helios, forever watching him cross the sky in his chariot after he left her—transformed into a sunflower, loyal and devoted, a symbol of pure and steadfast love. I want that. Pure and steadfast love.

And the sunflower's bright yellow hue and healing powers—symbolic of friendship, optimism, resiliency, hope. I will watch the botanical memories grow in garden box number 3. Transform from baby flora to gorgeous golden ties to the parents I have lost. There is a landscape of love and a reminder of hope in garden box number 3.

CHAPTER SIX

Cate sat at her desk late Friday morning and frowned at her cell phone. She knew that Meg frequently swam in the early morning, so she had put off calling her until she could find no further justification for procrastinating. She'd already decided not to involve Piper—Cate had Meg's phone number in her personal contacts, and what was more efficient than directly making the call herself?

Letting out a sigh, Cate continued to feel despondent. She knew that if she was being honest, she didn't want Piper's teasing input on this. She didn't want anything that might weaken her resolve. After a great deal of rumination last night, she'd decided the best course of action was to simply deal with Meg on a purely professional level and shut down whatever this imprudent connection was between them, this growing need she had for bringing this woman into her life. Hell, if she and Piper could name it The Meg Effect, it had gone well beyond anything she wanted to feel.

Cate finally picked up her phone and dialed Meg's number.

"Hi, Cate. I figured you'd be calling me one of these days." Meg's kind voice hit Cate hard. "I want to thank you again for Tuesday evening—you were a lifesaver. I was in a bad place and…well, you know. You were a real friend." Cate needed to get this over with.

"I only did what any decent person would do, and no more than that." Cate kept her delivery tone cool and professional. Shit, she might as well just guillotine the poor woman.

"Okay." Meg paused while she seemed to be digesting Cate's frosty rejoinder. "So, I should probably be asking if this call is professional or personal."

Cate could hear the vulnerability enter that charismatic voice. But Cate couldn't be a real friend—she didn't know how. "It's professional, Meg. Purely professional." Cate threw that last sentence in more for herself than Meg, as she fought to stand by her decision.

"I see," Meg said.

"I talked to Joe Gideon, and I'm convinced that Robert never stayed at Joe's place."

"I pretty much already knew that, but thanks for confirming things for me." Meg's voice had grown soft, as if Cate's obvious rejection was now layered on top of the confirmation of Robert's betrayal—and Meg was now buried beneath it all. "I guess if you don't have any more bad news for me, I should let you get back to your legal practice," Meg concluded in a subdued tone.

"Um, I'd just like to add that I'm not seeing any legal exposure in this for you. I talked with your personal accountant, and there don't seem to be any obvious issues there. You should probably make sure you have copies of your joint tax filings for your records." Cate paused, then finished. "I guess that completes our business. I am sorry." Cate suspected that Meg would think that she was sorry about delivering the final news about Robert, but she knew that a great deal of her own sorrow was about making it clear to Meg that their business was complete. Cate ended the call.

She sat for a moment. The call with Meg had left her nearly distraught. She'd done her job, and she needed to move on. But damn, it hurt. She drummed her fingers on her desktop, then decided to dial another number.

"Hi, Dad."

"Cate. How's my best girl?"

"Your only girl," Cate advised him. This was the usual script for their phone conversations. And there was comfort in that.

"So, what can I do for you, princesa?" her dad asked.

Was ice queen an elevation above princess? Cate wondered. Her father was descended from Peruvian immigrants who had come to California during the Gold Rush, and he spoke some Spanish. He had called her the Spanish word for *princess* for as long as she could remember.

"Just wanted to check in. To make sure you're doing okay. See what you're up to."

"Well, I'm eating three square meals a day. Playing poker with some new buddies. Going to an exercise class for old farts. And attending an art class offered by a wonderful woman named Meg. In fact, she's coming later this afternoon. She's going to turn us all into Picassos."

While Cate's dad chuckled, Cate kept her fragile control. Hell, there was no safe haven. She'd called her dad for distraction, and here he was, bringing Meg up and singing her praises.

Cate cleared her throat. "Well, I also wanted to let you know that I'm going to need to stay in San Francisco this weekend and catch up on some work." She hated to skip out on her dad, but she didn't want to tempt herself by being in Trinity Hills where Meg would be. She just wanted to be alone with her misery. She hadn't been this miserable before her encounters with Meg. This woman could kill her.

"Well, I'm going to miss you, princesa, but I hope you'll come see your old man the following weekend, then."

"Sure." Cate had mixed feelings because of Meg, but she knew she couldn't ignore her dad.

"Hey, Cate. You're sounding a little down. You okay?"

"I'm fine."

"Well, just don't work too hard. Life is short."

"Okay, Dad. I'll talk to you again soon. Love you."

"Love you too, best girl."

Cate hung up, not feeling any better. She ignored her emotions and dug back into the stack of work on her desk. That was the only way to get through this.

It was early Friday evening before Meg stopped to assess her day. She had paid close attention to the seniors in her art class that afternoon at The Terraces. There was a large recreation room where at least a dozen residents regularly attended the art class she volunteered to teach. While some of them were able to perform at a higher level than others, she enjoyed interacting with all of them. Most produced a piece of artwork every week, and their enthusiasm was contagious.

She had always enjoyed engaging with one of the seniors, Cliff, but hadn't registered that his last name was Colson until today. He was a handsome man with a slightly darker complexion than his daughter's gorgeous light brown undertones, and he had the same spectacular eyes—vibrant burnt sienna flecks gracing each umber iris.

He also displayed the magnetic warmth that Meg had experienced with Cate—she could see where Cate had acquired that concealed compassion. She had caught a glimpse of that Cate, and Meg had connected with it. She would have sworn that she had.

Meg was surprised at how crushed she'd felt all day after Cate's phone call. She felt a deep emptiness, a carving out. It wasn't the confirmation regarding the fabricated room at Joe Gideon's and Robert's lie because she'd already known that would likely be the news from Cate. It was Cate's demeanor. Like they'd never shared an afternoon talking about her grandmother and art, or that evening navigating her inebriated episode together. Meg felt hollow. And after Robert, she was beginning to believe that she had no clue how to read people. Because she'd certainly misread Cate.

❖

Later that evening, when Grace made an excuse to return a pie plate that she'd had for weeks, Meg knew she was actually checking up on her after the revelations of yesterday. Meg had leftover pizza and salad, but Grace insisted on bringing her a small pan of baked lasagna. Probably so Grace could come back over and collect the pan as an excuse to check on Meg again. While having such a caring friend lifted her spirits in one way, it also had Meg remembering how caring Cate had been. What had she done to cause Cate to pull back in the manner she had? Meg didn't know.

"So, what's got you so depressed this evening?" Grace asked. "Besides the week from hell. I've known you for years, Meg, and you are one of the strongest people I know."

"Cate called to confirm that Robert was not staying in that colleague's spare room, but I was expecting that. Her call was like a switch had been flipped, like we'd never shared a congenial moment together. She was in full-blown hard-ass professional lawyer mode without a hint of willingness to acknowledge we'd ever made a connection. I'm not sure what I did to destroy that bond."

"Can this old wise one offer some possible insight?"

Meg looked over at Grace and flashed her a hint of a smile. "Please, old wise one."

"I agree it was you, but not in the way you think. You scared the crap out of her, Meg. Cate Colson likes you—a lot—and she's afraid you're going to crack that armor she wears to protect herself. I suspect you started to do just that with those two encounters."

Meg considered this.

"I'd bet somebody broke her heart at some point, and she's not willing to let anyone else have a shot at that heart. She's feeling threatened. Afraid." Grace spoke like she knew what she was talking about.

Meg contemplated what Grace had just suggested. "Okay, if we go with your theory and it's more her than me, do I just write her off? I think I've got a bit of a broken heart myself, but I'm actually starting to think what's happened is a bit freeing rather than restricting."

"I think it's different for you, Meg. You and Cate are two different people with two different dispositions. And I suspect that you and Cate are in different places. That while his betrayal was a terrible shock, you'd already started to move away from any powerful hold Robert had on your heart—you're two years past his death. I also suspect that maybe you sensed that he wasn't fully invested in your relationship for a long time before that, and you had started emotionally letting go even before he died. I know that he hurt you very badly, but maybe not as badly as if you were crazy in love with him when he let you down." Grace stopped and studied her, probably hoping her insights were more helpful than hurtful.

Meg nodded as she digested what Grace had offered. "You're suggesting that someone Cate was deeply in love with, or committed to, hurt her so badly she won't let anyone else in."

"And she sees you as someone who could do that to her again because she's tempted to let you in," Grace suggested.

"That makes sense. As my kids would say, mad shrink skillz."

Grace snorted and then became serious. "I've fostered a lot of brokenhearted animals. It's about trust."

"So, what now?" Meg sighed. She was just starting to try to figure out who she was, and she certainly didn't want the heartache of a rushed relationship with the wrong woman. She was trying to recover from a marriage that she was discovering was way more broken than she'd realized. But Meg acknowledged to herself that she was drawn to Cate.

"First, give her time to decide what she wants. Whether she misses you or not. She won't begin to overcome her fears until she acknowledges to herself that she's willing to take a little risk in order to get to know you better. Willing to take the big risk of trusting you—with her heart. I imagine she's been in this mode for quite a while—growling, fear biting, running."

Meg laughed. "You make the beautiful Catherine Colson, Attorney at Law sound like an incorrigible mutt."

"She needs a dog whisperer," Grace advised. "Or in this case…a Cate whisperer. Maybe that's where you come in, Meg."

Meg felt better after Grace's visit. She didn't know how things would turn out with Cate, but she realized she needed to give her some space. In the meantime, she would do her best to go on figuring out and living her own life. She'd been thinking a lot about her life, her age, and mortality. She didn't want to be upset. Life was finite, and she wanted to appreciate the time she was given.

Meg wrote a blog before she decided to call Ben to see if she could drive up to Sacramento early the next afternoon and take him and his girlfriend, Sarah, out to dinner and maybe stay the night. Ben was delighted to hear from his mom and said that they'd love to see her. She texted Grace to tell her the plan and ask if she could drop in on Oscar and pill him. Grace responded with a heart emoji and a thumbs-up. Then Meg turned in with her book.

After her Saturday feline wake-up call, Meg decided maybe a morning swim would help her disposition. She put in her pool mile before packing a small bag. She did a little gardening and ate some lunch before heading up to visit Ben and Sarah. She was hoping Cate would come around, but meanwhile she was going to try to enjoy life and contemplate that challenge: Cate whisperer.

SLOUCHING TOWARD STARDUST WITH MEG THE UNMUZZLED

"Moments in Time"

Meg: Officially Known as Megalodon. Gargantuan, large-toothed shark for the ages. A top-of-the-food-chain ocean predator with a twenty-million-year run. Warm water aficionado with a ubiquitous range encompassing seas across much of the planet. Fossil teeth—all that remain. Extinct. Every being has its moment in time.

❖

Meg: Officially Known as Margaret. I'm at the pool most mornings between the predawn fanatics and the late-snoozing retirees, hoping to enjoy my own lane and the beauty of this piece of my day. My moment in time.

Today the water is perfect. Comfortable and clear. Some favorite oldies loaded by my middle child play on my SwiMp3 player, and I stroke to the beat as I complete the final portion of my workout. Doing a lap of backstroke, the cloud view offers an image of Mr. Magoo morphing into the face of God himself. The avian world in surrounding trees sports blackbirds and sparrows fluttering their morning rituals and friendly chatter. Look at those wacky humans swimming back and forth, back and forth, back and forth.

A flock of seagulls passes overhead, winging toward good pickings at the local dump. The moment couldn't be better as I stroke toward the wall. At the final lap I roll onto my back, searching again for that face of God. But what I see is a single, late, low-flying gull frantically flapping toward the dump. Our lives intersecting for only this one instant in eternity. Sharing the cerulean skyscape. The same skyscape ancient creatures once owned in their tick of time.

I pause and reflect on this moment—a fleeting moment in the finite heartbeats of life. And while nothing is forever, I savor what I am given, the beauty of this piece of my day.

CHAPTER SEVEN

After the hour-and-a-half drive to Ben and Sarah's apartment in Sacramento, Ben carried Meg's suitcase to their office, which doubled as guest quarters, discussing dinner plans as they settled her in. A visit with her youngest child and his girlfriend seemed to be a good antidote to her brooding. She was happy to see them both. Then they headed out to an early dinner.

After agreeing to share shrimp tempura rolls and a few chicken and fish à la carte main dishes, they settled in to visit. Ben and Sarah affirmed that their jobs were going well for both of them. Ben was in his first year of teaching math at a Sacramento high school, while Sarah was in her first year of teaching third grade. After discussing their professional lives, Ben asked his mom about her life.

"Well, I had dinner with Jessie and Luc when they came to pick up the old camping stove. Jessie is doing great at the tattoo business where they work, and Luc is focusing on their EMT program. Has Jessie done any new tattoos for you, Ben?"

"Nope. I'm sticking with the ink they've already done for now," Ben replied. "How about you, Mom? Any ink for you?"

"You might be surprised, but this old lady is seriously planning a small tattoo done by her middle offspring—once I find exactly what I want."

"Way to go. You always surprise me," Ben said. Sarah smiled too.

"I've undergone a lot of change in my life in the past two years, and it looks like boredom isn't in my future." Meg wanted to be careful what she told Ben about her personal life because she had no plans to upset him about Robert, and nothing else was well-defined.

Ben studied her. "I think you need something that symbolizes new beginnings. Change, self-realization, and happiness. My tattoos mean a lot to me personally, and I suspect that's what you're looking for too. Something with meaning for you."

"You're a smart kid. That's exactly what I want, something personal. And discreet. Not a full sleeve," Meg joked.

"You'd look cool in a full sleeve," Sarah teased as she joined the conversation.

Meg laughed. "And then I think I'd want a motorcycle. Maybe a big, loud hog."

Ben rolled his eyes. "Okay, Mom. That might be embarrassing. Focus on the tattoo."

"All right, Ben. I might embarrass you one of these days, but it won't be as a Hell's Angel." As Meg was figuring herself out, she'd already contemplated the issues she'd likely face with each of her kids—and probably not the same set of issues with each one.

They continued to discuss world affairs, family members, memories of holidays, and an assortment of other topics. After they finished their main courses, they sat and sipped their iced green tea lattes and then decided to go miniature golfing. Meg hadn't been miniature golfing since the kids were living at home. She made a hole-in-one and waved her hands above her head in a victory dance, declaring herself the champion. Ben and Sarah dubbed her achievement a megahit.

They watched a movie together, went to bed, and then shared a Sunday brunch of mom-cooked waffles and fruit before it was time for Meg to head home. The visit with her youngest child had been good for her. It was just what she needed before diving back into the activities and challenges of her daily life.

❖

"Hey, boss." Piper tapped on Cate's partially open door the following Wednesday morning before she charged in, barely able to contain her excitement. Her wild hair flying, her unbridled enthusiasm filling the room, Piper skidded to a halt in front of Cate's desk.

"And to what earth-shattering piece of news do I owe this interruption?" Cate asked as she considered that she was probably not in the mood to hear what her exuberant paralegal was going to impart.

"Maybe this will cheer you up," Piper told her.

"Do I look like I need cheering up?" Cate could hear the irritation in her voice as she addressed Piper.

Piper didn't respond to Cate but finished what she'd come to say. "I just emailed you a link. *Bay Area Heartbeat*. Check it out."

Cate let out an exasperated sigh before giving Piper a challenging look followed by a head nod toward the door. Piper knew nothing about what had happened after her Tuesday meeting with Meg, but Cate's reaction had her exiting Cate's space. "And shut the door, Piper," Cate ordered.

Once Piper was gone, Cate sat for a bit, collecting herself. Then she pulled up the website on her computer screen. The link took her directly to Carol's article: "The Legacy and Beauty of Generational Art: Collected watercolorist Josie Burke passed on not only her love of art to her granddaughter, but also her mastery." Cate read the article and studied the photos of Meg's work alongside her grandmother's paintings.

There were paintings of a creekside landscape, a still life of a wildflower bouquet in a glass canning jar, breaking waves on shoreline boulders. All watercolors by Josie Burke. Cate appreciated the mingling of color, the unique play of light through pigment, and the emotions they elicited.

And then there were the pieces by Meg. A moody watercolor of an ancient wooden barn, backdropped with a turbulent gray sky that connected with Cate's state of mind. A loving graphite study of a sleeping cat curled up in a big round cooking pot. Oscar. Cate remembered Meg talking about her old cat with such fondness. A stunning still life watercolor of a cut glass vase with light playing off its intricate faceted topography—and protruding from the vessel was a single sunlit white peony, tinged in pink and yellow hues. And another engaging watercolor of an outdoor garden box filled with the golds and greens of sunflowers stretching toward a blue sky. Tears welled in Cate's eyes. Oh God, Meg was so talented.

But it was the last page of the online article that undid Cate. There was a painting by Meg's grandmother of a beautiful blond girl about three or four years old, a hint of blush in her baby-soft cheeks, a suggestion of magic blue sparks escaping the slits beneath long curved lashes, and her head thrown back in the most joyful of laughs—it was that picture that unlocked the anguish inside Cate. *Margaret* was the word written under the photo. *Margaret*—what her grandmother had called her.

Meg. Didn't she know how amazing she was? And Cate meant amazing in regard to so much more than her art. The ache in Cate's chest grew to a stabbing sorrow. It was difficult to breathe. The deep pain for everything she'd walked away from streamed down her cheeks faster than she could wipe it away. For what had happened with Laurel—her role in deciding her professional life was more important than her personal life—and the consequences to her heart. For what she now refused to consider. For a woman who painted for herself.

❖

Cate remained miserable for the remainder of Wednesday and Thursday. Pete called her on Friday morning. Cate debated whether she even wanted to take the call. She knew that he wouldn't let her alone, and she really didn't want to talk about Meg. After the third call from Pete, she finally relented and picked up.

"Unless you've got a hell of a good excuse, I'm taking you to lunch today," Pete began the call.

"I'm busy." She cut him off before he could say any more.

"Nope. I don't buy it."

"You can't buy it. Who said anything was for sale?" Cate clenched her jaw.

"Come on, Cate. I want you to tell me that you've talked to Meg in the last week." Pete was using his soothing tone.

"I've talked to Meg in the last week." She threw his words back at him.

"When?"

Cate huffed. "Last Friday."

"And?" Pete wasn't giving up.

"And I told her exactly what I told you. Robert never used Joe Gideon's spare room. But there seem to be no legal issues for the firm or personal issues for Meg either, from talking with their accountant."

"So, you've completed the legal aspects of your relationship with Meg?" Pete asked.

"I have."

"And now?" he prompted.

"That's it. Done. Done with Meg. Done with this conversation." She let out a long sigh.

"I'm at your law office. Just entered your reception area. Let's not do this in front of Piper."

Cate remained in her office and on her phone with Pete. She could also hear his muffled voice through the closed door, but she liked the barrier between them. Needed it. He was too astute.

"Damn, Pete. Sometimes you're a pain in the ass." Cate continued to talk into her phone.

"But you love me anyway. Come on. Grab your purse and let's go." He was persistent.

"Grab my purse? Now you're expecting me to pay? You're the rich CEO."

"Nope, I'm paying. But you need your license—in case they decide to card your forty-two-year-old gorgeous mug. I'm not only springing for lunch, but a glass of wine too."

"I can't drink. I've got an afternoon of legal work to do." Cate knew Pete wanted to have a talk about her personal life. About Meg. And she didn't want to talk about Meg.

"Come on. It's Friday. You're not that busy. Piper shared your schedule, and you don't have any appointments."

"Tell her she's fired," Cate snapped.

She could hear Pete through the door telling Piper that she was fired in his teasing voice. And of course, Piper thought it was hilarious. "It must be the tenth time she's fired me this month. Without me, she's gonna be the one sitting out here smiling at clients and watering the plants. *So* not Cate."

Cate shook her head, picked up her purse, and opened her office door to face the two conspirators—the dark-haired, handsome Pete in a tailored business suit, and the indomitable, rebellious-haired Piper. "I haven't fired you more than three times this month. But it should have been more. I certainly wouldn't be grinning like a Cheshire cat when I greeted clients—and the only plant that might survive me is that spiky thing."

❖

Pete hailed a cab and directed the driver to a restaurant where he knew the owner. A place where Antonio would manage to find them a secluded table. The fact that they were seated alone in a far corner did not escape Cate.

"I take it you have an agenda," she said.

"I might call it a come-to-Jesus lunch, but while I know you're very spiritual, you're not organized religious. So, a come-to-Meg moment might be more appropriate."

"Pete…" Cate was so tired of her misery. She didn't need more. And she hated the thought of being emotionally exposed.

"Let's eat first, and then we'll talk," he offered. "I don't think you've been keeping up with your calories."

Cate nodded. Pete ordered fettuccine con pollo because he often tended toward the chicken pasta dishes, and she ordered a chicken chopped salad and minestrone soup. She had to admit that she was hungry—she hadn't felt much like eating in the last several days.

After they'd finished their meals, he ordered each of them a glass of red wine. Cate pulled hers across the table so it was directly in front of where she sat. She needed something to hold and sip while Pete had his come-to-Meg moment.

"So, let's get this over."

Pete shook his head. "I'm deeply wounded. I just want to ask you some questions."

"Why do I think this is going to feel like dental surgery?" She grimaced at him.

"More like cardiac surgery. I want to talk about your heart."

Cate frowned. Her heart had been off-limits for years. She didn't want Pete going there.

"Are you happy? I mean honestly happy. Not just getting by," he asked in earnest.

Damn, Pete should have been a therapist. Cate needed a couch. She took a sip of her wine. Stalled. Pete waited her out.

Clearing her throat, she decided to get this over with. "Happy enough."

"Really, Cate? Enough? Does that just mean going through the motions of living?"

"What do you want from me?" She frowned at him.

"I want you to be able to tell me that you are can't-wait-to-get-up-in-the-morning happy. Deliriously happy. Over-the-moon happy. Or at least you tried. No regrets." Pete studied her.

Regrets, Cate mused. He certainly had a way of going for the jugular.

She picked up her drink and drank the entire wineglassful, one swallow after another, until it was empty. Pete cocked an eyebrow.

"Fortification," Cate told him, nodding at the empty goblet. Then she dove in. "Yeah, I have regrets. I regret that I didn't make more room for Laurel in my life. That I made her so miserable. So miserable that she left me. Because I did love her. I just didn't know how to show it. To do a successful relationship. And I'm afraid I still don't." She fought the moisture gathering in her eyes.

"So why not try?" Pete asked gently.

"Because it hurts so bad when I fail." Cate could hear the grief in her voice, and she hated it.

"So instead, you do no-strings hookups. No chance of pain."

"Exactly." She gave him an honest, carefully controlled response.

"And are you even doing that anymore? Or is that too unsatisfying too?"

She hated that Pete was getting so close to the truth. "I'm not talking about my sex life."

"Or current lack thereof," he suggested. "You might be excellent at one-night stands—the meet, the greet, the sex, the polite good-bye. But you're deeper. A person who needs personal connection. Who is good at it—I know. I've been your friend for decades. You need more to be happy. Really happy."

Cate considered whether Pete had insulted her or complimented her with his *excellent at one-night stands*. Nope, it was definitely an insult.

"Your point?" Cate demanded, ready to conclude this conversation about her life.

Pete was relentless. "You're afraid the next person you care about won't be a long-hauler. Won't stay through thick and thin. So, you've limited your encounters. No strings. No attachments. No good times and bad. No chance of a personal long-term relationship."

Cate took a deep breath and craved another glass of wine so she could empty it again.

Pete continued, "You've limited your encounters to people who have no chance of getting close to a Cate who learned a lot from her relationship with Laurel—not just about broken hearts. But how to probably do it better next time if she'd just give a next time a chance."

She waited, absorbing every word of what Pete was saying, but focusing on her empty wineglass.

"You're afraid, so you avoid real relationships to avoid the hurt. I get that. It's not that you don't want a long-term relationship. You do. But you're afraid that the other person won't be a long-hauler." Pete smiled sadly at Cate. She hated his sad smiles.

"You should have been a lawyer. But what if I think a person is a long-hauler and they're not?" Cate wanted Pete to understand.

"It's a chance we all take. But let's get specific. Let's define Meg. Would you say she's not a long-hauler? Twenty-eight years with a guy like Robert, and she wasn't the one to end it. I have no clue about a lot of things about Meg, whether she's straight or not, but I know that you usually aren't off with your gaydar, even if she doesn't know. She's the epitome of sticking a relationship out. And she's mature, charismatic, beautiful, kind, funny, smart, honest, probably a hell of a friend, single, sexy…"

"Shut up." Cate had to smile.

"Okay. Case rested. But think about giving some sort of a personal relationship with Meg a chance. Even if it's just a long-haul friendship. She'd be good in your life. You spent less than twelve hours with her, and I suspect several of those hours were really great. You made a connection. So you purposely killed that connection out of fear, and now you're miserable."

She looked at Pete. Wiped her eyes with her napkin—she decided it must have been the wine.

"That's all I'm going to say." Pete reached for the bill and started to stand up. "I love you, Cate. I want you to be happy. Not just happy enough."

❖

It was late Friday afternoon, after another senior art class at The Terraces, and a week since Meg had been hurt by Cate. A week since Grace had psychoanalyzed the situation down to the concept of a Cate whisperer. Meg had been giving the idea a lot of thought all week but wasn't about to make the first move. She'd decided to sit down at her computer and focus on her visit with Ben and Sarah last weekend. On their conversation about tattoos. She'd recently written a related blog after thinking about skin. About the role it played in people's lives. In Jessie's livelihood as a tattoo artist. And now as a symbol in her life if she could find what she wanted. Meg was exploring Pinterest, looking at various tattoo designs and locations for herself—definitely not a sleeve. And not in a location that would embarrass her or Jessie. Then the phone rang. Meg picked it up and took the call.

"Hi, Meg. It's Carol from *Bay Area Heartbeat*. I wanted to make sure you knew the article has posted. Did you see it?"

"I didn't. But I'm at my computer, so I'll look at it as soon as we hang up."

"It's getting a lot of great commentary. I think it does both you and your grandmother proud."

"I'm glad. I just wanted to pay tribute to my grandmother," Meg said.

"It does that. Not just the written article. The art is fantastic. You are your grandmother's legacy."

"I don't know about that, but I appreciate you taking the time to do the piece. And for calling me. Thank you."

"You have a good weekend, Meg."

"You too, Carol. And thanks again." They ended the call. And Meg looked online and read the article.

SLOUCHING TOWARD STARDUST WITH MEG THE UNMUZZLED

"Skin"

The body's largest organ. Three layers: 1) epidermis 2) dermis 3) subcutaneous fat layer. With so many physiological functions—protective, storage, regulation, sensory, production of vitamin D. And an illustration of the destructive bigotry of humans. The societal pain of melanin, pigment produced by melanocytes in the epidermis.

The skin as a human canvas. Ink injected into the middle layer—the dermis—because the outer epidermal cells are regularly shed. Those ink particles taken up by macrophages and fibroblasts, clumping between collagen.

The significance of a tattoo. Not just the visual, but the emotional, the personal. The tattooed numbers of Auschwitz survivors—the depraved, involuntary inking of an innocent soul. Or the voluntary inking of chosen art that declares This is who I am. *A chosen tattoo is soul on skin, an ode to self.*

When I find my ode to self, I will have it injected in ink into my dermis. Onto my canvas. A selection of modest artistry for a mature woman still defining herself. And the artist matters.

Because if you're going to wear someone's art for the rest of your life, the artist matters. I know that artist. I am still searching for that ode to self.

CHAPTER EIGHT

Cate woke up on Saturday morning feeling both exhausted and unsettled. She'd left work early yesterday afternoon—something she never did. Piper had noted her distress when Cate came back from her lunch with Pete. Cate felt numb. Pete sure knew how to implement a come-to-Meg moment.

And of course, the conversation Piper had witnessed between her and Pete before they left for lunch would have given even the densest person a hint that something was going on, and Cate knew Piper wasn't dense. She'd assured Cate that the legal practice was in good hands, that Cate should go and have a good weekend. Piper had even patted Cate on the back. Cate had suggested that maybe the plants needed some fluids, especially that barbed one.

Cate knew she needed to go see her father this weekend, so after she was up and showered, she dressed and then packed a small bag. She had some clothes at his house. She wasn't sure if she'd spend Saturday night there or not. She decided that she'd take him to lunch at a restaurant of his choosing. But seeing her father was not the big decision. Talking to Meg was. If Meg would even see her.

The trip across the bay to Trinity Hills was uneventful. It was the weekend, and so she wasn't dealing with commuter traffic, only people heading east to get out of the city for a break. Cate pulled her Audi into The Terraces' parking lot a little before noon. She had called her dad from the car to let him know she was coming. He'd been happy to hear from her and was waiting in the common area when she arrived.

"So, how's my best girl doing?" Her dad pulled her into a big hug. Cate normally didn't think much about those hugs. But she was fragile today, and she let him hold her longer than she usually tolerated. Just for a moment longer.

"Hey, Dad. I'm fine," she assured him. And then tried to assure herself.

"Probably not my business, but I can tell you've got something going on." Her dad studied her.

"Can't a best girl just come see her old man without the third degree?" Cate bumped her dad's shoulder. "Come on. Let's go get some lunch."

Her dad decided he wanted Greek cooking. The restaurant was small, the tables worn, but the staff was friendly and the food was superb. It was cuisine that her father didn't get at The Terraces. They chatted about Cate's legal practice and life at the assisted-living facility. Cate was grateful her dad didn't bring his art teacher up—she already had Meg on her mind without his innocent commentary. After she dropped him back off, she headed to her dad's house.

She hadn't been there in a few weeks, but Cate had arranged for a yard service, and there was an automatic watering system, so everything looked good. Cate needed to catch up on some work-related reading and consider what she might say to Meg. Work up the courage to talk with Meg. Damn, she had no idea what to say, and she was rarely at a loss for words. When in doubt, put up a good front and don't give an inch—that had been her motto. Self-protection. Boy, had Pete done a number on her. To be fair, he'd made her realize that there were some truths in his urging that it was time to face her feelings about what had happened with Laurel, or her misery would never go away.

It was approaching eight o'clock, and Meg could hear her three young adult dinner guests talking and drinking beer out on her back patio—Jessie, Luc, and her nephew Aaron. She wanted to give them some space to talk, so she was sitting in the family room with Oscar, thumbing through an art magazine when her doorbell rang. She wasn't expecting anyone, and when she swung the door open, there stood Cate. And damn, she looked good. She was not in the impeccable business attire that Meg had experienced in the past, but instead, Meg surmised this was the casual Cate. Tight-fitted black jeans that hugged her hips, a black lace-trimmed camisole under a loose, partially unbuttoned white overshirt with the sleeves rolled up to midforearm, and black flats. And her mahogany-hued hair in a ponytail.

"Well, this is unexpected. Is it professional or personal?" Meg asked with a bit of trepidation. Cate's rejection still stung. Studying Cate more closely in the porch light, Meg could see that she exuded uncertainty, rather than her normal in-charge persona. She'd never seen Cate unsure of herself. They stood and looked at each other. Meg waited.

"It's personal, Meg. Very personal. I'm sorry for interrupting—it looks like you might have company. Maybe I should talk with you some other time." Cate looked like she wanted to bolt. Like if she left, she wasn't coming back.

Meg shook her head. "Now's fine." An urge gripped Meg, to grab the obviously unsettled woman and hug her. To hold her because she was drawn to her. But Grace was probably right. This woman needed a Cate whisperer—a slow and trustworthy approach. So Meg stepped back and motioned her in. She led her to sit on the family room couch, held up a finger signaling Cate to wait, then walked over and pulled two goblets from a cupboard and opened the refrigerator in the adjacent kitchen to pour them each a glass of wine. Meg mused that Cate was not going to believe that she rarely drank, but she'd decided they both might need some wine for whatever reason Cate was sitting on her couch.

While she was getting them the drinks, she tried to keep an eye on Cate. She didn't want Cate to spook and leave. And while her back was turned, Oscar wandered in. By the time she'd turned around, he had hopped up on the couch and settled onto Cate's lap. That was the way to schmooze her. Meg could have kissed the cat. It was nice to know that he approved—he was a good judge of character. And maybe Oscar was a Cate whisperer.

"So, you're a cat person?" Meg asked, almost laughing at the initial shocked reaction Cate exhibited when the orange tabby made himself at home on top of her. She set one glass of wine on the coffee table in front of Cate and kept the other.

"Never had a cat in my life. My mother was allergic and wouldn't allow pets." Cate cautiously scratched the top of his head, and Oscar leaned in to her.

"Could have fooled me. Grace and I have been his only fully approved people, and we've put a lot of effort into achieving that status. Oscar's very picky about who he's willing to associate with. And my astute powers of observation suggest that you have his stamp of approval. And that you like him too." Meg smiled. Oscar was the best icebreaker she could have asked for.

"It must be the claws. We have something in common," Cate responded dryly.

Meg looked over the top of her wineglass at Cate. "I'm not going to argue. You wounded me last week." Meg put her free hand over her heart.

Cate took a sip of her wine. Swallowed. "I'm sorry, Meg." She whispered it so softly Meg could barely hear her. At least she wasn't biting.

"I'm sorry too. I'm not sure what I did."

"Honestly, Meg. Nothing. It's me."

"Well, that's a relief. I'd hate to have to admit I ever did anything wrong." Meg grinned as she sat down on the couch next to Cate and her cat, sipping her wine as she listened to the chatter and laughter floating in from the back patio.

"Your kids?" Cate asked.

"Jessie and their partner, Luc. And a couch-surfing nephew who showed up unexpectedly this afternoon. He needed a bed for the night, and I'm just the aunt to provide one. I worry about him." Meg wasn't naive—Aaron had issues. But he'd been a personable kid, and she wanted to treat him like she'd want a relative to treat one of her own children.

"So, I'm not the only stray to darken your doorstep tonight," Cate commented.

"But by far, the best-looking one." That likely wasn't part of the role of being a Cate whisperer. But Meg couldn't help herself.

Cate was now stroking Oscar's back. Meg reached over and rubbed the area behind the feline's ears with her free hand—he deserved a reward. And then Oscar suddenly jumped off the couch, giving Meg what she would have sworn was the cat version of a smirk as Meg's hand dropped into the unanticipated space devoid of a feline body and landed on top of Cate's hand.

The contact was electrical, a charge that Meg saw pass up into

Cate's eyes too. They both sat frozen, hands touching, trying to just figure out the moment, their next move. Meg was now feeling rather confident that she hadn't misread the good night hug in her hotel room. What would a Cate whisperer do? Meg wondered. Then she sat back, gently holding Cate's hand, and slowly sipped her wine. It felt right.

❖

Cate didn't know what to think. She'd never done anything as impetuous as just showing up on someone's front porch, uninvited. Not only rude, but a huge risk of rejection. And yet here she was in Meg's gorgeous home. In her comfortable, lived-in family room. Sipping wine and holding her hand.

She had come to make amends. To grovel—as if she knew how to do that. Not to pet a damn cat. And yet…she liked the cat. Especially now that he'd orchestrated this moment of hand-holding on the couch—and it almost felt like he'd done it on purpose. No way.

Meg's breath had caught when their hands had touched. But she hadn't pulled away. Cate had felt the potency of the intoxicating contact too. It felt good. It felt natural.

Cate cleared her throat. Smiled at Meg. "I saw the *Bay Area Heartbeat* article."

"You did?" Meg seemed surprised.

"I could confess to spending my time in my legal practice combing the internet for interviews with amazing artists, but it was Piper who screeched into my office, aflame with the news that the result of your meeting with the journalist was now online."

Meg blushed. "You liked my artwork?"

Cate collected herself before she spoke. "It made me cry, Meg. So goddamn beautiful. *So* you. And the painting of you as a child by your grandmother. I want to know you better." That was more intimate than Cate had been since Laurel. Maybe she was capable of moving on, of building trust. With this woman.

Meg paused at Cate's words, then gave Cate a teasing look with an eyebrow waggle. "Let me show you my etchings," she suggested.

Oh hell, she was toast. Cate really wanted to know her better. "I'd love to see your etchings, but I've crashed your evening, and you've got your kids here. I should go home to Dad's place."

"The kids will be leaving early in the morning, probably before I'm even up," Meg said. "Why don't you come over and have brunch with me midmorning after I finish my beauty sleep. And I'll show you my studio then."

"If you're sure. I'd love to see it."

"I don't usually share my art, but I'd like to share it with you. Since we've already reached the intimate stage of talking about my orange blobs and all."

Cate laughed. "The legendary orange blobs. I'd like that, Meg. What time?"

"Whenever you get here. I'm not going anywhere. But maybe make it after nine o'clock—a girl has to have time to look her best."

Cate continued to hold Meg's hand. She contemplated leaning over and giving Meg a kiss on the cheek before she left, as close to Meg's mouth as she dared—for both of them. Cate had come out a long time ago, but she still wasn't sure how Meg felt about herself, who she was, what she wanted. She needed to take this slow. Meg was not one-night-stand material—and they hadn't actually even had a first date where they'd agreed to meet. But she was drawn to Meg, and so she leaned toward Meg, sitting on the couch holding her hand. But before her lips grazed the laugh lines at the corner of Meg's mouth, Jessie walked in. Shit, now she'd embarrassed Meg.

Jessie cleared their throat and grinned. "We're heading up to bed, Mom." Jessie was taller but had the same lean build as Meg, a similar face with deep blue eyes, and honey-blond hair. Their hair was cut in a fade, leaving a full curly nest on top. A botanical tattoo in fine black outline and pale colors emerged from the bottom edge of Jessie's T-shirt sleeve and spread down along their left arm to the elbow. It was an engaging piece of ink work. A touch of nature.

Meg seemed to be more relaxed than Cate expected—she didn't relinquish Cate's hand. Maybe because it was Jessie.

"I'll see you in the morning, babe—but before you go upstairs, I want to introduce you two. Cate, this is Jessie, my middle one. Jessie, this is Cate, my friend."

"I'm happy to meet you." Jessie smiled at Cate, then gave their mom a nod.

"I'm thrilled to meet you too, Jessie," Cate replied. Maybe Meg was risking even more than she was.

Slouching Toward Stardust with Meg the unMuzzled

"Adrift"

He tells me he is a pirate. Not quite the image of a pirate: gray and fluorescent orange tennies, dress slacks butchered into shorts, a long-sleeved white blouse with large lace cuffs layered over two tie-dyed T-shirts. Those cuffs flapping out beyond the sleeves of a seen-much-better-days Men's Wearhouse blazer. He makes sure I know it's a Men's Wearhouse blazer. That seems important to him.

Put your seat belt on, I say as I scoop this emaciated, shaved-headed, twenty-four-year-old nephew up out of the BevMo parking lot. Tough guy to find: over an hour of searching, after a truncated phone call—pirates don't carry phones, only use someone else's. He pulls a tattered brown paper sack from his backpack and shows me an apple. Treasure, he boasts. Apple and banana in good shape, found behind a store. Ate the banana. Saving the apple. Do you want some wine? he asks. No thanks, I say as I drive him to my house.

I offer him some dinner. He doesn't turn it down. His skin-and-bones body consumes two plates full. He doesn't turn down a hot shower either. Or clean clothes. Or a night's sleep in a real bed. Let's develop a plan, I suggest. He agrees.

But the next morning is a different day. He has to see the ocean. The ocean. The ocean. It is stuck in his meandering mind. There is no dissuading that wandering pirate's mind. I will find a long-lost friend, he says. Become a rock star. Join the army. Move on to LA. You need to find your long-lost self, I say. He walks to the door. He will walk to the water, if he must. So, his cousin drives him to the ocean. And at the ocean, he floats off into the beachfront town. He is gone. The pirate. The wanderer. This homeless young man who does not want to be found.

CHAPTER NINE

Cate arrived at Meg's house for brunch at half past nine. She'd informed her dad that she had plans for part of the day but that she would see him in the afternoon before she left to return to San Francisco.

"Good morning." Meg waved Cate inside. "Great timing. I did some work on the compuuter after the kids left, coffee's made, and I've figured out what I can offer you for food."

Oscar came out from the family room and executed a right-sided chin-to-hip rub against Cate's lower legs before turning and repeating the sideswipe maneuver with his left side, achieving a whole-body massage.

"It looks like you've made his preferred-people list. I don't know how you did it. Grace and I constantly bribe him with delectable gourmet cat food. What's your secret?" Meg teased.

"I told you last night. Oscar and I are comrades in an elite Clawed Combatant Clique. And maybe there's the mutual recognition of a fellow member of the Meg Mullins Fan Club."

Meg turned and headed toward the kitchen, looking back as Cate followed. "I vote for the Meg Mullins Fan Club. Now let's go in the kitchen and see if I can stay on your good side with a little delectable gourmet bribery."

"So, are you telling me that you invited me over for a meal that requires a can opener?" Cate joked as she noted that Meg looked as good in her Sunday morning sweatpants and scoop-neck T-shirt as she did in her designer clothing.

She loved the casualness of Meg's bare feet with her tan ankles protruding from the elastic cuffs of her fleece wear. She even liked the au naturel look of Meg without any polish on her nails—maybe because daily swimming wasn't compatible. Or with family life, it had fallen off her calendar over the years. Cate's professional lifestyle had her visiting a manicurist and pedicurist on a regular schedule. She appreciated that while gorgeous and complex, Meg was not high-maintenance—she didn't seem to be trying to impress anyone. Cate rarely encountered women that met those criteria. It was enticing.

As they reached the cooking area, Meg gestured for Cate to take a seat at a small dining table, then moved over behind the counter so she could finish the brunch preparations.

"I'm making us cheese and mushroom omelets, unless you don't like cheese or mushrooms, with a fruit side and croissants. And I've got coffee and juice," Meg said. "Sorry, but the can opener belongs to Oscar."

Cate chuckled. "That sounds delicious. I hope you had a good night."

"I did a bit of tossing and turning. Thinking about a little hand-holding." Meg pressed her lips together, but there was a hint of a smile.

"A bad thing?" Cate asked as she considered Meg's expression.

"Not at all. But a bit complicated. Or maybe just novel," Meg offered.

"I get it, Meg. I'm only dealing with me. You've got a lot more people to consider."

"Yeah, but I've been doing that my whole life. Now, nobody is dependent on me."

"And?" Cate prodded.

"And now it's my time to figure out who I am, what I want. And I'm hoping you'll be a part of that."

"At your service, ma'am," Cate sassed.

"Don't *ma'am* me," Meg warned as she wielded the spatula at Cate. "Fifty is old enough without making me feel over the hill. Not with you." Meg stopped, then added in a reflective tone, "I think maybe I'm trying to pick up where I left off at twenty."

"At twenty," Cate repeated. "But with three kids and a conniving cat."

"Exactly. And a few more gray hairs."

"So, we take it slow." Cate took a deep breath. "I've only got me to consider, but I come with baggage. Baggage that makes me skittish as hell. But I want to be happy, and how I'm living my life right now isn't ever going to get me there." Cate paused.

"You don't have to tell me, Cate. The baggage—it's not my business."

Cate sat and scrutinized Meg for a moment, then dove in. "Her name was Laurel. I loved her. But I was a lousy partner. Too busy establishing my law practice. Self-absorbed. We spent nine years together. I was twenty-eight when we met. And then five years ago she gave up on me. I deserved it, looking back." She paused. "I hope I've learned something. But I worry that I haven't learned enough. And I worry that I've been too terrified of the pain to try again."

"Aren't we a hell of a pair? But I like you. And I'm not Laurel. I'm fifty, in case you didn't catch it when I said it a minute ago. Lots of disadvantages to fifty, but one advantage is maturity. And patience. I suspect I can handle your schedule—if I could handle Robert's." Meg swallowed. "But if we start to take this somewhere, please don't cheat on me. Just tell me you need to move on."

"I'm not a cheater. I'd tell you. I confess to very short, no-strings-attached liaisons, by mutual agreement. But I'm forty-two years old and self-absorbed. A workaholic. Rather high-maintenance. And I have claws."

"Now there's an endorsement," Meg responded with a chuckle. "So, shall we agree to just take this slow? As I figure myself out. As you figure out if you even want to put up with me trying to figure myself out. It's important to me that my physical involvement doesn't get way ahead of my emotional involvement. I've learned a lot about myself, and I know that I need the emotional component to keep pace. To make the right decisions for me." Meg took a deep breath with that confession.

"I hear what you're saying, Meg. I'm an impatient sort. I haven't wanted a relationship in years. I don't know what I want, but I guess I'm here for a reason." Then thinking of Pete, Cate quietly added, "I hope so."

Meg set the plated food on the table. "Can I get you coffee or juice?"

"I had coffee when I got up. A small glass of juice would be perfect. This looks wonderful." Cate watched Meg pour herself a cup of coffee and add soy milk.

Glancing out into the family room, Cate asked, "Why don't you have a lot of paintings on your walls?"

Meg sat down and stirred the soy milk into her coffee. "Robert's taste in art was completely different from mine. Large, loud, abstract. I took it down after he died—it was expensive, so I donated it. I've recently repainted and updated many of the rooms to a style I'm happier with, and I'll add the art when I'm done with that." Meg took a sip from her mug.

"That makes perfect sense. I'd just love to see your taste in art hanging on your walls." Cate smiled at Meg.

And with that, they turned the conversation to talking about the kids leaving earlier that morning, and Jessie not seemingly bothered by Cate's presence last evening. Meg shared that it wasn't Jessie or Ben that she was worried about so much as she came to terms with who she was, but it was Natalie and her evangelical beliefs. Meg told Cate that her nephew, Aaron, had insisted on heading to the coast instead of inland to his parents' home. They discussed Cate's job, and the scope of her work in her legal practice. That she volunteered time to do some pro bono legal work for people who found themselves needing help with IRS issues but unable to afford a lawyer. And when they had finished eating, they cleared the table and headed to the back of the house—to view Meg's *etchings*.

❖

Oscar led Cate and Meg down the hall to the back room that Meg had converted into her art studio. As they entered, Meg took in what she knew Cate was seeing for the first time. With its white walls, high ceiling, and wide, north-facing window, it was perfect for an art area. Across the room from the door, there was a long art table against the wall with a chair, the table covered with a few in-progress projects and paints and brushes. A large oak chest rested against the wall to the right, more art supplies on top. And shelves to the left of the door were filled with containers of additional paints, brushes, pencils, and other equipment, as well as books. A six-drawer flat file was tucked back in a corner next to the large oak chest. A few framed works were stacked against empty wall space around the room, and a few unframed studies were tacked on the walls and stacked on an easel.

Framed and hanging on the wall to the left was the original painting of Meg as a child, painted by her grandmother. Meg watched Cate pause and focus on it.

"This is the Josie Burke watercolor from the *Bay Area Heartbeat* article," Cate noted as she blinked a few times. "To be honest, this portrait helped lead me here today. It adds such a touch of joy to your studio. It's so beautiful."

As Oscar jumped onto the far-right end of the art table and settled into his cat bed, Meg was pleased with Cate's words about her childhood portrait, not because the image was her, but because she thought the beauty was in the love the painting represented. Her grandmother's love.

"So, what do you think?" Meg asked, waving her hand at the room.

"I think I want to see more of your art," Cate answered. "You're amazing. And I want to get to know the woman that the girl in the painting has become."

"Well, let me start by telling you about my studio," Meg offered. "I've never shared my studio with anyone except Grace and the kids, and the kids only stick their heads into the room when they're looking for me. This was an office space that I converted about a year ago into my own dedicated art area." Meg was so thrilled that Cate was interested in her art—Cate was not like Robert. And then there was the fact that Cate had the Golden Gate watercolor hanging in her office. Meg couldn't believe that art seemed to be another connection.

She took a deep breath and continued the tour. "You can see some of my pieces sitting around the room. Here on the table, I have a painting I'm just starting—a botanical effort of some drying leaves that I wanted to try. Lots of character, and it will be a good challenge in an array of browns, golds, yellows, and maybe a hint of a few other hues too. I'm also doing an anatomical study—a sketch of the bones in the human hand. Just an interest from the little biology I've had," Meg explained. "I've been working hard to educate myself about the composition of various organisms. A personal interest and helpful for improving my art."

Cate slowly turned around, taking in the room, nodding her appreciation of Meg's studio. "I'm glad that you're updating the rest of your house to your personal tastes, but this studio is what really reveals who you are. It feels like your heart and soul."

Meg loved that Cate understood the importance this room played in her life. She grinned at Cate, then continued the tour. "Over here I have a collage I've just about completed, and if you follow me to my flat file, I can show you some finished pieces." Meg pulled out a large stack of watercolors from one drawer, including those in the online article, as well as landscapes of hills, vineyards, and the coast; still life paintings ranging from flowers, to fruit, to glassware; and animal studies including birds, farm animals, and wildlife. Meg opened another drawer and revealed some ink drawings. Then she pulled a spiral notebook from a drawer in the large oak chest and flipped through pages of graphite drawings of local scenes and animal sketches.

"And that concludes the grand tour, Cate," Meg told her. "My hobby."

"For yourself," Cate murmured, repeating what Meg had told her about her art when she'd first been in Cate's office.

"Yeah. For myself," Meg affirmed.

"I get that you do the art for yourself. But it's so good…you should be sharing it with the world."

"That boat has sailed. And I'm at peace with that." Meg looked away from Cate. She wanted to be at peace with that.

"And now for those etchings." Cate grinned, giving Meg a hip bump. Meg appreciated that she was lightening the mood.

"Oh, you're smart enough to know that's always a ploy to get the beautiful woman alone in a studio." Meg winked at Cate.

"Well, in that case…" And Cate leaned in, took Meg by the shoulders, and gently planted her lips on Meg's lips. Meg closed her eyes and kissed her back for a long moment, then moved her lips across Cate's jawline in a soft featherlight caress.

Meg heard Cate moan and then inhale before Cate pulled back unhurriedly and said, "Thanks, beautiful woman. If we are going to take this slow, I need to get out of here now. Before I can't."

Meg took a step back and shook her head. "Damn. I'm glad there's one adult in the room."

Cate laughed. "It's probably a first for me. I'd have pegged you for the adult in the room. Although I'd kind of like to hope that maybe you're not. At least sometimes."

"The last date for me that included a first kiss, I ended up pregnant," Meg replied with a chuckle.

"Well, I don't think that's an issue. You're the biology expert, though." Cate gestured toward the anatomical hand study that Meg had left out on her art table.

"I do need time to figure things out, Cate. I don't want either of us getting hurt. We're just starting to get to know each other better, and I need that emotional relationship. Be patient with me," Meg implored.

"I'll try. I haven't done anything for a long time except be impatient and self-gratifying. A person who called the shots with no strings attached, for the past five years. I probably need to figure things out too. But you need to know, today's been amazing."

Those were words Meg wanted to hear. She felt the same way. She took Cate's hand and led her back to the living room. They hugged each other, and Cate promised she'd call Meg in the upcoming week when she had some time and would plan to see her the next weekend when she came back to town to see her dad. Then Cate winked and slipped out the front door.

Meg leaned back against the door and realized she was feeling a lot more like a teenager than a mature fifty-year-old woman. Oscar sauntered back down the hall and rubbed against her bare ankles. Meg picked him up and scratched his head. "Life is complicated, but looking up, old man. Looking up." Meg danced around the living room with the cat, then waltzed him back down the hallway to her art studio where she'd just shared the most promising kiss of her lifetime, with exuberant expectations for more. She spent the rest of the afternoon laying down the sky for a landscape she planned to paint. And then she spent some time after dinner writing a blog about that sky. Not a blue sky, but a sky tinged with the sweet, sweet glow of hope.

❖

When she arrived back at her apartment in San Francisco that evening, after seeing her dad and stopping at the grocery store, Cate took a deep breath, picked up her phone, and called Pete.

"And to what do I owe the pleasure of this call, Counselor?" Pete answered on the second ring.

"I just wanted to thank you for orchestrating the come-to-Meg moment." Cate waited for Pete's reaction. She knew he'd probably gloat.

"Whoa. Is this Catherine Colson, Attorney at Law actually offering me a thank you?" Pete asked.

Cate cleared her throat. "It is."

"So, you must have talked to Meg."

"I did."

"And it went okay?" Pete asked.

"It did." Cate repeated her succinct response.

"This must be the dental surgery phase—after the cardiac surgery phase, huh? Like pulling teeth." Pete chuckled.

"Okay, I owe you. What do you want to know?" Cate had known that Pete would give her the third degree when she placed the call. But she was indebted to her old friend—pain in the ass that he was sometimes.

"Did you see her?" Pete asked.

"Yes, I saw her this weekend. I went to see my dad and saw her too." Cate paused, then added, "Twice."

Pete whistled. "Twice?"

"Yes, Pete. She had kids there on Saturday evening when we first talked, so I went back on Sunday morning and she cooked me brunch." Cate knew Pete was enjoying this.

"Brunch is good," Pete offered. "So, are you going to see her again?"

"I am."

Pete whistled again. He was just so damned pleased with himself.

"We talked about things. My issues regarding Laurel. Meg figuring out who she is. Taking it slow. Just up your alley. Touchy-feely." Cate knew Pete would love that.

"Touchy-feely. I like the sound of that," Pete teased her.

"Oh, shut up." Cate smiled as she admonished him. Pete was incorrigible.

"You're telling me you have hopes of a love life. And after all I've done, you're going to owe me every detail."

"Not happening. I never kiss and tell. You know that," Cate scolded him.

Pete whined into the phone, "I bought you lunch. A glass of wine. Remember? I want details."

Cate laughed. "You'll just have to interpret the bounce in my step. The twinkle in my eye."

"You're killing me. How will I know you don't just have a rock in your shoe? Soap in your eye?"

"Can't help you out there. But I do want to thank you. I owe you lunch. And a glass of wine," Cate offered.

"That you do. Just name the date. And I'm happy for you, Cate. And proud of you—you bona fide heartless bitch." Cate could hear the teasing in Pete's voice.

Cate had the feeling that this was going to be Pete's signature sign-off from now on. He was still laughing when they ended the call.

SLOUCHING TOWARD STARDUST WITH MEG THE UNMUZZLED

"After the Blue"

Watercolor is my therapy. My therapists are Daniel Smith, Da Vinci, Holbein, Sennelier, Winsor & Newton. All tubes of pigment suspended in a gum arabic binder.

I want to paint a sky. Life is looking up—so not the storms of the past. Not the aching depths of blue. I want a caress of warmth. A glow of hope. A reflection of joy. So, I select quinacridone rose along with ultramarine and cerulean blue...a kiss of red for that mingle of love by the end of the journey.

First, I dip and load the sable-hair brush in the bowl of clear, clean water. This bristled instrument of the heart, a sacred heirloom from my grandmother. Creating puddles of pigment where the bristles will drink before leaving those strokes of heaven.

From the heights, I spread the mix of blues, left to right, across the tilted page. I reload at each completion, catching the bead of the previous swipe as I build each lower layer. Every step of the pilgrimage dependent on the previous.

I work my way down the page toward the horizon, adding more water, grading the wash, weighting the ether hue. As I descend the upper atmosphere, richer at the home of the stars, paler at the hem of the sky, I acknowledge the layers of blue I have known. Needing something different. Striving for something more.

And after the blue, as I prime each brushstroke with quinacridone rose tinged water, I drop that caress of warmth into the sky. Wet into wet. With a careful touch, the heavens display the blush of mild rose tint—a subtle, but significant change. A glow of hope. A reflection of joy. And a mingle of love dances on the page. My grandmother would have been pleased.

CHAPTER TEN

Cate came into work early on Monday morning and put a new little cactus on Piper's desk. She'd seen it in the floral section of the grocery store the night before when she'd stopped to buy a few items, and she couldn't pass the tiny plant up. She hated to define the purchase, but she knew it was an offering for what her paralegal had to put up with, and for her efforts to take care of Cate last Friday after the lunch with Pete. Cate couldn't go so far as to bring herself to buy some lush, ornate, scented plant because she had an image to maintain, but she hoped Piper might appreciate her gesture for what it was. She didn't leave the gift in the reception area but took it back to the desk in Piper's personal office—she wanted Piper to know that it was a hand-selected offering from Cate without having to work out what to say. Cate had never done appreciation well at work—it was so much easier to just be the boss. After depositing the offering in the center of Piper's desk, Cate headed into her own sanctum to get some work done.

Cate was deep into an opinion letter for a client when she heard Piper arrive about a half hour later. Nobody ever arrived at the legal office with the unique entry of Piper—the whoosh of the door at Piper's breakneck entry, the noisy clomp of her boots, the soft hum of her voice. Cate continued to work as she listened to Piper move around, water the plants after a long weekend, check the area where Cate sometimes left requests or work for her. Then she heard Piper's boots retreat down to her office.

A loud squeal followed before the clamor of footfalls landed Piper at Cate's door. "Did someone just hurt a pig?" Cate asked, without raising her gaze from her paperwork.

"No, Cate. Just me."

Cate. Not *boss*. That was encouraging, if only because it meant Piper liked the little plant.

Piper swung the door open from its partially closed position and walked in, a huge grin on her face. "I know it's from you, Cate. You don't have to fess up. But it's perfect. Thank you. And I hope you're feeling better."

Cate looked up from her work. "I have no idea what you're referring to. But I'll take credit. I've recovered from whatever ailment caught up with me—did anything of notice happen on Friday afternoon while I was out?"

"Nope. I managed just fine. I wasn't sure if I should come in today or not. Since you fired me on Friday…again." Piper chuckled as she stood there.

"I think you have a new needle-infested twig to place out in that jungle before you get on with it," Cate responded.

"Oh no, boss. That little baby is going to stay on my desk. To remind me that you've got a heart the next time you fire me."

Oh God, now Piper was accusing her of having a heart. Was that another result of The Meg Effect? Cate found herself biting her cheeks to keep from smiling. What had Meg done to her?

And it was only Monday morning. Meg was several days away.

❖

It wasn't until Tuesday afternoon when Grace caught up with her—to pick up the lasagna pan—that they had a chance to get together.

"Sorry I've been so busy," Grace said as she entered Meg's house. They headed into the family room and sat on the couch. "This weekend—no rest for the wicked. Ashley came home to introduce her new boyfriend to us, John's parents came through town and took us to dinner Saturday night, I had to handle two open houses on Sunday." Grace stopped to take a breath. "How are you doing, sweetie?"

Grace set Oscar down after she'd placed him on her lap for some love. The cat had charged over from his family room bed as soon as he'd heard Grace's voice. Once the feline was back on the floor, Grace stopped to study Meg.

"You're looking a lot better than last time I saw you. What gives?" Grace smiled.

Meg wanted to play things low-key. "My nephew Aaron came through Trinity Hills Saturday, and I spent a while driving around to find him so he could spend the night. Remember Robert's sister, Martha? Aaron is her son—twenty-four years old. He's been a drifter, as the kids say, for a while. Jessie and Luc drove over from Santa Clara to see him. They all spent Saturday night, and then Jessie and Luc ended up taking him to Santa Cruz when he refused to go home and insisted on the beach instead."

"Well, that couldn't be what has you looking so ravishing. Or should I say ravished?" Grace gave Meg a pretend leer.

Meg laughed. "Damn, no secrets from you." Meg had never been one to go into explicit detail regarding her sex life, but just the memory of kissing Cate created a need at her core.

"So, what gives?" Grace demanded. "We haven't been friends for this many years without learning how to read each other."

"I don't think it's just friendship that's trained you in people reading. I think it's those impressive foster animal skills," Meg told her.

"Ah...so was the Cate whisperer at work this weekend?" Grace guessed.

"If there's a Cate whisperer in this house, it's my cat. You'd have thought Oscar had a degree in matchmaking."

Grace reached down and picked Oscar up again. "So, what did you do, ol' boy?" When Oscar didn't answer, she turned to Meg. "Okay, spill."

"Cate came by Saturday evening. While the kids were out on the back patio visiting and drinking a little beer." Meg smiled as she remembered all that had happened with Cate over the weekend: her arrival, the hand-holding, brunch, sharing her art, the kiss.

"Well, looking at you, I'd say that was good," Grace commented. "Did you kiss and make up?"

As Meg felt her face flush, Grace chuckled and declared, "You did. Literally."

"As I said, damn, no secrets from you." Maybe no secrets, but Meg wasn't about to spill the specifics. It had been so good, but private.

"Okay," Grace prompted. "Talk to me."

"Oscar got us sitting together on the couch Saturday night, but it was chaotic with the kids. So she agreed to come over for brunch on Sunday and we talked. And you were right—she has her baggage, but so do I. Her shutting me out was a reaction to that. Anyway, for whatever reason, she says she wants to get to know me better. Take a risk. We talked a long time."

"Well, hot damn." Grace was elated.

"Remember, Grace—you promised you'd let me run my own love life from now on." Meg exchanged a look with Grace, one that implored her to understand.

"I did, sweetie. And I will," Grace responded. "But can't I be happy for you?"

"I'd hope so," Meg said. Meg welcomed Grace's happiness for what had happened. She just wasn't ready to talk about what had been a personal, special moment. That was between Cate and her—and Oscar.

"We both agreed to take it slow, get to know each other, because we've barely spent any time together. And I've got to figure myself out. Consider three kids."

"I get it, sweetie," Grace said.

"I do think the art, my grandmother's paintings, and the article connected with her. I showed her my studio. My work. And she liked it." Meg couldn't help but smile at her memory of their time in her studio.

"Hey, what's not to love? You're amazing, Meg."

"Says my best friend." Meg chuckled. "Anyway, it was a good weekend."

"I'm glad. I think waiting for Cate to come to you was the right move."

"I agree. I think Cate's figuring things out, just like I am. Quite a pair," Meg offered.

"Yeah, quite a pair." Grace chortled as she grinned at Meg.

"And to change the subject, I haven't felt the desire to buy a new dress in a long time. I haven't had a need for one. I need help picking something out that doesn't flaunt my fifty years. I'm thinking I'd like to go shopping. Do you have time to go with me?" Meg asked.

"I don't think you're changing the subject. The subject is still Cate. And I'd love to go shopping with you. For a Cate acquisition dress. What are best friends for?" They agreed to go shopping the next afternoon.

❖

Wednesday evening, Meg stopped to reflect on her weekend interactions with Cate. She'd seen Cate totally vulnerable and so unsure of herself when she'd arrived on Saturday evening—a side of Cate that she never exposed. That had taken guts. The connection she'd felt after Oscar's stunt on the couch—Meg had not felt that kind of physical attraction in years, if ever. Just a touch of the hands. Their talking over brunch. Cate's genuine interest in her artwork. Meg liked Cate. She was both personally and physically attracted to her—and the feelings only increased the more they interacted.

Meg also understood that rushing things could be a disaster, at least for her. She couldn't stand to be another one of the many no-strings-attached encounters that seemed to have become Cate's modus operandi after her breakup with Laurel. Meg knew she wanted strings. At this stage of her life, she needed strings. Cate sounded like she'd come to terms with the risk of strings too, at least intellectually. Meg needed a strong emotional bond before she slept with Cate. She needed her heart to be involved, for Cate's heart to be involved. She'd just have to make sure her body didn't overrule her head when it came to Cate. The woman was sexy as hell.

Meg's logical side was pleased with their discussion—that she had managed to make no promises, just that she was willing to try to figure herself out, and to get to know Cate, to build a relationship with a strong emotional component, the very thing that Cate had avoided for years. So, Meg acknowledged again that the course they'd agreed upon—learning more about each other, seeing how each of them might fit into the other's life—was what she required, and hopefully Cate would feel she was worth it. But that didn't mean that building those strings couldn't be fun, a touch of flirty, and a bit of slow burn as they explored the relationship. Meg needed that too. But damn, fifty was a lot more complicated than twenty.

Later that evening, after writing a blog, Meg decided to get out her phone and send a text. She didn't want to disturb Cate, but she'd like to build those strings if Cate wasn't busy. Because she missed Cate.

Meg: *Thinking about you. How are you feeling?*
Cate: *Regretful.*
Meg: *I'm so sorry.*
Cate: *No, you idiot. Regretting that I was the adult in the room.*
Meg: *Thank God you aren't regretful. And someone had to be the adult.*
Cate: *But I don't want to be.*
Meg: *Hey! Did you just call me an idiot?*
Cate: *No ma'am.*
Meg: *There's that ma'am again. Maybe I'm too old for you.*
Cate: *No way. You're perfect. Smarter & wiser. Giving us a chance for something to grow.*
Meg: *Smarter. Wiser. Tell that to my kids.*
Cate: *And Oscar. How's Oscar tonight?*
Meg: *Oscar says he misses you.*
Cate: *I miss that conniving cat too.*
Meg: *Conniving? How do you know I didn't train him?*
Cate: *Because he's a cat.*
Meg: *There is that.*
Cate: *I want to hear some purring.*
Meg: *Mm-hmm.*
Cate: *Do a little back stroking.*
Meg: *Mm-hmm.*
Cate: *That, and more—with his person.*
Meg: *Mm-hmmmm.*
Cate: *Seriously. But I know I need to be careful with you. I'm a serious person.*
Meg: *And a boss.*
Cate: *You're right. Forget the adult in the room. I like being a boss better. I'm good at bossy.*
Meg: *Mm-hmmmmmmmm. You're good at this.*
Cate: *Now you're making me crazy. Good night, Meg Mullins.*
Meg: *Good night, Cate Colson...until next time.*

Slouching Toward Stardust with Meg the unMuzzled

"The Appraisal"

I wasn't usually one to dwell on my age. But lately I'd been feeling the passage of time—not that time hadn't been passing at the same rate my entire life. No, it was more the stacking of years, one on top of the other. As I looked in the dressing room mirror, I saw every flaw. And at age fifty, there were many...the slight pooch of my abdomen that emphasized I'd had multiple kids, the hint of crepe papering on my arms, the downward shift of my bustline, the wrinkles on my face. Hell, the person in the mirror was looking more and more like my mother.

As I stood there after dwelling on my mortality, my friend knocked on the dressing room door. "You doing okay in there? How does the dress fit?"

I opened the door and my friend grinned at me. "Gorgeous," she said. "You're gorgeous."

"I'm old," I told her.

"No, you're not. You've raised three amazing children, you have the laugh lines to prove you've known joy, you've grown from teenage perfection into a work of art that is so much more interesting than flawless juvenile beauty. So much deeper. You're a ten," my friend told me. "An absolute ten."

"I think I'll take the dress." I smiled.

CHAPTER ELEVEN

Thursday morning Meg's Oscar alarm head-bumped her until she was wide awake. She kissed the ochre boy and crawled out of bed. Once she had fed him, she headed to the pool and swam her laps. Afterward, as she sat in her kitchen at the counter sipping her smoothie, Meg realized that Cate was occupying more and more of her thoughts—she couldn't get Cate out of her head. She had told Cate she wanted to progress slowly, to get to know each other better. And the more she knew Cate, the more she liked her. Their relationship was evolving, and Meg liked where it was going. She already knew that Cate was making her consider the things she'd begun to consider decades ago but never pursued after she became pregnant and the subsequent marriage to Robert.

There was no doubt in Meg's mind that she loved her kids—that she wouldn't change the course her life had taken because of them. But she was now coming to terms with this major shift in herself, a change precipitated by Cate. She finally had the luxury of reexamining what she wanted—it wasn't what she'd had with Robert, and it wasn't being alone. She was relieved that she no longer wanted to just do what was best for her family, as she had done for thirty years, but that it was now time to do what was best for herself. Meg's grown children were a huge piece of who she was, but she couldn't let them dictate her life now that they were independent and living their own lives. She was finding peace with this shift, with the increased desire to try to build a new life with Cate in it.

Meg recognized the chemistry she had with Cate, how she felt when they were together. She acknowledged that they were very different people. Cate was eight years younger than her. She was a stunning, smart, very successful lawyer—with claws at times, but so much compassion too, although Cate often seemed reluctant to reveal that side of herself. Meg suspected she could tame the claws, not that she didn't appreciate a little attitude. Hell, she'd lived with Robert for twenty-eight years, and he was the incarnation of claws—she could handle Cate. That epiphany of a life with Cate as a partner was really taking hold if by some miracle Cate really wanted that too.

The only advantage to being fifty was that it brought some maturity. Some insight. Meg knew that this was not about all the what-ifs. Not about all the other people in her life. This was between Cate and her. That was the insight she needed to focus on—where fifty years had led her. She knew what she saw in Cate, what she was feeling about Cate. But what the hell did Cate see in her? Meg had never had a profession—Cate was the epitome of a professional woman. Meg had only had a domestic life with three kids who could deeply mire a relationship with Cate if they made an effort to do so. Meg couldn't let that hinder what was happening between Cate and her. And these were the things that Meg was contemplating when the phone rang.

She glanced at her vibrating phone's display: unknown caller.

"Good morning. This is Meg Mullins."

"Margaret Mullins, granddaughter of Josie Burke?" inquired the pleasant voice of an unknown woman.

"That's me. But you can call me *Meg*."

"Hi, Meg. My name is Olivia. I'm co-owner of Legends Art Gallery here in San Francisco. We're the gallery that represented your grandmother on the West Coast. She also sold paintings across the country out of other galleries—she had a great reputation as an artist. But we worked with her here in San Francisco."

Meg's interest was piqued. "I remember your gallery from when I was much younger. I know it's an important San Francisco gallery. How can I help you?"

"I saw the article in *Bay Area Heartbeat*. I loved it, and I want to talk to you in person. Not over the phone. Is there any chance we can meet here at the gallery sometime soon?"

Meg was curious. Could there actually be a chance of becoming a professional? The Mona Lisa Meg that Robert had kidded? Meg didn't want to even think about it, in case that was not what this call was about. At least Cate had taken her art seriously.

Trying not to get her hopes up, Meg responded, "How would next Tuesday around two o'clock work for you?"

"That would be perfect. I'll see you Tuesday at two o'clock, then. I'm looking forward to meeting you."

"I'll see you then. And thank you, Olivia." Meg ended the call and just sat for a bit, placing Oscar on her lap and scratching his ears. Could her life possibly be picking up where she'd left it thirty years ago? Well, not exactly—deceased husband, three kids, one old cat.

"Well, Oscar, what do you think? I know it's almost too much to desire: Cate and a little recognition of my art. But I'm hoping."

Oscar purred and rubbed his head against her clavicle. Then he gave her his amber-eyed stare before finally wanting her to set him down.

"I take that as agreement, old man. I'm glad you're on my side." Meg smiled as the feline wandered off.

❖

Cate realized that she was overwhelmed with work by Thursday afternoon. She had an important appointment with one of her clients next Monday morning, and she had a large stack of associated materials sitting on the desk in front of her that she hadn't studied yet. She needed to spend the weekend working so that she'd be prepared. It was part of her personal code—she was always prepared. That's what made her great at her job.

However, there was Meg to consider. And her father, although he understood her schedule and her priorities. But it was Meg who infiltrated her thoughts. Who pulled at her heart. And who derailed her professional drive. Meg would probably be pleased with the first two— but derailing her professional drive? It was memories of Laurel that made Cate consider the last. *Cate, you're an insensitive, work-obsessed jackass.* Those were Laurel's final words to her as she had walked out the door. She didn't know how to do relationships, how to balance her legal life with a personal life. Oh hell, how could she be so deep into Meg and not admit it would only end badly? Cate continued to fret.

"Hey, boss. I know you'd like an update on how that needle-infested twig is doing. Anonymous donor and all. Status report: magnificently." Piper sauntered into Cate's office and gave her an appraising look. "What's up with you today anyway?" Piper asked as she unloaded some additional paperwork that Cate had requested. "You can't be stressing over a simple client issue."

Cate frowned. "It's complicated."

"So, you're not just your usual grumpy self. It must be Meg if it's complicated," Piper mused. "You don't find legal work complicated."

Piper was too damn aware for her own good. "Don't make me fire you again today," Cate growled.

Piper laughed. "That's your answer to everything. But you can't fire Meg. She doesn't work for you. She just likes you."

"So, what's your answer, smarty-pants?" Cate nailed Piper with a glare.

"Simple, boss. Talk to her. You're so good at talking law. I think you need to learn how to talk love."

What the hell? "Have you ever seen me do love?" Cate demanded.

"Maybe it's not love yet, boss. But I don't think you'd suck at it. Just talk to her."

"Out," Cate ordered as she pointed at the door. "I pay you to be my paralegal. Not my therapist."

"It's called adulting, Cate. Do the adult thing. Just talk to her." Piper headed out of the office and closed the door most of the way.

Damn. *Adult*—there was that word again. And from Piper.

She drummed her fingers on her desktop. It couldn't be that easy. She didn't know how to do easy. But she might as well get this over with. Cate picked up her phone.

"Hi, Meg. It's Cate."

"Hey, Cate. I'm hoping this a *personal* call," Meg drawled.

God, she loved the sound of Meg's drawl. "It is personal, but probably not what you're going to want to hear. I'm calling about this weekend. I feel terrible. I've got a big meeting on Monday and a weekend worth of work to do," Cate explained.

"So, you're not coming to Trinity Hills this weekend?" Meg asked.

"I can try to make it out Saturday night if I get enough done. See you a bit, and my dad too. But it depends on how much I accomplish here." Cate couldn't keep the unhappiness out of her voice.

"Can I offer a solution?" Meg inquired.

"Sure," Cate responded. "What are you thinking? I really do want to spend time with you. I'm just not good at this."

"Hey. I lived with Robert. I *am* good at this. But if you two-time me in a side apartment, they'll never find the body," Meg wryly advised.

"Then I'd better behave." Cate chuckled. Meg was making her feel better already. "So, what's your proposal?"

"Well, I just had a call from someone named Olivia at Legends Art Gallery in San Francisco. That was the main West Coast gallery that showed and sold my grandmother's work. She wants to meet with me. Uh...after the *Bay Area Heartbeat* article." Meg sounded uncertain.

Meg must still be having doubts about how good she was. "That's wonderful news." Cate knew how good she was.

"They just want to talk to me. So, I'm not sure what their agenda is. But I'm coming to San Francisco on Tuesday to meet with this Olivia in the afternoon at two o'clock."

"Wow. This sounds promising," Cate enthused.

"I'm waiting to hear what they want before I get excited." Meg's tone remained low-key.

"So, what about this weekend? I want to try."

"I'm thinking you stay in the city this weekend. I'll come in Tuesday morning, and maybe we can go out to lunch if that works for you. And if you're okay with it, I'll take your dad out to lunch one day this weekend. I like Cliff, and he knows me from the art class—it should be fun for both of us."

Holy crap, this woman was too good to be true. "Are you sure? I don't want to blow up any chance of a relationship," Cate responded.

"I get it. You're a busy person. There's a law practice you're juggling, and I have three grown children that I have to juggle a bit too. We have to cut each other some slack or throw in the towel right now. And I don't want to do that," Meg stated. "I want another kiss," she quietly added. "And more."

"Well damn, where have you been all my life?" Cate was feeling a surge of optimism. Maybe they could make this work. Meg certainly wasn't Laurel.

"So, we'll text or talk this weekend. I'll catch up with your dad, entertain him a bit. I like him. And I'll plan to see you late Tuesday morning about eleven o'clock at your office if that's okay. Then we can go to lunch. Does that work for you?"

"It's perfect. Thanks. I feel so much better," Cate told her.

"Good," Meg said. "I'll talk to you soon, then."

"Hey, Meg?"

"Yeah?"

"Not soon enough."

❖

On Saturday just before noon, Meg headed into the assisted living facility and collected Cliff. She was looking forward to spending some time with Cate's father, getting to know him better. She noted how handsome and self-assured he was for a man who was in his mideighties. He was casually attired in comfortable tan khakis and a blue button-up shirt that complemented those Colson eyes that she loved—that umber iris with the captivating flecks of burnt sienna.

She led Cliff to her car and made sure he was strapped in before they headed out of the parking lot. "I hope you're okay with this," Meg said, glancing over at him.

"You don't know how pleased I was when Cate called me and told me the plan," he told her.

"I'm happy to have lunch with you. I enjoy going out to eat—and with the Picasso of my class. Can't beat that," Meg responded.

"I love your art class, and I'm positive lunch will be fun. I kind of feel like teacher's pet. Can't complain about getting ahead of the other art students." Cliff chuckled.

"Hey, don't think this is an automatic A, putting up with me and all. I'm a hard grader. Gotta see if you're up for a hamburger first," she teased him.

"I'd love a hamburger," he told her. "With lettuce and tomatoes, and french fries on the side."

"You've got it." Meg reflected on the fact that Cate's dad was fun to be with. She was enjoying herself.

"Just don't tell Cate about the fries. She'd make me get apple slices, or something healthy," Cliff divulged.

"It's our secret. I won't tell if you don't tell," Meg promised.

When they arrived at the restaurant, they walked inside together and were seated. Since they had agreed on hamburgers already, it only took a moment to place their orders. The waitress brought them each the water they requested, and as they were waiting for their food, Cliff cleared his throat.

"Can I talk to you, Meg?" Cate's father had sobered.

"Sure. What is it?"

"I know that Cate is a lesbian, but I'm not sure about you. I think you have a family."

Meg suspected where this was going. "I'm a widow with three grown children."

"Are you straight?" Cliff asked. He wasn't a man to beat around the bush.

Meg choked on her water. This was the first time she'd had to face the hard questions. In their conversations, Grace hadn't cornered her with specific questions about her sexuality, and she was pretty sure Jessie had an inkling after last weekend that she and Cate weren't simply friends, but they hadn't talked. She might as well not shy away from the topic.

"I don't think so. I've been trying to figure myself out, especially since I met Cate. I don't want to say anything she might not be comfortable with, but I will say that I want to know her better," Meg replied.

"And how does Cate feel?" Cliff studied her.

Meg understood that he was worried about his daughter, wanted to better understand Meg and Cate's relationship. "I think she wants to know me better too," she told him. "But to be honest, I'm wondering what Cate sees in me. I'm older, have never been a professional, and have three adult children to complicate things."

"I like you, Meg. Before I even knew that you and Cate had something going on. I just want to say that she's fragile. I've never seen her with another woman since, uh…"

"Since Laurel." Meg finished the sentence.

"That's good. She's talked to you about Laurel, then?" Cliff let out a deep breath. He seemed to be struggling with trying to find the appropriate level of inquiry into this topic.

"She has." This conversation was an indication of just how concerned he was about his daughter. He loved Cate. Just as she loved her adult children.

Cliff looked into Meg's eyes. "Just don't break her heart."

"I'll do my best not to. I really like your daughter, and I want more."

"Okay. Just so I had my say." Cliff seemed to relax a bit.

"I hear you. I don't want anyone's heart to be broken. This is not a game for me. Okay?" Meg smiled at him. She was glad Cate had a father who had her best interests at heart.

"Good. Here's our lunch. I hope there's ketchup for those fries." And with that, Cliff changed the subject, and they enjoyed their food while talking about The Terraces, baseball, Cliff's former occupation as a landscaper, and how the area had changed since he was a youngster growing up in the Bay Area. She enjoyed the time they spent together.

Afterward, Meg dropped Cliff off at the assisted living facility and headed home to finish some weekend chores. It had been a good encounter, and she'd promised him that they'd do it again. She'd had fun on the one-on-one lunch date with Cate's dad. And it had given her a bit of insight into Cate's family.

❖

On Tuesday morning, Meg left Trinity Hills after an early swim and arrived in the city in time to make it to Cate's office by eleven o'clock. She parked her car in a nearby garage, and on her walk to Cate's work, she attracted a stray dog that followed her to the legal office. Meg arrived with the dog in tow because she couldn't just leave him out there on the street. Cate brought Meg and the mutt into her office past Piper, closed the door, and assessed the dog and Meg. Then leaning into her, Cate gave her a prolonged hug. Meg apologized for bringing the stray along, but she hadn't known what else to do. Cate told her that she was happy to order sandwiches and share an intimate lunch at her desk with Meg. Cate left for a bit, returning with a bowl of water and a towel that she put on the floor, and the dog curled up and slept. Cate sat in her office chair, and Meg sat across the desk in the same chair she had used during her prior visit.

Piper gave a loud knock before opening Cate's door and inquiring about the dog, then reached down to pat him on the head, but only after she had given Meg a smile and turned to Cate with a wink and a thumbs-up.

"He looks like a stray," Piper offered. "Even lost a leg somewhere on his journey, the poor guy."

"Yes, he looks like he needs a home," Meg responded.

"My mom's been wanting a mature dog and not a rambunctious pup. Would it be okay if I called and left my number at the local humane society and rescue groups with a picture of him, just in case he does have an owner, and then see if my mom is interested?" Piper asked.

"That would be wonderful. I've got Oscar, and I'm not ready to take on a dog right now, but I couldn't leave him out on the street. I'll take him home if I need to," Meg said.

"I can also see if he has a microchip tomorrow," Piper added before she snapped a picture of the dog with her phone and went out to get to work on making sure he was taken care of.

Cate leaned back in her chair and gazed across her desk at Meg. "It's been a hell of a long week and a half. I've missed you."

"I've missed you too. How did your meeting go yesterday?" Meg asked.

"It was fine. But you certainly helped me out this past weekend—I couldn't have done it without you. How's my dad?"

Meg smiled. "Your dad is great. We had a good meal and visit. I enjoyed myself." Meg told Cate about her lunch date with Cliff.

Then they chatted until the food was delivered. When Meg realized there were four sandwiches, she cocked her head and studied Cate. Oh God, this was the moment she would call it love. The revelation flowed through Meg in a physical wave—pausing her breath, speeding her heart rate.

"It looks like they doubled my order. I guess we'll just have to give one sandwich to Piper and the other to the mutt," Cate murmured.

"You're such a liar." Meg needed to touch this woman. This stunning, contrary, compassionate woman. Meg went around the desk behind Cate's chair and put her arms around Cate from behind. "Just fess up. You ordered four sandwiches."

"Well, I can't have anyone starving in my office. It would be terrible publicity for my law practice. A horrible headline." Cate chuckled, but there was a hint of defensiveness in her voice.

Meg rolled her eyes. "I know, you've got an image to maintain. Especially here in your legal world where weakness isn't an asset. But guess what? I'm astute enough to recognize your many facets. You've dared to expose them before. And I see right through you, you old softie."

Cate shook her head and pretended to growl her response. "Who are you calling a softie? And did you call me old?"

Meg laughed into Cate's hair. "I know what I see in you. But I'm still wondering what you see in me."

Cate turned her face upward and laid a trail of gentle kisses along Meg's throat up to her chin. Meg felt Cate pause and inhale the floral scent on her neck. Then Cate rotated her chair so that her lips could brush Meg's before Meg was captured in a kiss that grew more ardent. Meg hoped that Cate was letting down her guard because Cate had realized she could be herself with Meg. Even in her professional world.

Then Cate answered her question. "I see someone who makes me want to appreciate Piper. Feed a hungry dog. Cry over a beautiful painting. Damn, Meg. I want this to work."

"Me too," Meg answered as her heart hammered in her chest. As her lips responded to Cate's soft warm lips, tasting and teasing in a long and arousing kiss. "Me too."

SLOUCHING TOWARD STARDUST WITH MEG THE UNMUZZLED

"The Rescue"

I had driven into the city for a lunch date with my favorite lawyer. As I exited the parking structure into the urban hubbub, I looked up and down the busy street. Cars coming and going. People biking and walking, paying no attention to anything except the path to their destination. I could understand that. It was the best way to get to that endpoint.

But as I gazed left again, I saw a dog. A black dog with a white chest. A tuxedo appearance. Male. Back left hind limb missing: tripod. A sad, matted mutt. I tried to look away. I wanted to ignore the creature—I had an important lunch date. But he locked eyes with me. I'm such a sucker for eyes. The connection with that damn dog—it was a soul lock. I saw his history of heartbreak. And he saw mine.

I bent down as the pooch approached me. I petted his filthy pelt. "You need a bath," I said. "Hell, Tux, you need a lot more than that." I dug into my purse and offered him a protein bar. He gulped it down.

Then Tux followed me as I tried to scoot away. I turned and locked eyes again, then moved on, feeling guilty. The dog followed with its uneven gait. As I approached the building, I turned back, ended up holding the door for the mutt. What was my favorite lawyer going to say? The canine launched himself into the elevator with me, rode the box three stories up to the law office. I took a deep breath and entered the firm's door, the dog on my tail.

That impeccable lawyer of mine was out by the receptionist's desk. I hesitated. Looked at her as she studied the begrimed mongrel. Then the encumbered me. She and I have developed a connection. A complicated relationship. What was she thinking?

"Got a new dog?" she inquired, lifting an eyebrow.

"No," I insisted, then gave up. "I think the poor thing has me."

"I've always liked you," she mused. "Now I know why."

"I've ruined our lunch," I apologized.

"As if we can't order in," she countered.

Maybe not so complicated, I thought, as Tux thumped his tail.

CHAPTER TWELVE

M eg left the diner around the corner from the gallery, where she'd written and posted a blog about the dog over a cup of coffee. She was pleased she'd made productive use of the unexpected free hour after Olivia had texted apologetically that she was running late for their meeting. But Meg now stood at the entrance to the gallery. She remembered the front of Legends Art Gallery from the visits she'd made there so many years ago with her grandmother. Stepping inside the door and looking around, Meg admired the art. The large open gallery displayed paintings throughout the expanse, as well as sculptures on tables and pedestals. This was how she recollected it, except for better lighting and fresh paint. It was an attractive, upscale space. As Meg took in the exhibition room, a middle-aged woman came from a side room.

"You must be Meg. Thank you for putting up with my delay. I recognize you from your photo in the *Bay Area Heartbeat*," the raven-haired woman said in greeting. "I'm Olivia. My father owned this gallery when your grandmother showed with us, and now I own it."

"Hi, Olivia. Yes, I remember this gallery from years ago when I came with my grandmother, both to deliver her art and at least a few times for her shows. I was always in awe of the entire art scene here."

"So, why don't you come into the office and we can talk. Let me get you a glass of water."

"That sounds good. I'm not quite sure why I'm here, and I have to admit that I'm curious," Meg said, following Olivia into the office and accepting a glass of sparkling water.

Olivia smiled. "I only offer representation to artists I know can be professionally successful. That was Josie Burke, along with all the other notable names hanging on our walls. I don't need, nor do I want, to promote and sell art that collectors will not be interested in. That said, I saw the *Bay Area Heartbeat* article, and I knew immediately that you have what it takes. What I want."

Meg just sat and took in this information. *Oh my God, I must be dreaming.*

"I'm sure you have questions, and I'm happy to answer them. But let me answer one question you might have. Yes, the fact that you are Josie Burke's granddaughter is enticing, but your art is amazing. You may get other gallery offers, but the fact that Legends represented your grandmother and that it's a premier upscale gallery makes me hope that you will show with us. The generational factor will only enhance the allure, but have no doubt that your art stands on its own, without the Josie Burke legacy."

Meg's eyes welled with the emotions Olivia's words evoked. This was beyond her wildest dreams. Olivia was offering Meg the opportunity to legitimize a love that she had held her entire life, but buried beneath Robert and her children. This was taking a piece of her identity and validating it.

Olivia smiled and offered Meg a tissue. "I rarely have artists cry in here," Olivia stated with a chuckle, "unless I'm giving them bad news, that we can't represent them. I'm assuming these are happy tears. I suspect this has been a long time coming, Meg."

"It has," Meg responded. "I'm having a hard time believing this is actually happening. It's rather overwhelming."

"Well, it's real," Olivia said. "And there are business realities you'll want to consider. I'm assuming you probably have other works of art that weren't featured in the article, and I'd be interested in seeing those. Then we could help you get pieces matted and framed. And there's a contract that you might want to run past an attorney."

Meg smiled. She knew a lawyer, and she suspected that Cate would be happy to advise her.

"So, if you're interested, I'll give you a copy of the contract. I can assist you in choosing the pieces to be shown if you decide this works for you. I'm happy to help you navigate this. When we're all ready, we'll set a date and have an opening show here at the studio, where I'll invite our collectors and anyone else either of us thinks would be appropriate to invite. How does that sound?"

"That sounds perfect," Meg responded.

"Okay. Let me get you a copy of the paperwork, and then I'll give you a tour of the gallery."

Olivia offered Meg the contract and then they toured the gallery, looking at the pieces of several known artists that Meg recognized, both paintings and sculptures scattered around the establishment. Meg was in a daze. Meg could not believe she was being invited to show her work here. Mona Lisa Meg was hitting the big time. Meg was most pleased because her grandmother would have been thrilled for her. It was a tribute to the time her grandmother had spent helping Meg fall in love with art. It was a tribute to the grandmother she had loved.

When they finished, Olivia thanked Meg for her time, and Meg promised to call Olivia so they could move forward. Meg left the shop feeling better than she'd felt in ages. While she told herself that at her age she should be past the need for it, the fact that she would be validated as an artist thrilled her, maybe because Robert had always relegated her to the role of family support, and her art had never been recognized as an important part of her identity. And while she knew that Cate had been attracted to her as she was, Meg felt better about herself for believing that her art had just been elevated to a professional level. Maybe she would pick up where she had left off at twenty in a number of ways. She called Cate.

"Hi, I'm done here."

"Will you come by the office and tell me about the meeting?" Cate asked.

"I'd love to," Meg responded, wanting to share the news with Cate.

"How about a hint? You know I'm the impatient sort."

"No way." Meg laughed. "I want to tell you to your face."

"Well, if that isn't a hint, I don't know what is."

"I'm not good at secrets," Meg replied.

"I don't know. You've kept a few for thirty years. I'm just happy to be on this end of that timeline," Cate told her.

"I'm glad you are too."

"Well, get yourself over here, and you can share your news officially. Maybe it will deserve a celebration."

"Maybe a hug," Meg teased.

"Or a kiss," Cate countered in a seductive tone that registered low in Meg's pelvic region.

"What are we wasting time on the phone for?" Meg asked. "I'm on my way."

❖

Meg took a cab back to Cate's office. By the time she arrived, it was almost five o'clock. When she walked in, Cate and Piper were waiting in the reception area.

"Okay. Now we're face-to-face. Let's hear what Legends Art Gallery wanted," Cate said.

"My, my. You're an impatient sort, aren't you?" Meg scolded as she suppressed a smile.

"Damn right. Spill," Cate demanded, while Piper watched them interact.

"Well, first things first," Meg said. "Do you know a good lawyer?"

"Lawyer?" Cate questioned, lifting a perfectly sculpted eyebrow.

"Yup. I've got a contract that needs to be reviewed by a good lawyer." Meg held out the contract.

Cate's eyes twinkled with humor. "I might just know a lawyer who could help you out. But she'll want her fee in trade."

"Are we talking Sunday brunch again, or something more intoxicating?" Meg asked.

"Like champagne with that brunch?" Cate joked. Piper was grinning ear to ear.

Meg put her finger on her chin, pursed her lips, and cocked her head while she pretended that she was taking this under consideration. Cate leaned forward and kissed her on the mouth.

"I was thinking something more intoxicating. Over *easy*. With a side of *hot* sauce," Meg informed her.

"I'm shocked." Cate put on an air of false indignation, but it was obvious to Meg that she was suppressing her mirth. "On a Sunday morning when you should be in church? And the word *easy*—that's downright insulting. I want some effort. But the *hot* sauce could work for me."

Piper laughed out loud at them. She looked at Cate. "I think that

The Meg Effect is on full display. I'm happy for you, Cate." Then she added, "You too, Meg. I don't know who's gonna get the better deal on this one. I think you both might end up winners."

Meg smiled at Cate and Piper. "It's been an amazing day. They want to represent my work at the gallery. The gallery where my grandmother showed. Help me have it matted and framed. Have an opening show with collectors. I can't believe it."

"Believe it. Your work is amazing. I'm so pleased for you." Cate beamed, reaching out and wrapping Meg in a hug, not letting go.

"Not to interrupt the party, but I need to go see my mom about a dog. Let me grab him out of Cate's office and leave you two to whatever devious activities this contract deal leads to. Just don't do anything I wouldn't do." Piper waggled her eyebrows. "And you aren't even close to the things I'd say this contract deal calls for."

"I don't think I've fired you yet today," Cate advised Piper with a chuckle as she continued to hug Meg.

"Well, I'm out of here before you do." Piper's merriment played across her face as she turned to walk into Cate's office to collect the dog.

"Thanks so much for helping me rescue this fellow," Meg told Piper from Cate's embrace as she and the dog headed out. "If there are any issues, let me know."

"I will, Meg. See you tomorrow, Cate." Piper pointed her index finger at Cate, gave her a nod of approval, then headed out and closed the office door as she left.

❖

Cate continued to hold Meg. She hadn't had such a good time in… ever. That was sobering. Laurel was in the rearview mirror. One-night stands were good for some things, but Cate was enjoying getting to know Meg so much she wasn't missing what Pete had so indelicately summarized as *the meet, the greet, the sex, the polite good-bye*.

"I could stand here forever with you holding me," Meg said. "But I've got a cat I need to get home to, sometime today."

"And that conniving cat has been so helpful up to this point. Can you at least have a quick dinner with me before you head home? We can leave now if Oscar will put up with it," Cate inquired.

"Let me text Grace and see if she can swing by to check on him and give him his evening pills—then we can take our time," Meg responded.

"Okay, Meg. You do that while I take care of a few things and get ready to lock up." Cate headed into her office to collect the dog towel and bowl of water, as well as put a little paperwork away. She'd finished the chores before Meg was done texting. Cate stood and watched as Meg typed while her lips twitched upward until she broke into a full smile with whatever Grace was responding. The thought crossed Cate's mind that she could really get used to that smile in her life.

Meg: *Hey. I'm in SF. Gallery wants to represent me. Cate wants dinner with me. Is it convenient for you to check and pill the old boy this evening before I get back?*

Grace: *Gallery wants to represent you—YES!!!!! Go have a celebratory dinner with Cate. I've got Oscar covered. Spend the night if you want.*

Meg: *I'll be home tonight. I'm seeing a sleepover in the future but don't want it rushed. I'm enjoying the flirting too much.*

Grace: *So glad you've got your flirt back on. Can we catch up tomorrow? I want to hear about the gallery—and other things.*

Meg: *I must have a pan or plate that you need to collect. There's probably a lasagna or pie in your future that's calling for a drop-in tomorrow. Thanks for the Oscar check-in service. You're the best.*

Grace: *John has been asking for lasagna or pie—tomorrow. Just happy for you. It's about time. Is midafternoon after work ok?*

Meg: *On my calendar: Grace collecting nonexistent pan or plate tomorrow afternoon.*

Grace: *Ha! Ha!*

Cate went back into her office and came out with her purse. "Ready?" she asked.

"I am," Meg responded. "Grace has Oscar covered, so he'll be good until I get home later tonight. Where shall we go?"

"Let's go someplace close, where we can walk, if that's okay with you. That will give us less time working out transport and more time to relax and eat."

"Perfect," Meg answered, giving Cate a smile.

"That dog distracted me, but I wanted to tell you that you look great in that dress," Cate said. "Is it new?" Cate's expression was filled with appreciation as she took in Meg's formfitting dusty-rose dress with its above-the-knee hem and hint of cleavage.

"This old thing? Yeah, it's new. Grace went shopping with me. She called it a Cate acquisition dress."

Cate laughed. "Well, I'm flattered. It's beautiful on you, but you'd look beautiful wearing anything...or not." As Cate spoke, her eyes turned even darker than usual and her pupils dilated.

"Or not?" Meg felt her face warm as she considered how her body had changed over the years. "You haven't seen this fifty-year-old body yet. It's got mileage."

"I love it when you blush. You're perfect, Meg. Don't doubt that. Inside and out."

Meg didn't know what to say, so she changed the subject. "I'm ready to go to wherever you're going to lead me."

"Oh, I have some suggestions, but I think that you're meaning dinner," Cate said, teasing her.

"I am. When I follow you somewhere else, we're not going to be on a deadline."

Cate took Meg's hand and led her outside to a small restaurant a few blocks down the street. They shared some hors d'oeuvres and then each ordered a dinner salad. They spent the time chatting and laughing. Because Meg did not want to drink and drive, she and Cate toasted goblets of sparkling water in celebration of her gallery offer. As the clock approached nine, Meg knew it was time to head back home. Cate walked her to the car and gave her a hug.

"It's been the best day. Thank you so much." Meg held Cate in an extended embrace.

"A dog rescue. A fun lunch. An offer from an art gallery. A wonderful dinner. You lead a boring life, Meg Mullins."

"You forgot contract negotiations with my favorite lawyer—left up in the air at over easy and hot sauce, but still negotiable," Meg added.

"I'm not done negotiating. As a lawyer, it's one of my strengths."

"As the mother of three, it's one of my strengths too. This ought to be fun." Meg laughed.

"As Piper indicated, there probably won't be any losers, whatever price you have to pay," Cate said with a grin.

"You're on, Counselor Colson. Let me know your plans for the weekend."

"I will. Drive safely."

Meg started her car, backed up, and blew Cate a kiss as she pulled away. *I'm falling for her.* Falling hard.

Oscar greeted her at the door when she arrived home. Grace had left a note informing her that she'd been by and pilled Oscar. Meg was wide awake and decided to do some writing before she turned in. It had been an amazing day, one of those landmark days she would remember. A day when she woke up in one reality and went to bed in another. Her dream of becoming a professional artist was materializing. The miracle of a relationship with Cate was feeling real too. Fifty was feeling damn good.

Slouching Toward Stardust with Meg the unMuzzled

"Love"

Love: Deep affection, fondness, tenderness, warmth, intimacy, attachment, endearment, devotion, doting, adoration, idolization, worship, ardor, passion, desire, lust, yearning, infatuation, adulation, besottedness.

Now there's a gambit of emotions, not all equivalent, but appropriate when fifty years of living offer a person an array of relationships. A smorgasbord of feelings. A spectrum of love. Fifty years have taught me that love is personal. Unique. Life enhancing. Often complicated. Sometimes inconvenient. Unpredictable. And nothing that a person can coerce. Love is a wild beast.

I'm half a century old. With a deceased husband, three adult offspring, and an old boy feline who inhabits an exclusive place in my heart. I would confirm that love has been a factor in all of these relationships to some degree. As one synonym or another. And I would contend that love can mature or morph or even dissipate. So, I find myself newly consumed by the connection of chemistry, the inferno of sparks, the ache of attraction—falling into love. A new love. A different love. An unlikely love. A love that seemed so inconceivable until it decided to grow on its own.

How did you get to this place? I ask myself. Yes, I nurtured the relationship. Gave it a chance. But true love doesn't grow through decree. It's an independent entity, germinating from the unplanned moments that are throwing me into the abyss: witnessing the covert compassion of feeding a hungry dog, the unaccredited leaving of a small gift, the unsolicited support of my passions. And the building of trust—the growing belief that my breakable heart is in honorable hands.

So, here I am. Acknowledging that I'm falling in love. Because two people deserve the opportunity to see if love will grow. Everyone deserves that chance when it comes along. Even when complicated. Even when difficult. Even when challenged. I need to embrace this miracle. I wouldn't stop this plummet if I could. Love is too precious.

CHAPTER THIRTEEN

G race arrived a little after three o'clock. Meg stopped her sorting in the studio to let her in, right behind Oscar, who tore down the hallway straight for the front door. Somehow, he knew it was Grace and wasn't going to miss a chance for an ear rub greeting when she came in.

"Well, if it isn't the soon-to-be world-famous artist, Meg Mullins," Grace pronounced as she scooped up the cat in one arm and held Meg in a hug with the other.

Meg shook her head at Grace's *world-famous* characterization of her new prospects as an artist. She could always count on Grace. "Thanks so much for coming by last evening to take care of the old man."

"I'm so glad that you texted me. I'd have been very upset if you'd passed up the chance to have dinner with Cate," Grace told her. "Oscar and I had a good visit. But enough of that. My God, you're going professional. So deserved," Grace gushed as she stepped back from Meg.

Meg had to smile at her friend. She was tired from working so many hours in the studio, but Grace's enthusiasm was contagious.

"I have to keep pinching myself. I'm afraid I'll wake up and it will just be a dream," Meg confessed.

"Believe it, girl. It's about time," Grace responded.

"At this point in my life, I'd accepted that my art was just for me. That was enough. In fact, there's a whole lot to showing with a gallery—lots to do that's going to require some time. I've got to organize my works so I can show them to the gallery owner, Olivia, whom I met with yesterday. A contract. Matting and framing. A gallery opening." Meg rattled off the chores on the list.

"Well, at least you have plenty of pieces to show her. All these years of what you considered therapy. I've never known anyone whose therapy was going to go professional, sweetie."

Meg grinned. "I never thought of it that way. My life has taken so many interesting turns in the past weeks."

"So how are you and Cate doing? Inquiring minds want to know."

"We're good. Better than good. I'm falling for her. She's got so many layers, but under it all…she's a hidden gem, but with enough attitude to never be boring. And while both of our pasts are making us take it slow, I think our histories are also giving us a better chance at this relationship," Meg confided. "More willing to know what counts and work past all the crap in our lives. And unlike Robert, I think she may have matured into a decent perspective on work-relationship balance. Robert grew into someone who only took me for granted. I'm hopeful that Cate sees me through a different lens."

"I get it." Grace nodded. "To speak ill of the dead, Robert was such a bastard in the end. You deserve so much more. I'm pulling for Cate."

"And I think we're both having fun. At least I am, and I'd lay money on Cate finding our chemistry working too. To be honest, I'm wondering where Robert and I would have landed if I hadn't gotten pregnant. This just feels so much freer with Cate. No pressures, like a pregnancy pushing the outcome."

"What about the kids? That's going to be something you'll have to deal with. You marry Cate, they'll have a stepmom," Grace warned.

Meg hadn't even considered that. "Oh my God, now there's a thought. But you're getting ahead of things. Don't think I haven't worried about the fallout from telling them I'm having a relationship with a woman. Hell, I think I'm starting to fall in love with her."

Grace smiled at that news. "You deserve someone you love and who loves you, Meg. It's your life, and it doesn't belong to your kids anymore."

"Natalie is the one who concerns me the most—I don't know that there's any room in her religious world for me to love Cate. To be happy. I'm not telling Nat anything until I need to. Until I'm certain that this relationship is going somewhere." Meg massaged her temple as her anxieties about Natalie surfaced. "But I do need to call her and just keep our lines of communication open. She's my daughter, and I love her. But I'm at a point in my life where I can't let her opinions control the rest of my life, if it comes to that. I just hope Nat loves me enough to understand."

"I'm glad you get that. It's time for you to be happy. Be in love with whomever the good Lord leads you to. I think maybe you took a big detour with Robert," Grace suggested gently.

"Well, it's certainly been a journey that's brought me to this place. It's the fifty-year-old me now, and I'm coming to some significant acknowledgments," Meg declared before she changed the subject. "How about a glass of iced tea with me? And if your excuse for checking in is a lasagna pan or pie plate, I can probably locate a spare one for you."

"Tea sounds good. And yeah, you can give me a plate or pan—then I'll have a reason for bringing it back and getting the next installment in the life and times of Meg Mullins. It's the most interesting part of my life," Grace admitted with a chuckle.

"Well, that's downright sad." Meg laughed as she led Grace out to the kitchen.

❖

Cate came into the office on Wednesday morning to find Piper already there, working at the receptionist's desk. Cate knew that Piper was going to engage her regarding Meg, so she decided she might as well get it over with.

"How did your mom do with the dog?" Cate asked, figuring that was as safe a topic as any.

"We gave him a shower. He's a whole new dog. A three-legged dog, but awesome. I haven't found a prior owner yet but contacted all the organizations I could find online. He's not chipped. And Mom and that dog—she didn't want to finalize a name until we're sure he'll be hers—they're already heading toward true love."

"Well, that's good," Cate said.

"And how did you do with Meg?" Piper grinned. "When I left, my prediction was that you two were heading toward true love too."

"Well, that's a little presumptuous," Cate replied. "And as I've told Pete, I never kiss and tell."

"Maybe you don't, Cate, but my eyes don't lie. And I'm pleased to report that my boss doesn't need kissing lessons," Piper sassed.

Cate felt a wave of embarrassment, though it was good news that she'd measured up.

"And, boss?"

"What, Piper?" Cate braced herself.

"I'd make a hell of a bridesmaid." Piper winked.

Damn, Piper. Cate knew she wouldn't leave yesterday alone. Cate made a show of looking at the clock in the reception area. She nodded toward her office. "We're wasting time. Work is waiting. For both of us."

"I'm happy for you. Meg is wonderful. And perfect for you."

"I know." Cate made the rare overture of admission.

"Just don't blow it. Meg will take a lot of your attitude—probably even enjoys most of it—but I bet she has her guard up about some things."

"Did you go to paralegal school or couples' counseling training?" Cate asked, trying to suppress an upward twitch of her lips.

"Well, the paper on my office wall says *paralegal*, but you'd have to admit that I'm not a bad couples' counselor. You know, the recognition of The Meg Effect on my part and all. If I get fired from my current job, I have a backup profession."

Cate bit the inside of her cheeks to keep from outright smiling and encouraging Piper to offer her more advice about her growing relationship with Meg.

"Maybe I need a pay raise." Piper's brows rose above her dancing eyes. "Extra workload. Dual job duties…"

"Well, neither of us is getting the job done that we should be doing. I'd hate to have to fire you before nine o'clock." Cate suppressed a laugh. What the hell was happening to the professional decorum around here?

"Paralegal it is for this morning. But just call me if you need love life advice. I won't steer you wrong."

"Piper?"

"Yes, Cate?"

"Thanks." And with that, Cate turned around and headed into her office to get some actual work done.

❖

It was early Thursday evening before Meg took time to sit down and call her daughter. Her love for Natalie resided in her chest, but the complexity of their relationship always lodged in her gut, and that surfaced whenever she picked up the phone to call her.

Natalie and her husband, Gus, rarely traveled to the Bay Area, and Meg hadn't been down to LA in several months, but Meg called her every few weeks to stay in touch. She wasn't going to lose her daughter if she could help it. But she knew Cate was going to complicate their relationship. Hopefully, not beyond repair.

"Hi, Nat. It's your mom."

"Hi, Mom. How is everybody?" Natalie sounded pleased to hear from her mother.

"We're all fine. How are you doing down there in LA?" Meg inquired, picturing her slender daughter twirling a strand of her long blond hair around her finger as she talked.

"Good," Nat replied. She was never much of a talker, so Meg carried the conversation.

"Are you busy at work these days?"

"Yup. I'm working on a couple of projects."

"Well, that's good. Jessie and Ben are busy too," Meg told her.

"Uh-huh," Nat responded.

"How are your cats?" Natalie had adopted a couple of abandoned neighborhood cats who had moved into her backyard, and Meg knew they would draw her daughter into the conversation. "Is it Midnight and Mr. Jolly?"

"Yeah. They're doing okay. I had to get some medicine for a cough Mr. Jolly had, but he's doing better now. And Midnight has finally put on a little weight."

"I'm glad. Oscar is his obnoxious, wonderful old self."

Natalie chuckled. She'd been in her last year of high school when they'd adopted Oscar, and she'd spent some summers at home working when she was in college. "Is he still your alarm clock?"

"That he is. More reliable than a store-bought one. As long as I want to get up when his stomach goes off," Meg responded.

Natalie laughed. Meg loved to hear that laugh. It wasn't often enough.

"How's Gus?"

"Good." Natalie didn't elaborate, which Meg had come to accept as just part of Natalie's way of keeping her newfound religion separate from her former, more outgoing lifestyle.

"Any vacation plans?" Meg asked.

"Not really," Natalie answered.

"Well, I'm hoping to get down to LA to see you one of these days soon if you're not coming north. I haven't spent any time with you in ages."

"That would be good, Mom," Natalie said. Meg had stayed in a hotel on the rare occasion she had visited them, as Natalie and Gus's house was small and had no guest room. That was fine with Meg. She hadn't always lived in a large house either.

"I'll let you know when it looks like I can come down, and I hope we can make a plan because I'd love to see you," Meg told her daughter. "Oh, and I just heard from a San Francisco art gallery that wants to carry some of my art. The same one that carried Great-Grandma Burke's paintings."

"Hey, that's great," Natalie replied. Natalie used to love art before all of her time was taken up by work and her church. She had talent, and Meg had been sorry to see her give art up because when she was younger Natalie often had a painting or drawing project she was working on. But Meg knew that you had to let your kids figure out their own lives. And maybe Nat's architecture career was fulfilling her creative needs.

"At some point, the gallery will have an official opening for my work, and maybe you'll be able to come." Meg tried not to sound too hopeful.

Natalie didn't respond, so Meg knew there was not much chance of that.

"Well, I'd better let you go. Have you had your dinner yet?"

"Nope, it's in the oven and Gus is waiting."

"Okay, then. I love you, Nat," Meg said.

"I love you too, Mom. And we're praying for you."

They hung up, and Meg felt like she always did when she talked with her daughter—full of love, but miles and miles away, both literally and figuratively. As for recent developments, Meg could only imagine that conversation about herself and Cate. And she still planned to keep quiet about Robert's transgressions—that discovery should not burden her children. But just as she did her best to let Nat live her chosen life, she was now determined to do the same for herself.

"God and Meg"

There is an enduring book by Judy Blume, published over fifty years ago, dedicated to the author's mother. What if Blume hadn't just stuck to the realities of a girl contemplating religion along with a number of other adolescent issues? What if Margaret was growing into the exploration of being attracted to other girls? Or not feeling female? Sexual orientation questions. Gender identity questions. All hell would have broken loose.

❖

Is that you, God? Margaret here (you can just call me Meg—most everyone else does), wondering about some people. Wondering about your role in the world. I worry for humankind—the judgment, the division, the hate, the harm. I worry as an individual. I worry as a mother. I love some LGBTQIA+ individuals. And I love some religious individuals who are focused on their own standards for eternity. All part of the family. Family who grew up loving each other.

Your followers, God. Evangelicals. No one has revealed that some members of the family don't measure up to the salvation standards of others. Not rocking the family boat. Avoiding the preaching. Avoiding the judgment in your name. Probably wrong, but what's the right answer, God?

Don't they all know that you don't make mistakes? You're supposed to stand for love. So, if you're actually up there and overseeing this place (and I have my major doubts, or you'd be tearing your tresses out), you should have been a little bit clearer, God. Go with the bumper sticker: love is a terrible thing to hate.

Or send a new memo, God: love is love is love.

CHAPTER FOURTEEN

On Friday morning, Meg was thrilled to receive a text from Cate. She could picture Cate at her desk, maybe even glancing at paperwork in the wait as the messaging played out. A call or FaceTime might be faster, but Meg loved their text flirting, and she suspected that Cate was getting a kick out of it too.

Cate: *Hey pretty woman. I'm hoping the professional artist is having a good week.*

Meg: *Tuesday was exceptional. Loved our time together.*

Cate: *Me too.*

Meg: *I'm hoping my favorite lawyer is coming to town this weekend.*

Cate: *You might be in luck. Your favorite lawyer makes house calls to a limited & select few. I believe there's a contract that needs a consultation.*

Meg: *And payment to work out. Looking forward to that.*

Cate: *The negotiation or the payout?*

Meg: *Both.*

Cate: *Do you want to go to lunch with Dad & me tomorrow?*

Meg: *Would love to but maybe I should keep working here & you could come to dinner instead. Jessie & Luc are coming. I can introduce you and me and see how it goes if you're agreeable. Jessie already has a hint.*

Cate: *I've been out for years, so this is up to you. I'd love to join you all for dinner.*

Meg: *Let's do it then. My place tomorrow evening at 5ish.*
Cate: *I know this is a big deal. I like the you and me. See you then.*

Meg decided that Saturday's dinner was going to be another one of those landmark moments for her, one that she would always remember with regard to the before and after times. Coming out to Jessie and Luc was probably going to be the easiest part of coming out to her family. And she'd already admitted to Cate's dad, Cliff, that she wasn't straight. *So here goes*, Meg silently encouraged herself.

❖

As the time neared for everyone to arrive for dinner, Meg was a little nervous but pleased that Jessie and Luc were coming. She knew her short wavy hair swirled upward at the tips where the steam from her recent shower had teased the blond curl into full display. She'd applied a little makeup and wore nice gray dress slacks and a formfitting blue blouse that she'd selected to accent the azure in her eyes. After slipping on some black flats, Meg had just headed to the kitchen when a couple of knocks landed on the front door before it swung open.

"Hey. We're here," Jessie and Luc called out.

"Hi, you two, come on back into the kitchen. I'm making vegetarian lasagna, salad, and French bread." Meg looked up as the two entered the kitchen, Jessie carrying Oscar. They looked good—Jessie in a button-up sage-green shirt that set off the green leaves in their botanical arm tattoo and tan pleated khakis. Meg noticed, as always, how much Jessie resembled her. And Luc wore an ivory button-up shirt that set off their dark hair and golden complexion and new blue jeans.

"That sounds delicious. We brought some red wine. And Luc made their famous key lime pie, as promised. You look gorgeous, Mom."

"Thanks, Jessie. Your pie is the best, Luc. Thanks so much for making dessert. I'll put it in the fridge. We'll eat in the dining room. Four of us for dinner," Meg informed them, hoping her casual delivery would play down the magnitude of the event for her.

Jessie glanced over at Luc and the two locked eyes for a moment. Obviously, they'd discussed this after Jessie witnessed the hand-holding a few weeks ago.

"I'll stick the pie in the fridge," Luc said.

Meg nodded and then cleared her throat. "Cate's coming to dinner too. I want you both to meet her."

"Didn't I meet her two weeks ago?" Jessie asked.

"You did. But this is official. I'm just going to say it—we're seeing each other. In a dating way. I really like her. And you're the first of you kids I'm telling." Meg waited nervously for Jessie's response. She needed this to be okay with Jessie, her child most likely to accept her revelation.

"It's cool. You deserve to be happy. I know Ben and Sarah will want the same for you. Now Nat might be another story."

"Thanks, babe. You're making this easy. Probably a lot easier than Nat will make it, but this is practice," Meg admitted to Jessie.

"We're on your side, Mom."

"I'm just hoping you kids don't have to take sides." Meg knew her tone was injected with the worry she felt. "But I'm not naive."

"I know. You wouldn't be introducing us to Cate if this wasn't important to you."

Meg smiled. "And I have other good news."

"Besides a love life?" Jessie teased her.

"Yeah. Legends Art Gallery in San Francisco, the one that sold your great-grandma's watercolors—they're going to represent me." Meg felt a wave of fulfillment course through her as she shared the information, tying her own art to her grandmother's art in a professional way.

"Wow. A love life and a professional life. You're full of surprises."

"And don't you forget it. I'm not totally over the hill yet," Meg advised with a chuckle.

"Yes, ma'am," Jessie and Luc said in exaggerated unison. They both knew that *ma'am* pushed her buttons.

Just then the doorbell rang, and Meg and Oscar went to the door to let Cate in. Jessie and Luc officially greeted Cate, and she seemed comfortable with the two. After the introductions, Meg set the food on the table while Jessie opened and poured the wine. They all sat down to dinner, Meg and Jessie at each end of the table, and Luc and Cate across from each other on the sides. After some discussion about Cate's law practice, Luc's EMT program, and how Meg and Cate knew each other through Robert's former business dealings, the conversation turned to Jessie's profession.

"So, I hear you went to the California Academy of the Arts, Jessie. I guess the art gene is alive and well in the next generation," Cate said.

"Yeah. I got my degree from CAA, and now I'm a tattoo artist."

"That's what your mom told me. Are you liking your profession?"

"I love it. I know it's not what Dad had in mind when he spent the big bucks, but sometimes you've just got to follow your heart."

"In more ways than one," Cate muttered.

"Exactly. Mom needs to follow her heart too," Jessie told her.

"Well, I guess that completely broke the ice," Cate noted.

"We're cool with you and Mom. We want her happy, and she's smiling and laughing more than I've seen her in years." Jessie grinned down the table at Meg. "So, good job, Counselor." Jessie clearly liked Cate.

"You and I are going to get along just fine, Jessie," Cate responded. "You need any free legal advice, I'm the one to see first."

"Free legal advice," Meg interjected, looking at Cate. She shifted her gaze to Jessie. "We're still negotiating the fee payment for Cate to look over the contract that the art gallery gave me. I offered Sunday brunch."

"Well maybe you've met your match in a lawyer, Mom." Jessie chuckled, then turned to Cate. "She's a tough negotiator. Don't let her off easy."

"I won't," Cate promised, looking at Meg with a twinkle in her eyes that only Meg noticed. "Collecting payment is what we lawyers are famous for."

"Okay, you two. No ganging up on me," Meg warned them, "if you want any of Luc's famous dessert." Then she changed the subject, directing her next comment to Jessie. "I want to get a tattoo. A small one. I talked to Ben, and he suggested something that symbolizes change. A new beginning. I'm also thinking self-realization."

"How about a dragonfly? It symbolizes those things. I can do whatever size you decide. Maybe low on your ankle or the top of your foot," Jessie suggested.

Meg smiled. "That's exactly what I was thinking after a lot of online research."

"Well, you think about it, and I can do it next weekend if you want. I can schedule you in late Saturday afternoon. Special mom discount rate…free."

Luc pulled up their sleeve and revealed a gorgeous, delicate dragonfly tattoo just below their right shoulder. "Compliments of Jessie," they said.

"Luc, that's beautiful," Cate noted.

"I've got a mom's girlfriend discount rate too," Jessie told her. "You want one, it's free for you. You can come along with Mom."

Cate looked like she was giving it some thought. "Let me take it under consideration. I've never seriously thought about getting a tattoo, but now that I know the artist…and a mom's girlfriend discount rate is something I've never been offered before." She winked at Meg.

"You're welcome to just come watch Mom get inked, or get your own. Next Saturday, I'll block out time for two. And it can go either way. No problem."

"You're a good kid. Your mom is lucky to have you." Cate smiled at Jessie.

"Enough of the lovefest. It would be wonderful if Cate wants to get a tattoo with me next weekend or just comes to hold my hand. But right now, I'd love some of Luc's signature key lime pie," Meg declared as she stood up to clear the dinner plates from the table.

Everyone helped clean the kitchen, then they all sat down to eat pie and drink coffee. It was close to ten o'clock before Jessie and Luc departed with a promise to hopefully see both of them in a week at the tattoo shop in Santa Clara where Jessie worked.

After they were gone, Meg, Cate, and Oscar sat on the family room couch. Oscar sat in Meg's lap.

"How's Cliff today?" Meg asked.

"He's good," Cate said. "He wants to go to church late tomorrow morning, and I promised I'd take him to see his old congregation rather than The Terraces' service. I hope that's okay with you. I can come over in the early afternoon after I spend time with him at his church. I'll look at the contract before I head back to the city in the late afternoon."

"That's perfect. Olivia is coming on Tuesday, and I haven't finished sorting out my art for her, so a free morning will work out well," Meg responded.

"Dinner was delicious. And Jessie and Luc are amazing. You're so lucky."

"I know. And my coming out couldn't have gone better with them. Ben should be okay with it too. But Natalie…that will be tough. I'll have to work up to that one." Meg let out a sigh as she thought about talking to Natalie.

"I don't think I've talked to you about my mom, have I?" Cate inquired, letting out a sigh of her own.

"No, you haven't told me." Meg set Oscar down from her lap and paid full attention to Cate.

"My mom and dad are both religious. But my mom was way more judgmental. When I came out in college, she told me I was going to hell. And she never forgave me," Cate revealed. Meg took her hand. "It was hard, but I knew who I was at that point. My dad never let me down, and Pete was a wonderful friend. I'm sorry my mom died without ever accepting me for who I am. But I've come to terms with the fact that it was her decision and not mine."

"I'm so sorry too. Religion is already straining Nat's and my relationship. I'm just hoping this doesn't sever it. But I can't live for Nat. I spent thirty years living for all of them, not that I resent a single day, but it's time to finish my life on my terms. Finding and accepting who I am," Meg told her. "And you play into that." Meg leaned over and gently teased Cate's bottom lip with her thumb before hugging her closer for a deep kiss. Then she pulled Cate's earlobe into her mouth and skimmed her tongue back and forth across it before breathing into Cate's ear, "I want more of you." Meg felt the arousal of a deep desire to show Cate exactly how much more. The area at her feminine core was aching for increased contact with Cate, intimate contact. Cate made her feel so alive.

Cate shifted sideways and pushed Meg back against the pillow at the end of the couch, leaning onto her and pinning her there with her warm, solid body. Flecks of golden heat burned in her umber eyes. She locked those smoldering eyes with Meg's to make sure that she was okay with the intimacy, and Meg pushed her pelvis into Cate's in response. Cate exhaled into Meg's hair before tenderly trailing her lips from Meg's forehead to her jawline.

"I'm going to take you to bed one of these days, Meg Mullins," she declared in a husky voice. "And it won't be just about sex."

"Really? And just what will it be about?" Meg asked.

"Oh, there will be a little body worship for sure," Cate told her as her fingertip traced a line from Meg's throat to the swell of her breast. Meg sucked in a jagged breath and closed her eyes. Then Cate trailed her tongue across the smooth flesh at the opening of Meg's shirt, pausing to kiss and savor the upper curves of exposed cleavage before pulling back. Moving up, her lips barely skimmed each of Meg's closed lids and moved to her ear. "I want to show you how much I care. That we have something important growing between us. Something sustainable. I want to worship the real Meg Mullins. The mom. The artist. The person. The woman. But only when you're ready," Cate whispered into her ear.

Meg groaned, "Damn, Cate. You need to tell me these things when I'm not lying here under you, ready to peel off every stitch of clothing we both have on. I have only so much willpower. But I don't ever want there to be any regrets for either of us—I know a lot more at fifty than I did at twenty. And while I can't get pregnant with you, I could certainly lose my heart." Meg knew she already was, and she hoped Cate was too. "When I know we've put in enough time on our emotional relationship to make this work for the long term." Meg did not want to make a mistake that would hurt both of them, no matter how much her hormones were speaking out.

"Me too, Meg. Me too. So, kiss me good night, and your attorney will be here early tomorrow afternoon. After church." Meg heard the desire in Cate's voice.

"After church," Meg repeated.

Cate chuckled. "I don't think I've ever uttered the word *church* at the same time I was contemplating taking someone to bed. I'll see you tomorrow."

"I'm counting on it, Counselor. For several billable hours."

"Yes, ma'am," Cate drawled as her gorgeous dark eyes danced with mischief, and Meg affectionately whacked her on her shapely ass before they both got up and saw Cate to the door for a prolonged good night kiss.

Cate arrived about one o'clock the next day and spent over an hour studying the Legends Art Gallery contract, while Meg continued to putter around the studio and Oscar curled up in his bed. There wasn't time for any serious teasing about contract consultation fees by the time Cate finished reading and clarifying the terms of the document to Meg, so they laughingly agreed to serious negotiations later. They both agreed they were comfortable it was a fair offer.

Before Cate left, Meg insisted on sharing a quick bite of warmed-up lasagna so that neither of them would need to worry about a substantial meal later. After a productive afternoon, Meg walked Cate to the door, and they promised to talk during the week, to make a plan for the next weekend and the tattoo date. Then, with a quick kiss, Cate was off to San Francisco and Meg had time to do a little writing, reflecting on a good weekend with Cate and the fact that she'd at least managed to reveal to one of her kids the changes she was making in her life. Positive changes.

SLOUCHING TOWARD STARDUST WITH MEG THE UNMUZZLED

"The Journey"

I've trekked through a topography of longing for many miles now. Not that I haven't detoured for times into the hills of hope, the coastlines of calm, the grasslands of gratitude, even the deserts of delight. And I have stood at moments on the mountaintop of love. For who could not find these respites with the birth of their children? Or the visit of a friend? Or even in the mirage of a mediocre marriage?

But the landscape of longing has persisted through the years. Buried deep in my heart. For places on this journey, for paths I have never traveled, left in the past. For the pieces of myself that I have never found. And now, after all these years, I am leaving that landscape of longing behind.

Whether it's fifty years and maturity, the lottery of luck, or the collision of both, I find myself in the territory of fulfillment. At the validation of pursuits, at the destination of self-discovery. In this amazing passage called life, I am finding myself. Finally.

CHAPTER FIFTEEN

After swimming on Monday morning, Meg spent the rest of the day preparing for Olivia's visit. When the raven-haired gallery owner arrived on Tuesday morning, Meg greeted her and led her back to her studio. Olivia entered the room and scanned the space. Her dark eyes immediately landed on the hanging portrait that Josie Burke had painted of Meg when she was just a child.

"This is the watercolor called *Margaret* that was in the *Bay Area Heartbeat* article. It's absolutely gorgeous," Olivia enthused. "That photo didn't do it justice. It's a portrait portraying the epitome of childhood joy. I'm so glad you have it, Meg."

"Yes. It's probably my favorite painting by my grandmother. Not just because it's of me, but because it reminds me of her unfaltering love whenever I look at it."

"There's something about a grandmother's love, or a mother's love, isn't there?"

"There is," Meg said, as she reflected on what lay ahead with Natalie, and maybe Ben. "Although I don't know that I appreciated the depth of her love until she was gone. It left a huge void."

"Well, shall we see what you've got for me to look at here?" Olivia suggested.

With Oscar observing from his bed, they spent a few hours going through the artwork that she had organized for Olivia's consideration. Olivia selected several pieces to take back to San Francisco, mostly watercolors, and a few sketches. And then there was a collage that Olivia loved. A collage that was not Meg's normal fare, but Olivia was sure it would entice a few collectors she knew.

Meg had not done many collages, but creating that one recently had been a good experience. She considered the process she had gone through in making the piece of artwork. It had given her an outlet, allowed her to assuage some of the emotions she was feeling after learning about Robert. She didn't mind selling it. Its purpose had served her well. Meg thought back to her art teacher's telling the class, *Art is my religion*. She took a moment to consider this. For Meg, art was her therapy.

"These pictures will be perfect for the opening," Olivia said. "I'll work with my framer to get them prepared for hanging. And if you would keep these additional pieces set aside, we can decide about them after these first ones are sold."

"Well, I guess this confirms that you like my work well enough to move forward with this gallery proposal," Meg offered a bit shyly. She was still feeling overwhelmed at the events in her life. "I'm so flattered, and happy."

"You deserve this. You have your grandmother's talent. And the gallery is thrilled to have the opportunity to represent you. With the collectors I'll invite, I think we'll have a very successful opening. If it works for you, we can schedule the opening for the middle of next month."

"That should work fine," Meg agreed. "Just let me know the exact date. And I almost forgot. Here's the signed contract. I reviewed it with my attorney—actually, she's my girlfriend." Whoa, that had just slipped out. Meg decided it was because this was a day for change. Her art. And publicly referring to Cate as her girlfriend. Meg took inventory of her feelings. She felt good.

Olivia didn't blink at the word *girlfriend*. Meg considered that maybe the gallery owner thought she'd said two words—*girl friend*. Or maybe the art scene in San Francisco didn't give Olivia any pause regarding romantic relationships between two women. This was all new territory for Meg. But she was determined to move forward.

"Thanks, Meg. Let's get this art secured and loaded into my car, and I'll be out of your hair."

Meg helped Olivia package and load the pieces into her car, promised to stay in touch as they moved toward the gallery opening, and then she headed back into the house.

❖

That evening, the phone rang, and the screen showed that it was Ben. Meg had an inkling what the call might concern after Saturday's dinner with Jessie and Luc. She hadn't asked Jessie not to say anything about Cate, and she knew that Ben and Jessie talked. She wasn't ashamed of her relationship with Cate.

"Hi, Ben. What's up?"

"I hear you've decided on a dragonfly tattoo," Ben said. Yup, he'd talked to Jessie. "Nice choice."

"Just a little ankle or foot one. No sleeve. No motorcycle. I'm not going totally wild on you." Well, that denial ought to have given him an opening to bring up Cate. Might as well get this over with, Meg told herself.

"Speaking of wild, Mom…" Bingo.

"I was going to wait until I saw you, babe, but I guess we can do this over the phone for now, since you've spoken with Jessie."

"They told me about Cate. About how happy you are. I know how difficult life was for you before Dad passed away. I wasn't clueless. And after he passed away…you've been lonely. I think Jessie broke us in regarding having an LGBTQIA+ family member. I'm going to be good with it. I love you."

Meg sniffed. The emotions of the moment hit her. "I love you too. How about you and Sarah come down soon and meet Cate?"

"I have finals coming up in my classes and there will be a lot of grading to do, but as soon as I'm through with that, we will. Jessie really liked her. So I'm sure I will too."

"I'll talk to you soon. You're my favorite youngest child."

Ben snorted. "Your one and only. You're my favorite mom too."

"Good night, Ben."

"See you soon, Mom."

Meg hung up the phone. Well, that had gone well, thanks to Jessie. She silently offered gratitude to her middle child. Meg understood that Ben would have to process the information. That it was a lot to digest. But she hoped that she had assured him that nothing had changed between the two of them. She thought that was the most important thing she could offer each of her children. That her love for them would never change. If only her relationship with Natalie could weather this.

She decided to text Cate after talking with Ben. She'd love to hear her voice, but she knew Cate was often busy with her demanding job, even in the evening. A text would allow her to respond when it was convenient. And Meg was enjoying their texting. It was growing their relationship in ways that a call or FaceTime probably wouldn't. It was allowing her to see a lighter side of Cate. Meg drew a breath, got her flirt on, and started typing.

Meg: *Hey. Are you done for the day?*
Cate: *Marinating. But behaving myself. I miss you.*
Meg: *Get all of the behaving yourself out of your system while I'm not there.*
Cate: *Yes, ma'am.*
Meg: *Ma'am! That's not behaving yourself.*
Cate: *But you're so much fun to tease.*
Meg: *I have other ideas for fun.*
Cate: *Care to elaborate?*
Meg: *How about being my date the middle of next month for my gallery opening?*
Cate: *That sounds like fun, but what if we plan to extend the evening and you come to my place to see my etchings afterward?*
Meg: *You have etchings?*
Cate: *A soon-to-be-famous artist once told me that's always a ploy to get the beautiful woman alone in a studio.*
Meg: *Giving away the trade secrets.*
Cate: *You've never seen my place. And I have a spare bedroom you can use if my etching ploy falls short.*
Meg: *I'm more inclined to think that it won't if I end up in your studio.*
Cate: *Inclined? Reclined is more what I had in mind.*
Meg: *Can I say maybe for now? Life is moving at such a fast pace. Ben called.*
Cate: *And?*

Meg: *He knows about us. He's going to be okay with it. Now Natalie!*

Cate: *I wish I could help.*

Meg: *If it goes south be there for me.*

Cate: *I will. I know it's hard.*

Meg: *Speaking of going south I'll probably head down to LA to tell Nat in person soon. I'd invite you along to meet her but I think I need to break the news first. Probably be a very short visit. Just lunch or dinner.*

Cate: *I get it.*

Meg: *And I'd better confess that I went public. I told Olivia that my contract lawyer is my girlfriend. Sort of slipped out. I hope that's okay.*

Cate: *Hallelujah! You're making progress. I think there's hope for us, girlfriend.*

Meg: *I'm optimistic too. Will I see you this weekend?*

Cate: *Hey we have a tattoo date. I've got a mom's girlfriend discount rate and it's valid too. Now that you're officially my girlfriend.*

Meg: *No pressure on the tattoo but at least come hold my hand.*

Cate: *I'll be there, girlfriend.*

Meg: *Now I'm wondering if you're just using me for the discount.*

Cate: *I have ideas about using you but a tattoo discount isn't half of it.*

Meg: *Counting on it. Good night, Counselor.*

Cate: *Good night, Meg Mullins...until next time.*

❖

Meg wasn't surprised when Grace came by for a catch-up on Friday afternoon, returning a pie plate as her stated pretext. She hadn't seen Meg or Oscar in over a week, so there was a lot of catching up to do. After she and Oscar had their tête-à-tête, Grace settled in at the kitchen table with a glass of iced tea.

"Well, it's been over a week. Are you going to update me on the next installment in the life and times of Meg Mullins? I told you it's the most interesting part of my life," Grace said.

Meg laughed. "If you insist."

"I do. How's the art profession going? And I want to hear about Cate."

"Olivia from the gallery came and selected some of my pieces, and the opening is planned for the middle of next month. Cate is wonderful. I had Jessie and Luc over to meet her at dinner on Saturday and it went better than I could have hoped," Meg said. "Jessie told Ben, and Ben called me. Now he knows and seems to be handling it okay." Meg considered all that had happened in the past week and a half as she related her news to Grace.

"Cate is going with me to Jessie's shop in Santa Clara so I can get a dragonfly tattoo on my foot or ankle. I'm not sure if Cate will get a tattoo or is going to just hold my hand."

"So, you're finally going to do it. And a dragonfly."

"Yes. It was Jessie's idea, to symbolize change and a new beginning. It can also mean transformation and self-realization. Pretty much what I want in a tattoo."

"I'm proud of you." Grace smiled. "You've certainly taken control of the reins of your life."

"There's plenty with all this change that I haven't instigated. This new art opportunity just fell into my lap. And while I'm very optimistic that a relationship with Cate is heading in the right direction, I guess I probably have Robert to thank for that initial meeting," Meg noted, as she considered Grace's praise.

"Well, that bastard certainly owed you something," Grace replied. "It's one thing to be offered something, and it's another thing to maximize that opportunity. A different person wouldn't have ended up where you are now."

"Yeah. Fifty years old, coming out to my kids, a new girlfriend, starting a career." Meg looked up at the ceiling as she shook her head.

"Exactly," Grace said with a chuckle. "And with all that, I believe this is where you're supposed to be."

"Well, I still have Nat to deal with. Maybe I'll fly down in the next week or two because things are moving so fast."

"Just let me know when, and Oscar can come pole dance at my house."

"You're the best, Grace. I don't know what I'd have done all these years without you."

"You deserve to be happy. And to be honest, I'm enjoying the hell out of watching you bloom." They continued to catch up while finishing their iced teas and then promised to try to talk to each other during the next week.

SLOUCHING TOWARD STARDUST WITH MEG THE UNMUZZLED

"Seeking Inner Peace"

Watercolor is my medium of choice. It's often transparent. It frequently has a mind of its own while accepting input from the artist. Some colors play well with others and some do not. It lets the light in, then offers a piece of itself before returning that light to the eye of the beholder. And the end results can certainly be beautiful. If not a love story, there is most assuredly a relationship between the artist and the medium, the artist and the creative process. There have been complicated times in my life when I've needed more than watercolor. When different materials and an alternative process offered exorcism. A pathway back to inner peace. A cleansing of the soul.

The perfectionist in me struggled as I stained the Japanese rice paper with a swath of dragon's blood. Take that, and that, and that! Then I added undersea green and charted a road map in walnut ink. I gnashed my teeth and plucked some sacred feathers from their perch. After securing the avian offerings with shots of mucilage, I attacked an outdated weekly tabloid, severing a now-former prime minister from his latest lover. Studying him for a moment, I decreed decapitation was in order, then skillfully executed the sentence. Finally, selecting the torso rather than the noggin, I captured the entire mess beneath a bombardment of archival critic-proof varnish. Victory declared. Masterpiece complete. Mission accomplished.

CHAPTER SIXTEEN

After a lovely lunch with Cate's dad, Meg and Cate headed to Jessie's tattoo shop.

"My favorite ladies. Follow me." Jessie led them back to one of the separate rooms set up in the shop for tattooing.

"Almost feels like the doctor's office," Meg noted as she looked around.

"We strive for a comfortable, clean space. We need to keep things sterile," Jessie said. They turned to a notebook Jessie had selected. "So, let me show you a few dragonflies I have, and you can see if there's one you like, and then you can decide on location."

Meg looked through Jessie's options and immediately pointed to a delicate example done in fine line black ink with a mix of pale blue and sienna watercolor-like shading that added to its appeal. A sienna like the flecks in Cate's eyes.

"I'd like it on the top of my foot," Meg told Jessie.

"That's a beautiful choice and a good spot," Jessie said. "Perfect size for your foot, and you can cover it with a shoe if you choose. It'll always be out there in the water when you swim. I'll give you written aftercare instructions, but you'll have to stay out of the pool for a few weeks. Minimal showering is okay after twenty-four hours." Meg nodded her understanding as Jessie turned to Cate.

"And are we doing you today too, or is this just hand-holding?"

"I'll have the same," Cate told Jessie as she smiled at Meg.

"Matching tattoos. Almost like getting engaged," Jessie joked.

Meg understood the significance of Cate's decision. This was a big step for both of them. But it felt right. She leaned over and kissed Cate.

"Well, let's get to it, then. We'll start with you, Mom, and Cate can hold your hand and distract you. It's gonna hurt."

"Now you tell me," Meg quipped as she climbed onto the table and stretched out on her back.

Jessie pulled up their work chair. Cate sat near Meg's head, held her hand, and talked to distract her as Jessie worked on her foot.

Meg had been nervous about the tattoo, and initially, reclining on the table and the close proximity to Cate had the combined effect of escalating her tattoo anxiety as well as causing her to reflect on the intimacy of the moment. Being stretched out on her back with Cate's sweet fragrance filling her nostrils sent her thoughts to more passionate places. Meg wasn't sure which one was causing the pounding in her chest, or maybe it was both. But as Cate clasped her hand and carried on chatter about mundane topics, Meg began to relax and just enjoy the moment. The significance of Cate's willingness to get a paired tattoo along with Cate's efforts to distract her only escalated her feelings for her. As Cate talked about her dad and then Meg's art and then Piper's plants, Meg thought about Jessie's *practically engaged* joke. Meg knew they were just getting to know each other better, but matching tattoos certainly felt right.

It took almost three hours for Jessie to complete the tattoo. Meg was thrilled with it when it was finished, although the skin was fairly red around the art. She knew it would take time for the inflammation to subside. After inspecting Meg's new ink acquisition, Cate declared she was ready for her turn. By the time Jessie had prepared sterile equipment and she and Meg exchanged places, almost another three hours had passed with Meg trying to offer Cate the tenderness that Cate had just offered her.

It was after nine thirty by the time Jessie was finished and had given them aftercare instructions and lotion.

"Are you sure we can't pay you?" Meg asked.

"Hey, what are moms for if you don't get to torture them once in a while," Jessie answered with a laugh. "And a girlfriend twofer. How cool is that?"

"Would you at least let us buy you some dinner?" Cate offered.

"I need to get home to Luc. We're watching some superhero

movie they've been wanting to see tonight. But I'll take a rain check," Jessie advised them.

So, following the hugs and good-byes, they decided to pick up takeout on the way back to Meg's house. After all, Oscar was waiting.

❖

Cate leaned back on the couch and studied Meg once they were back at Meg's place with their carb-load pizza order. At eleven o'clock, the only one not exhausted was Oscar, who was thrilled with the company and crawled into Cate's lap as she and Meg sat on the couch eating dinner from the box and drinking beer. It had been a very long day. As they relaxed in companionable silence, the magnitude of not only the events of the day, but the place that Meg now occupied in her life hit her. Cate examined those feelings for Meg first. Not just the sexual attraction, because while that was certainly present and had been all that she'd considered with women since Laurel, it was this new growing emotional connection that she felt for Meg that she was thinking about.

Gazing out toward Meg's front door, Cate realized that it was not only a literal door, but also a metaphorical door to a major shift for her. The first time she'd knocked on it, the evening she'd taken the huge risk of rejection, she'd done so because she was finally ready to take that risk. And Meg hadn't ever tried to push her beyond what she was feeling—Meg was as cautious as she was. She appreciated that Meg wanted strings, didn't want to be hurt. Wanted the emotional component of a lasting relationship. Wanted to build on that.

Today's tattoo was something she'd considered all week. Examined. Debated. Presented oral arguments in her head, pro and con, since Jessie had made the offer last weekend. The cons had all come out as intellectual efforts that were grounded in her past. The pros were not just intellectual—they considered her heart and Meg's place there. The pros were grounded in her future, a future with Meg that included the huge step of sharing a tattoo. And thinking about it now, Cate knew that it had been the right choice. Meg was the woman she wanted in her future. It was what her heart was telling her. That was the biggest pro of all. If they could manage to make it work.

Oscar got up and walked over to Meg on the couch, pulling Cate from her thoughts. They finished eating and sat together holding hands with Oscar chaperoning.

"Do you want to sleep in tomorrow a bit and come for a late leftover pizza lunch?" Meg asked after several minutes of what Cate had enjoyed as companionable silence.

"That sounds good. I told my dad I probably wouldn't see him tomorrow, that I'd call him next week. He was good with that. And thanks for going with us to lunch today. I know Dad likes you, had a good time." Cate added Meg's rapport with her father to her growing list of why she was falling for Meg.

"I did too. All day long." Meg stifled a yawn and it was contagious. Cate yawned next, followed by the old cat. "I think even Oscar's ready to turn in," Meg observed.

As Meg walked Cate to the door, she put her arm around Cate's waist. "I think this tattoo is going to hurt for a while," Meg said.

"No pain, no gain, huh?" Cate winked.

"Thank you." Meg's beautiful blue eyes looked back at Cate as she gently leaned in and then softly brushed her warm moist lips across Cate's mouth.

"Who could pass up a twofer?" Cate joked.

"You could have," Meg replied.

"I didn't want to, Meg. This felt right."

"Yeah, it does," Meg said as they shared a more passionate kiss before agreeing to meet around noon for leftover pizza the next day, and then Cate headed to her car.

❖

Meg decided on Sunday evening after Cate had left for San Francisco that she would fly down to LA to talk to Natalie during the week. She felt the time had come. And she knew that their discussion probably wouldn't take longer than the span of a meal. Natalie would need time afterward to process the information, if she was willing. Meg was fairly certain an initial conversation wouldn't resolve anything. And she continued to worry what that resolution would be. In addition, she knew that Gus would likely come unless Meg made a point of expressing her need to talk to just Natalie—she wanted a one-on-one, so it didn't turn into a two-against-one.

"Hi, Nat. How are you today?" Meg said, opening the conversation.

"I'm good, Mom. What's up?"

"I'm coming to LA this week and want to take you to lunch or dinner. I have something I need to tell you." Meg was glad Natalie couldn't see that she was nervous. She kept her voice calm.

"Okay, what day are you planning?"

"What works for you?"

"I've got meetings all Monday and Tuesday afternoons, so any day but those," Natalie replied.

"How about Wednesday, then? I'd like it to be just the two of us." Meg could only hear silence on the other end of the line.

Finally, Natalie responded with a deep sigh and then, "If that's what you want."

"Good. So, would lunch work better for you than dinner?" Meg wanted to be as reasonable as possible, but still have the opportunity to talk to Natalie alone.

"Yeah. I always have dinner with Gus."

"Do you want me to pick you up, or do you want to meet somewhere?" Meg asked.

"How about that little deli around the corner from us, since I'm working from home on Wednesday? It has a nice patio. Do you remember the place? Lou's Deli."

"Sure. What's a good time for you?" Meg inquired.

"Noon should work."

"Noon it is, then."

"I love you, Mom."

God, she hoped so. Meg needed her daughter's love. Nat was a piece of herself. "I love you too, Nat. Always."

When Meg hung up, she made a plane reservation down to LA for Wednesday morning and back in the late afternoon. Then she reserved a rental car for the day. And after that, Meg tried to calm the unease she felt. She sat down and wrote a blog about being a mother. About her love for her children. About being true to herself.

❖

Cate owed Pete a lunch. She called him on Monday morning to see if she could take him out on Tuesday.

"Hey, Counselor Cupcake. What's up?"

"I think I owe you a lunch," Cate advised him.

"You owe me so much more," Pete informed her.

"Yeah, like for the tattoo I got this weekend." That ought to get his attention.

"Now I'm listening," Pete said. "You? A tattoo? Is it Meg's initials on your chest?"

Cate laughed at that image. Of course he was going to give her a bad time.

"If so, I want to see it. Firsthand," Pete said.

"Think a little lower."

"Oh God, no. Not a tush tattoo."

"Foot, Pete. Foot."

"Who puts initials on their foot?" Pete wondered.

"How did you get to be the CEO of an important investment firm?" Cate rolled her eyes, even if he couldn't see her.

"My charm and good looks," Pete offered.

"Must be. You are a handsome devil. So, to clarify, Meg's middle child is a tattoo artist and did matching dragonflies for Meg and me."

"And whose idea was that? Just wondering if it was the artist, Meg Mullins, or if you underwent a complete personality transformation." Pete chuckled.

"What? You think I'm too rigid for a tattoo?" Cate put on her best huff for Pete.

"Only if you're not falling in love."

"It was a twofer. A show of support." Cate wasn't going into her growing feelings for Meg with Pete right now. He'd want details about her emotions that she wasn't ready to share.

"Yeah. So, if I propose a *show of support* tattoo, you'll get one with me too?" Pete asked.

"Nope. My show of support for you is eating lunch with you tomorrow. So, where to?"

"How about that sandwich shop I like a few blocks from my office?" Pete asked. "With pastrami sandwiches to die for."

"Hey, I'm not ready to die for any sandwich, but that sounds good. Meet me there at noon?"

"You got it, lover girl." Pete laughed.

"Lover girl?" Cate knew that Pete must be smirking, but she was happy that he was keeping the conversation light. She wasn't ready to tell him how much she was realizing that she needed Meg in her life. Even if he'd been the one to convince her that was the case.

"Hey, it's a big improvement over bona fide heartless bitch." Pete hung up, laughing.

"Motherhood"

Three children, three distinct gifts of motherhood. So many ways to measure each. Not only the length, but the width as well. Each child unique, each connection a cord, each cord made of ties woven piece by piece. Love laced with the fragile elements of day-to-day living. And the unparalleled savoring of the height of each gift—inch by inch gains, the formidable bond, the incremental independence.

That independence. Expected of the progeny. Accepted for the offspring. But with the static assumption of the immutable mother. The heaviest burden she ever carried was the persistent cravings of a hungry heart—how to finally navigate this journey of mature motherhood with her independent offspring as she sought to finally nourish her own starving soul.

Now is her time. Not to walk away from motherhood, but to change her path while assuring her children that her love will never falter. And praying that her children will offer the same.

CHAPTER SEVENTEEN

On Wednesday morning, Meg waited in her seat in the airplane that would fly her from San Francisco to Los Angeles, where she would join her daughter for lunch. It was a little after half past eight in the morning. A few minutes later, the flight was in the air, and Meg figured she had about an hour and a half to collect herself and reflect on the growing feelings she had for Cate and the conversation she planned to have with her daughter regarding that relationship.

Apprehension squeezed Meg's chest with a steady pressure. Her stomach churned. She took a few deep breaths. She didn't want to lose Natalie, but she was determined that she wasn't going to let Nat's religious beliefs derail what she was finding with Cate. Meg was willing to acknowledge to herself that she was falling in love with Cate. And she knew Cate cared deeply for her too, whether Cate was ready to label it love yet, or not—Cate was cautious. She had been hurt before. A real emotional bond was forming between the two of them, and a very strong physical attraction too. Meg recognized that she had deep emotional bonds with several people in her life, but Cate had awakened the possibility of romantic love. And she hadn't felt this type of strong physical attraction in ages—she couldn't remember it ever feeling like what she was feeling toward Cate. Both were welcome surprises at age fifty.

Meg thought about her life up until now. The decisions she'd considered and made, complex decisions that had offered her many of the things she deeply valued in her life. She had no regrets. There had been some good times with Robert, but he'd never been the most attentive partner. Then things had changed over time for so many reasons. Thirty years ago she was beginning to explore who she was, but then she'd chosen her marriage and her family, and it had been the right choice. She knew that her recent attempts to date men hadn't offered what she wanted. She wanted to finally explore her attraction to women. To Cate. She wanted to nurture and grow what she was feeling for Cate. To see where it would lead.

As the plane cruised through the sky toward LAX, it didn't surprise Meg how much she was growing to want Cate physically. She had been feeling the heat of growing desire every time she and Cate touched, the need to physically express her feelings for Cate. Meg had been telling herself, and Cate, that she needed time to figure things out, to be sure their relationship was solid before they fully acted on their physical attraction. She had wanted a strong emotional relationship, not just a physical one. She needed that. And for that reason, she had kept their interactions to flirting, kissing, and a bit of touching—not that those actions with Cate weren't totally enjoyable. They had been. She knew Cate was ready for more. And she was willing to accept that she was comfortable with who she was finding herself to be, and with the strength of her relationship with Cate. She was ready for more too.

But the big acknowledgment that hit her as she sat at thirty thousand feet was that her current hesitation to making love with Cate was rooted in her need to inform her kids about the changes she was implementing in her life. And that was the reason for this trip. Jessie and Ben already knew. Now she owed Natalie the information, even if her religious beliefs would likely be at odds with anything she told her. Meg was not offering Natalie a say in the decision, but rather a heads-up about the truth of who she was because she loved her kids, and it was the right thing to do. Even if it would be a hard truth for Natalie.

❖

Meg arrived at the deli around the corner from Natalie's house at a little bit before noon. She waited in the rental car until she saw her slim, long-haired blond daughter approaching in dress slacks and a short-sleeved blouse.

She hadn't seen Nat in months, and she looked fine. Meg realized how much she missed her oldest child as she stepped out of the car and waved. Nat waved back as she approached, and then they hugged. Meg remembered when Nat was first placed into her arms, the tiny new life that created a devotion, an attachment, an overwhelming love unlike anything she'd known. She remembered Nat's first laugh, baby kisses, cartwheels, ballet recitals, prom nights, graduations, and eventually her marriage.

"Hi, Mom. You look good." Natalie smiled at her.

"So do you, Nat. Thanks for joining me." Meg smiled back.

"I'm not sure what this lunch is about, but I guess I'm going to find out."

Meg nodded and they went inside, ordered, and Meg paid before following Natalie outside to the awning-covered patio. They selected a table off to one side and made small talk until their food arrived and they began to eat.

Then Natalie cocked her brow and said, "Well?"

Meg inhaled and plunged in. "I've come to share some information about myself with you. Jessie and Ben already know, and I wanted you to know too."

"Okay." Meg could see that Natalie was on high alert now.

"First, I need to tell you how much I love you. All three of you kids. And the family we've built. Nothing can change that." Meg looked into her daughter's eyes. The same hazel eyes she'd known for thirty years.

"Now you're scaring me. What's wrong?" Natalie had stopped eating and was watching Meg.

"Nothing's wrong. There's a lot you don't know about me. Before I married your father, there were unanswered questions I had about myself. Things I put on hold about who I might be because our family was more important than that," Meg confessed. Her fear of losing Natalie's love lodged in her throat. She swallowed.

"What are you saying?" Natalie's hazel eyes widened with confusion.

Meg leaned back and wrapped her arms around her upper body before she continued. She knew that Nat's view of her would never be the same again. "I'm in a relationship with a woman. A wonderful woman named Cate. And I haven't told you kids until I felt comfortable saying I see a future and love involved between the two of us." Meg let out a deep breath as she watched Natalie stiffen.

"Is this about the fact that you were pregnant with me when you married Dad?" Natalie's voice had an accusatory edge to it.

"To be honest, I don't know what would have happened if I hadn't been pregnant. But I'd never change a thing. I love my family. And no, this is not about my being pregnant. This is about this point in my life. In being in a place where I'm finding out who I am now." Meg worked hard to remain relaxed and calm. She didn't want this to be a battle.

"You do know that you'll go to hell, Mom." Natalie's rejoinder was not surprising, but it was fast. There was no doubt in her response. She presented her beliefs as fact, and her proclamation caused Meg's chest to ache, but Meg did her best to remain outwardly unperturbed.

"I know that your church has taught you to believe that. I know some religious views have torn families apart, and I don't want that. But I can't live my life based on your beliefs, Nat. I'm a good person. I've devoted myself to our family. I never cheated on your father. I love you kids." Meg paused and held her daughter's displeased stare. "But I'm at a time in my life that I need to be my authentic self. To love who I love." Meg wanted to kiss her daughter and tell her that she was the same mother she'd always been, but she knew Natalie wouldn't accept that.

"And what do Jessie and Ben say?" Natalie demanded.

"They want me to be happy. Most love is not evil, and I don't believe Jesus would have condemned this. I know we disagree. But I can't live my life for you, even though I love you with all my heart. From the moment I knew that I carried you." Meg reached out and touched Natalie's cheek.

Natalie frowned. Meg could see the turmoil she was feeling. She could even understand it—Natalie had embraced her religion like a drowning person, and it seemed to have helped ground her. She had accepted what she had been told and had never had to confront the conflict her religion might bring to her life.

"I'm going to say one more thing. I was made this way. It's not an evil temptation. It's not always easy. But it's who I am, and I need to be who I am. And again, that has nothing to do with how much I love you."

Natalie shoved her plate away. Meg could tell she was done. With lunch. And probably with the conversation. All she could hope was that Natalie loved her enough to at least not sever their relationship, loved her enough to consider what Meg had said to her. She also knew that Gus and their church would put pressure on her to adhere to the religious beliefs she'd been taught. Almost a power struggle. And Meg did not know how to counter that.

"I accept that you think that I'm going to hell. I don't believe that. I want to say that what I'm feeling for Cate is a growing love. And I don't know what's wrong with loving someone when I'm not hurting anyone else. I won't stop loving Cate because you believe I'm going to hell. No more than I'd stop loving you. I do love you." Meg could feel her love for her daughter in the center of her chest.

"I love you too, Mom. And I worry about you because I love you." Natalie's voice was filled with emotion.

Meg felt some relief. At least her daughter didn't hate her. "I know, Nat. I know. But please don't let this come between us. I've accepted that you've become an evangelical. But I would have a very hard time accepting that religion could harm our love. Worry about me. That's okay. But keep loving me. And if you can, accept that I'm happy." Meg wiped her eyes, and so did Natalie.

"I've got to get back to work." Natalie stood up, ready to leave.

Meg hugged Natalie before she headed out on foot, and Meg got into her car and watched her daughter walk away. Meg wanted the little girl who wouldn't judge her, the girl who had not yet found a religion that would condemn her to hell. Meg sighed. Her family meant everything to her. She hoped this wouldn't sever the fragile ties she had with her daughter.

When Nat was out of sight, Meg decided to call Cate. She needed to hear her voice. The call went to voicemail, so she knew Cate was busy and left a message telling her that she was heading back to San Francisco. They'd agreed that she would fly in and out of SFO so that she could have dinner with Cate when she arrived back in the Bay Area early that evening. Grace had volunteered to stop by and take care of Oscar on her way home from work, so there was no rush to get home.

❖

It was close to six o'clock when Meg rode the elevator up to Cate's office. She'd picked up her Honda at the airport and parked it in the garage nearby. It felt good walking into the law firm after the long, difficult day. She needed to see Cate. Feel her embrace. As the elevator door opened and Meg looked up, Piper exited the office into the hallway and gave Meg a startled look.

"Hi, Meg," she muttered as she looked down and passed Meg for the elevator door before it closed. This was so unlike Piper.

"Everything okay, Piper?" Meg asked.

"Not sure," Piper responded as the door shut and she was gone.

That was strange, Meg thought, pushing the law office door open into Cate's reception area. As she entered, she could hear voices coming from Cate's office. One was Cate's. She didn't recognize the other voice—a woman's voice. Meg stopped where she was. She didn't want to interrupt but suddenly found herself eavesdropping.

"I'm so sorry for what I've put you through. But we had something. And I want it back. We were so good together, and it might have taken me five years, but I recognize that I was an idiot. I've matured, Cate."

"Laurel, I'll always have deep feelings for the years we spent together. For..."

The conversation muffled in Meg's head as the pounding of her heart drowned anything coming from Cate's office. *Oh my God* were the words that repeated in Meg's head as she stumbled and crashed into Piper's reception chair. She was just opening the door to leave when Cate charged out of her office.

"Meg. Wait!"

Meg continued across the exterior hallway to the elevator, rushed in as the doors slid open, and pushed the down button before Cate could catch up with her. She just wasn't ready for this.

Meg went to retrieve her car. Her phone was vibrating: call from Cate. She turned it off. Meg acknowledged that she needed to talk to Cate. But not now. Not tonight. It had been a hell of a day. Meg knew what she wanted. But did Cate?

Meg made it home and scooped up Oscar as she entered the house. She saw that Grace had already been by and fed him. He was thinner than he'd been in his youth. He was getting old, and that worried her. She needed her ol' boy. Really needed him. She kissed his head. Scratched his ears. Told him she loved him. He was so much less complicated than people were. Than Natalie. Than Cate. It had been a hell of a day. Meg threw her phone onto the mail table, noting nine missed calls from Cate. Not tonight. Then she headed to the shower. Afterward, in her favorite mid-thigh-length robe over cotton sleeping shorts and a low-cut T-shirt, she decided that she deserved a glass of wine, but she would not get drunk. She propped herself up in bed with the drink on the night table. She'd let her damp hair finish drying before she went to sleep, and maybe write a blog for distraction—about anything but Cate. Oscar joined her. Her good ol' boy. She took such comfort in his presence in her life. And she needed him tonight.

SLOUCHING TOWARD STARDUST WITH MEG THE UNMUZZLED

"A Letter to My Cat: Living with the Elderly"

Dear Oscar,

Having had a father-in-law carry the same moniker as you is sometimes confusing to the rest of us, but I don't think you actually give a damn, and I appreciate that. You, like my father-in-law was before we lost him, are getting up there in years. Geriatric.

At the end, he was acting his age in abbreviated flare-ups. Flare-ups: the hairs on the back raised up when help was offered, the hairs on the back raised up when help was not offered, the night howls to the kids—threatening to call the sheriff because too much living can make one sad and irrational. Too much living. It had led my father-in-law to wear his version of to hell with it—purposefully uncut hair, the same clothes day after day. And it has led you to wear your own version of to hell with it—slacking a bit on the meticulous grooming.

But Oscar, while you survived the streets through terrible times, you are the one who praises the simplest pleasures: being warm, safe, and well-fed in this hard world. You are the one who praises the simple pleasure of a small space to call your own. The simple pleasure of a short nap in the sunshine. Of a bird near the window. Of one more day.

Father-in-law and you—old age and health issues. I treasure that being on medications—for hyperthyroidism, acid reflux, chronic renal disease—hasn't jaundiced you. Never focusing on what has been taken from you—there is no bitter pill to swallow. No blame to blurt, no war to wage, no rage to roar. Instead, Oscar, you hug me close with your old feline body and praise the moment—a rumble of reverence for just being. The purr of pleasure. The purr of peace. The purr of satisfaction for what you still have. The purr of not giving a damn for what has been lost. And for that, Oscar, I love you.

Taking notes,
Meg

CHAPTER EIGHTEEN

It was close to midnight when Meg finally turned off the light. She was exhausted but afraid sleep wouldn't come. At least she could doze, and that was just what she was doing when a banging on the front door aroused her. She didn't know who it could be at this time on a Wednesday night. Maybe Cate? Meg threw on her short robe and trod to the door. She turned on the porch light and looked out through the peephole. It was Cate. Meg pulled the door open, fingering her hand through her now dry hair.

Cate looked at her, her gaze traveling up and down Meg's body. It felt almost as sensual to Meg as a physical caress. She could see the desire flash across Cate's face. Cate's eyes darkened to even a deeper shade than the gorgeous hues that always enthralled Meg. Then Cate straightened her stance. Bit her lower lip. They studied each other for a long moment.

"Can I come in? I tried to call, but you didn't pick up." Cate sounded a bit indignant.

"My phone is off." Meg didn't try for an apology. Just a statement of fact.

Cate waited. Meg stood back and waved her in.

"What are you doing here, Cate? Don't you have work tomorrow?"

"Nothing I can't cancel. And I'm here so this doesn't get out of hand."

"It's not my business what you and Laurel had to discuss."

"Are you kidding? It's absolutely your business. So get over whatever you're thinking and come sit on the couch with me."

Meg had always liked the bossy Cate. She let Cate lead her over to the couch. Let Cate put her arms around her in an embrace. Let Cate plant a kiss on her cheek. Meg began to cry, and Cate just held her.

Finally, Cate said, "Listen to me, babe." *Babe.* Meg sniffed and followed orders. "I haven't seen Laurel in five years. She just suddenly showed up. As you know, she put me through hell. Yes, I'll always care for her. For what we had. But as I told her tonight if you'd stayed and listened, she and I are over. You are my future. That is what I told her because that's the truth."

"I'm sorry, Cate. It's been an emotionally horrendous day."

"I'm sorry I wasn't there for dinner. For you—after Natalie."

"So am I. I needed you. And when I got Laurel instead, I just bailed. Hit my limit."

"Well, I'm here now," Cate said.

"At midnight. On a work night. That says a hell of a lot. Thank you."

"Yeah. Way past my bedtime on a work night. But I left Piper a note to cancel out the next two days, and I'll call her tomorrow. I haven't taken any vacation in ages. No vacation is a hazard of being the boss. But taking an unexpected few days off is a perk of being the boss." Cate chuckled as her lips swept Meg's cheek again.

Meg locked her gaze on Cate's hungry dark eyes.

"God, your eyes are gorgeous, Meg," Cate told her as she looked back. "Striations of light and dark blues."

Meg took Cate's face between her hands and gently captured Cate's mouth. She lingered until Cate softly asked, "How did it go with your daughter?"

"It probably went better than I'd thought it might. The word *hell* came up, but I got the word *love* into the conversation several times."

"That's good."

"It was an honest conversation. And I'm still running my own life. So, I'd have to say that's the good news." Meg knew the smile she gave Cate was a bit crooked.

"I know it was hard," Cate spoke in a tone that soothed her.

"Nat listened to me. And she loves me. But I've put her in a position of probably having to choose between her husband, her church, and me. I hate that."

Cate just sat and rocked her. Meg closed her eyes and breathed in Cate's delicious scent. This was exactly what she needed. "Natalie was the last of my kids I needed to tell. It was important to me to tell all my kids about you before we move on. I acknowledged to myself on the flight down that was a major factor holding me back from advancing our relationship." Meg leaned back and looked again into Cate's enticing eyes. "I'd decided that I know who I am. What I want. And that I wasn't afraid of you breaking my heart. And then I heard Laurel."

"But you didn't stay to hear *me*. I told Laurel that you're my girlfriend. And as Jessie said, we're practically engaged with matching tattoos."

Meg laughed through her sniffling. She lifted the hem of her shirt and wiped her eyes. Cate looked hungrily at her exposed abdomen. "Hey. Multiple births and I'm probably showing you the least sexy part of me," Meg told her as she noticed Cate's stare.

"Sexy as hell," Cate growled.

"Well, I was going to tell you tonight at dinner that now that I'm out to my kids, I think I'm ready to seriously consider seeing your etchings."

"God, Meg. Don't tempt me tonight. It's too late and you're too exhausted. When we do this, I want it to be perfect. With no rush."

Meg was a little disappointed, but she wanted them to take their time too. And not have their first time be when she was as exhausted and emotional as she was.

"I'm going to hold you to it, Counselor. I wish you'd stay and just hug me tonight."

"I don't have that kind of willpower. I want to see you naked. I want to make love to you. Worship your body. Ravish you until you can't take anymore."

"Now you're challenging my restraint," Meg said. "So, I guess you're going to your father's place tonight?"

"I'd better."

"Do you want to go out in the morning and get coffee? A little food? Since we missed dinner," Meg asked.

"That sounds wonderful."

"Shall we invite your dad?"

Cate shook her head. "You are the ultimate mom, always thinking of everyone. Yes, let's take Dad. He'll love it."

"It wasn't an ultimate mom thing. It was a chaperone thing, so we don't end up in bed before lunch," Meg grumbled.

Cate laughed. "Okay, babe. Okay."

And Meg laughed too. *Babe.* She could get used to that.

❖

Cate called Piper at the office at nine o'clock the next morning.

"You had me worried, boss. I saw your note. I hope everything is okay."

"It's okay," Cate assured her. "I just wanted to make sure you canceled appointments today and tomorrow. I don't think there's much on the books, luckily. I know that I have a few calls to make, but I can do those from here. And you can call me if you need anything."

"Is Meg okay? She was just coming in as I was leaving yesterday. And that lady who said she was your old girlfriend had just walked in before that. You sure do know how to live dangerously."

"Meg is fine. But I needed to come see her. Clarify a few things. I'm in Trinity Hills at my dad's place."

Piper cleared her throat. "Don't fire me, but here's where my love life advice comes in."

Cate had to smile. "So, let's hear it."

"Go with Meg. She's perfect for you."

"I'm glad we agree. I guess I won't have to fire you. Today." Cate didn't even try to suppress the humor in her voice or the affection she was feeling for Piper.

Piper laughed into the phone. "You're the best. Just don't do anything I wouldn't do."

"I ascertain that might leave me a lot of leeway," Cate responded archly.

"Hey, boss?"

"What?"

"Just don't get her pregnant."

"I'll see you on Monday, Piper."

"I'm holding the fort, Cate. Don't worry."

❖

An hour later, Cate picked up Meg. Cliff was already in the car. He was in the front passenger seat but suggested he could move to the back seat so Meg could sit next to Cate. Meg insisted on just hopping into the back of Cate's Audi.

"We want coffee and some food, Dad. So, where shall we go?"

"You want highbrow, lowbrow, or in-between?" Cliff asked.

"Well, let's not do McDonald's. But I think there's a nice little pastry shop downtown that would fit the bill. What do you think, Meg?" Cate asked.

"Lead the way. I'm easy."

"I already knew that, but where shall we eat?" Cate teased.

Cliff chuckled. "I'm so glad you two found each other."

"So are we, Dad. It's amazing what happens when you aren't planning it."

"That it is, princesa."

They ordered their coffee and food, then spent the next hour enjoying each other's company. Cate had to admit that she loved the way Meg welcomed her dad. A major perk of not being teenagers— they could date and bring Cliff along. It was obvious to Cate that he appreciated the attention, and Meg made it easy for her to spend time with her dad.

After they dropped Cliff off, Cate explained that she needed to complete some work-related business—the day off was unplanned, after all. Meg was fine with that. There were projects in her studio she wanted to pursue. And maybe a little blog writing.

They agreed to meet at Meg's house for dinner that evening at six o'clock. Meg knew that Oscar would be happy with the added company. Then Cate dropped Meg at her house and headed home to her dad's place.

At six, Cate arrived with a bag and headed to the kitchen with Oscar on her heels. She set the bag on the table and unloaded two chicken salads and an order of pot stickers. Meg laughed.

"In honor of our first unofficial date at your hotel." Cate grinned.

"You're so mushy," Meg drawled.

"I am not mushy," Cate retorted. "I just had an inclination to remember our first evening together."

"And why would that be?" Meg eyed her.

"Our first kiss."

"Now that is mushy." Meg came up behind Cate, put her arms around her waist, and rested her chin on her shoulder. Meg could feel her heart respond to the thoughtfulness of this woman standing in her embrace. Not only her heart—she responded lower as well.

"Nope. Just hoping for a whole lot more than a kiss tonight. Purely selfish. But if you want to call it mushy, I'm not going to argue. As long as there are results." Cate turned her head and trailed gentle kisses along Meg's jawline.

"I'm hungry," Meg said, knowing they'd miss the effort Cate had put into their special dinner if they didn't eat now.

"So am I," Cate replied. "For more than salad and potstickers."

SLOUCHING TOWARD STARDUST WITH MEG THE UNMUZZLED

"Eyes"

While the artist in me appreciates the hues, the patterns, the reflections, the spark of life that eyes portray, it's the anatomy of the eye that makes those features possible. The melanocytes of the iris create two melanins: a brownish-black pigment and a reddish-yellow pigment. Greater or lesser amounts of these pigments and greater or lesser collagen fiber density result in the vast and spectacular array of individual eye colors—brown, hazel, green, gray, blue—as well as color patterns in the iris: rings, bands, spots.

I love eyes. The many moments when our eyes met. Revealing. Intimate. Magic. Seductive umber infused with a salting of smoldering burnt sienna meeting the blue blend of deep river currents and expansive azure sky. The genesis of a kiss before it reached the lips. The yearning for a touch before it became an embrace. An invitation to unravel you in the silence of our rendezvous. A proclamation of passion without one word uttered. A place to get lost. A place to be found. The window to your soul. And I heard your soul whisper to my heart: I want you. I need you. I love you. And my soul answered back: me too.

Chapter Nineteen

They had just finished eating dinner and were still at the kitchen table when Cate looked up. "There are a few things we haven't discussed, and I think we should."

"This doesn't sound like it's going to be mushy." Meg felt a wave of uneasiness. "Should I be nervous?"

"No. I just want you to know a few things." Cate inhaled, and Meg noticed she was a little uneasy. Cate looked down. "I've had several short-term encounters, uh…since Laurel." Then Cate looked back up at Meg. "But not since we had dinner in your hotel room. I had myself tested for STDs because I want us to be safe." The corners of Cate's mouth quirked up as she offered Meg an anxious look.

Meg returned an indulgent smile. "Cate, we both know we each have histories. It's okay. And I love that you want us to be safe. If this is true confessions, I haven't been in bed with anyone since well before Robert died." Meg cast her eyes down. "He wasn't interested in me anymore, and we probably know why with that apartment. I must have had a subconscious clue about his activities because I had myself tested after he was gone, just to be sure I was healthy." Meg looked back up at Cate. She didn't want to think about Robert. She wanted to be here with Cate.

Cate let out a sigh of relief. "Thank you. For being willing to have this conversation with me. For sharing with me. Staying safe is important—for both of us."

Meg couldn't believe that she was fifty years old and discussing safe sex for herself. "The last time I had this conversation, it was with one of my teenage kids." Meg chuckled as she considered the situation.

"And the fact that you were willing to have it—that's mushy in its own way."

"If that's the case," Cate responded, "there's something else I want to ask you. Nothing like getting points for being mushy." Cate offered Meg an amused grin as she stood up and walked around to Meg's chair and pulled her up into her arms.

"Okay. Are we playing Truth or Dare?" Meg teased. "I'll take truth."

"I just wanted to know if you've ever been with another woman. I want this to be what you need. I want us to do it right." There was naked hunger in Cate's half-lidded gaze as she held Meg.

"No, Cate. I hadn't ever actually dated anyone seriously when Robert talked me into going out with him. And we know where that went." Meg shrugged slightly, and then her tone softened, "I haven't been with a woman, but if it helps, I'm not short on biology. Anatomy. As an artist…" Meg rambled.

Cate silenced her with a slow caressing kiss. "It's okay. Are you ready for me to show you how much I care? How attracted I am to you?"

"If we're still in the game, I'm taking the dare," Meg responded, allowing her mouth to turn up in the hint of a smile. She hoped she'd live up to Cate's expectations. "The dare—to show you what I feel for you too, Cate." Meg was tempted to tell Cate she loved her, but she didn't want to say it when Cate might interpret it as only a declaration made in the heat of an intimate encounter. It was too important. So, she'd make love to Cate now and make the declaration some other time.

Cate softly brushed her lips along the side of Meg's neck. Then she took Meg's hand and led her out of the kitchen to the living room, where she looked up the staircase with a raised eyebrow. Meg was already barefoot, and Cate slipped out of her shoes at the bottom of the stairs.

Meg stopped and studied the art they shared. Two dragonfly tattoos. The significance of the ink on their feet almost overwhelmed her as she thought about her journey to this moment. She felt at peace with where she was. This was where she was supposed to be. The symbolism associated with the small, winged creatures permanently represented on their skin was important to her, but it was also the act of sharing the experience of acquiring the tattoos and wearing them in unison that touched her heart. These tattoos represented both the emotional and physical bonds that she wanted in her life. Cate's commitment to Jessie's matching art only increased the desire Meg felt for her.

Meg shook her head to bring herself back to the moment. "There's a bedroom suite here at ground level as well as one upstairs. After Robert, I moved into the one down here and bought a new bed. Down the hall past my art studio." Her voice had become low and throaty.

Cate laced her fingers with Meg's as she led her to the bedroom—a large room with a king-sized bed covered in a cream-colored quilt and several cream and watercolor floral print pillows against the headboard. Cate turned to face Meg. She ran her hands through Meg's short thick hair, pushing it back behind her ears. Leaning in, Cate planted a quick kiss on Meg's exposed neck, then straightened. Meg shuddered and reached out to touch Cate.

Cate held Meg's hands down against her sides and whispered into Meg's ear, "Let me show you how much I want you. Worship you. Map out every beautiful square inch of you."

Meg nodded as desire coursed through her. This deep carnal need was greater than any she'd ever felt. But it was her heart that told Meg she was where she wanted to be.

Cate walked Meg backward to the bed, led her down to a sitting position with gentle pressure on her shoulders before moving her hands to the buttons on Meg's blouse. Meg closed her eyes as Cate leaned in and ran her lips lightly along her throat. Then Cate stepped back and began slowly unfastening those buttons, one by one.

Meg reached for Cate again. "Uh-uh," Cate murmured. "Let *me* show *you*," she repeated. "I want you to feel my touch everywhere. Show you what it's like to be with me. Until you can't take anymore."

Meg gave a soft strangled whimper as Cate finally freed the bottom button and pushed the sides of the top away from Meg's chest. Then, guiding Meg into a reclining position, Cate stretched out next to her. She rolled Meg onto her side, mapped Meg's lower back with light-fingered strokes, before she unhooked Meg's bra. A black silk bra. Cate rotated her again so she could free the undergarment and toss it aside. With one hand gently holding Meg's hands above her head, Cate's fingertip traced a line from the corner of Meg's mouth to the swell of her breast, alternating a light circle around the peak of one swell and then the other. Leaning in and teasing each dark aroused apex with her tongue, Cate whispered, "Beautiful, Meg. Beautiful."

"Jesus." Meg couldn't stop herself from moaning the word. "Please." She pressed her hips into Cate. She wanted so much more of Cate. "You're driving me crazy."

"That's the goal, babe," Cate advised her in a husky voice as her free hand skimmed down Meg's abdomen and she slipped her fingers under the waistband of Meg's jeans. Then she unzipped them. Meg tracked the path of Cate's hand as it explored the upper edge of her black silk briefs.

They were both so focused on their escalating passion that they did not hear the phone ringing out in the front of the house until Oscar jumped on the bed and shattered their perfect moment.

"What the hell," Cate growled. "Ignore it."

"Damn, I'm trying." But the ringing didn't stop. First it was Cate's ringtone. And then Meg's ringtone, followed by Cate's again. "I think you need to go answer your phone, Cate. I'm worried it's The Terraces. They're the ones who know we both see your dad, and they have both our numbers."

As Cate headed out to her phone, Meg pulled her unbuttoned blouse all the way off, ignored her tossed bra, and pulled on a T-shirt. She took a deep breath and struggled to put the overwhelming physical desire of the moment on hold. Then she followed Cate out to the living room and waited next to her.

"Yes. This is Cate Colson." Cate put the phone on speaker.

"This is Sue at The Terraces, Cate. Your dad was having severe abdominal pains, so we called an ambulance. They just took him to Trinity Hills Hospital to evaluate him."

Cate bit her knuckles and her eyes glistened. "I'll head to the hospital right now," she said. She hung up and looked at Meg.

Meg morphed into her efficiency persona. She'd had thirty years of running things. Handling one kid crisis after another. She grabbed her own shoes and offered Cate hers. She collected her phone, car keys, and their purses. As she handed Cate her handbag, Meg led her toward the front door.

"I'll drive so you can take any further phone calls," Meg told her. She grabbed Cate, gave her a hug, and said, "It's a good hospital, Cate."

She knew that she spoke with authority—she'd spent so much time there with Robert. But now wasn't the time to think about that. She needed to get Cate to Cliff. Then she gently guided Cate out through the door and locked it.

Meg drove through town at the maximum speed allowed, while Cate sat silently in the passenger seat. Meg looked over at her a few times, patted her thigh, but remained silent. There was little she could say until they had talked to a doctor. Meg told herself that she would do everything in her power to be there for Cate and Cliff through this. The two had become an important part of her life.

They pulled into the parking lot, and Meg found an empty spot near the entrance. Cate jumped out first, then waited for Meg. Meg took her hand as they hurried in through the automatic doors to the reception desk.

Cate hadn't said a word since they'd left Meg's house but cleared her throat now.

"My dad, Cliff Colson, was brought in by ambulance from The Terraces with abdominal pain. I'm Cate Colson."

"Hi, Cate. Go take a seat and give me a minute to see what I can find out for you."

Cate just stood there. Meg quashed her many memories of being here with Robert, then took Cate's hand and led her over to a chair. It struck Meg that while she had three kids and a cat, Cate's dad was her entire family. No wonder she was in shock. Meg continued to hold Cate's hand while leaning in just enough to touch shoulders. She was trying to give Cate some space to process the news while not smothering her. But she wanted Cate to know that she was there for her, however Cate needed her.

Finally, the receptionist came over to talk to them. "They're evaluating and running tests on your dad," she told Cate. "He's conscious and more worried about you than about himself."

Cate's face relaxed a bit and her mouth twitched. "That's my dad."

"As soon as they know something, one of the doctors will come out and talk to you."

Cate just sat there, so Meg thanked the receptionist and they both continued to wait. Meg considered what she would say to one of her kids in a crisis to soothe them—that was her territory. But what to say to her lover? *Lover.* That was something she had no experience with.

Robert had never needed or wanted her opinion or comfort in a crisis. Even when he became so sick. Meg decided that she just needed to be honest and make this about Cliff and Cate. She broke the silence. "Cliff is a tough guy, Cate. And this hospital has an excellent reputation." She squeezed Cate's hand. "He knows how much you love him."

Cate squeezed her hand back. They waited quietly with minimal conversation for two and a half more hours before a slender woman of about forty in blue scrubs came out from a closed door to talk to them. The doctor pulled off her scrub cap as she approached and a shock of dark curls emerged. She smiled as she approached.

"Hi, which one of you is Cate?" Cate stood up. "I'm Dr. Fallon. I've run some tests on your dad, and he's stable. It looks like he has a complete intestinal blockage. We need to get the official results of some additional tests we ordered, especially since he's eighty-four, but Dr. Pabst, the surgeon, doesn't want to put off addressing this due to the risks of waiting." Dr. Fallon gave Cate a moment to digest what she'd just said. "He'll go to surgery in the morning. In the meantime, we'll make your dad comfortable."

"What time are you planning the surgery and how long will it take?" Cate asked.

"He'll start pre-op about half past five, surgery scheduled at eight o'clock. It can take several hours, depending on what we find. We'll have him busy, so you won't be able to see him then. We'll get you in to see him for a few minutes now. Then go home and come back around eight o'clock in the morning. If there's any change, we'll call you." Dr. Fallon paused to make sure Cate was understanding, then continued, "Do you have any other questions?" She offered Cate a compassionate smile.

"None that I can think of," Cate responded. Meg could see that Cate was struggling to put on a brave face.

"Well, then. I'll send a nurse out to bring you to him, so wait here." After shaking Cate's hand, Dr. Fallon headed back in the direction she'd come from.

A few minutes later, a young male nurse collected Cate and Meg and led them to a room where Cliff was lying in a bed. He smiled when he saw them.

"I'm on pain meds, so no holding me to anything I say," he advised them.

"So at least they've alleviated some of the pain?" Cate asked.

"I'm feeling pretty darn good right now," Cliff said with a chuckle.

"I love you, Dad."

"You too, princesa. Did the doc tell you they're going to fix me in the morning?"

"She did. And Meg and I will be here waiting. In the meantime, you need to get some rest," Cate advised.

Cate hugged her dad, then Meg did the same. He was falling asleep from the medications as they left the room and headed back to the car.

❖

Cate was emotionally exhausted, but she doubted she could sleep. She trailed Meg into the house, Oscar waiting at the door. Cate was prepared to brood all night—how could she sleep with her father in the hospital, waiting for emergency surgery? She wasn't ready to lose her dad. Cate sniffled. Meg turned around, gently grasped her by the wrist, and led her toward the bedroom.

"We're going to get you a shower, and then you're going to bed—to sleep. No arguing. I'm in charge now. Your dad is going to need you over the next few days."

Through her fatigue, Cate had to smile. This was Meg—in her mother-in-charge mode. Cate let Meg guide her through the bedroom to the en suite and watched her turn on the shower water, adjust the setting. She let Meg efficiently strip her, push her into the warm water. As Meg started to close the shower door, Cate reached out and caught Meg's wrist. Cate gave her a pleading look and tugged her toward the running water. Meg toed off her shoes and stepped into the shower, fully clothed, her T-shirt slowly darkening and clinging to her body. Cate realized Meg had nothing on under the T-shirt. Her body surged, full of lust she couldn't control, as she raised her eyes to study Meg's face, then trailed her hungry gaze back over her soaking chest and swept down the rest of Meg's wet clothing, finally stopping at her bare feet. Toe to toe, the delicate matching dragonflies faced each other. The significance of the matching tattoos hit Cate. Meg was looking down too, studying the art that bonded them. Cate moved even closer to Meg, reached out to take control, but Meg shook her head.

"We can resume what we started when your dad is okay—with

you in charge. But tonight," Meg informed her, "you relax. Let me be in charge." Cate swallowed, fighting the heat—and not the warm-water heat. Meg focused the hand-held nozzle away from their feet to prevent soaking the new tattoos for an extended period. Meg held the soap in her hand and started lathering Cate. Front first, efficiently, then rinsed. Turned her and soaped her back, followed by another efficient rinse. Meg squatted at Cate's left ankle, then ran the sudsy body sponge up her left leg to her hip, avoiding Cate's inner thigh. Meg did the same with the right side. Cate's breathing deepened and sped up, and when Meg rose and looked at her, she knew that Meg had read her need. Yes, it was a need for release, but also for Meg. For her caring. For the connection with this specific nurturing woman. And a need to believe she would be okay as she worried about her dad.

Meg attempted a supportive chaste kiss on Cate's cheek, but no kiss of Meg's struck Cate as chaste.

"Please, Meg," Cate pleaded.

Meg smiled her understanding that she needed to finish what they had started earlier. Cate needed that. Meg reached through the warm, flowing water and touched her hand to Cate's core, waltzed her fingers into Cate's feminine folds. With that dance, the beauty of the bond with Meg slowly swelled and spread from Cate's center up to her pounding heart and hurled her entire body into spasms. Meg tenderly held her as the water rained on both of them, kissed each of her closed eyes.

"I wanted to do that to you tonight, Meg. I was supposed to be in charge."

"I love the bossy you, Cate, but another night. I'm fine. You've got to get some sleep. Cliff is going to need you tomorrow."

Meg turned off the water, reached out and grabbed a towel from a hook just outside the shower, and wrapped it around Cate, patting and rubbing her dry. As she led her from the shower, she quickly wrapped another towel around herself, clothing and all. Leaving damp footprints across the low pile rug, Meg guided Cate onto the mattress after turning back the bedding. Covering Cate, she kissed her on the forehead. Cate closed her eyes and felt herself drifting off.

"Now go to sleep," Meg ordered.

Cate tried to mumble her appreciation, but it came out in her exhaustion with only an audible, "Dreaming of you."

"Mushy." Meg's reply was barely a whisper.

Cate was aware that Meg changed from her soaked attire into her pajamas and robe. The last thing Cate heard was Meg carrying wet clothes and towels to the laundry room, then heading out to the living room to spend time with Oscar and her laptop. A little over an hour later, Cate resurfaced from her exhaustion for a moment when Meg returned to the bedroom, set a wake-up alarm, and stretched out next to Cate's warm body to get some sleep too. Cate took Meg's hand and laced their fingers together, feeling the squeeze of Meg's hand before she nodded off again.

"Dragonflies and Ode to Self"

The dragonfly: An ancient flying insect evolving about three hundred million years ago. Two compound eyes. An elongated ten-segment abdomen. Six legs. Four independent wings, layered with clear and iridescent chitin segments. Often with yellow, red, brown, black pigments and photonic cells reflecting the blue sky above or combining with yellow pigment to create green. Water to land, aquatic nymph to airborne adult. Spiritual symbol of rebirth, life balance, wisdom, energy, maturity, new insights.

❖

I once told myself, when I find my ode to self, I will have it injected in ink onto my canvas. A selection of modest artistry for a mature woman still defining herself. And the artist matters. Because if you're going to wear someone's art for the rest of your life, the artist matters. I know that artist. I am still searching for that ode to self.

And now, I have found my ode to self. The dancing, gossamer-winged, water-loving dragonfly. Magical, elegant, graceful. A symbol of my ongoing transformation in self-acceptance, self-perspective, positive change, courage, strength, and happiness. Injected in ink for the rest of my life, the artist my child. And what added layer of symbolism is represented when someone commits to place that same ode to self on their human canvas? Someone significant. Someone important. Someone I want in my life. Both of us wearing this permanent art that bonds us. I'd call it love.

CHAPTER TWENTY

Meg woke up on Saturday morning at six o'clock when the alarm went off. As she rubbed her tired eyes, following a night of sleep that had been much too short, Oscar ambled into the room. "Good morning, old man. Where is Cate?" The other side of the bed was empty.

Meg combed her hair, brushed her teeth, then pulled on undergarments, a T-shirt, and a pair of jeans before she wandered toward the kitchen where she could hear Cate moving around as she drew closer.

"How did you sleep?" she asked Cate as she approached her at the coffeepot.

"Better than I expected, thanks to you," Cate said before she cleared her throat. "Thanks, Meg. For yesterday…all of it." Cate held Meg's gaze. Then she shifted the conversation, saying, "I'm feeling better about Dad this morning. We've got to get through this, but I think he's going to be okay."

Meg walked over and took Cate in her arms. "I think so too." Then she leaned in and spoke into Cate's ear, keeping her tone gentle. "Glad I could help."

Meg hadn't fully processed their interrupted lovemaking, and she knew that she needed to focus on helping Cate through the surgery this morning. But for her first time with a woman, for her first time with Cate, and with the medical emergency last night, it had been so much better than she would have predicted. Things hadn't gone as planned, and she was looking forward to the time when things did, when there wasn't a crisis, because she had no doubt that bossy Cate in bed would be amazing—she'd sampled that before the call interrupted them. Meg was looking forward to that time, and it wasn't just the tightness of her nipples or the need between her legs as she held Cate now. It was these strings of connection. The strings that she needed.

"I think your debt for the contract review is paid in full," Cate said, a touch of humor playing across her face.

"Well, that's no fun. I was looking forward to negotiating," Meg responded with a chuckle. Cate looked better this morning than she had last night after the news of Cliff's medical condition. That was likely because Cate knew the cause and that action was being taken, Meg reflected. Cate was a woman of action.

"Shall we have a cup of coffee and toast, then hit the road for the hospital?" Meg asked.

"That sounds good. If we leave soon, I should have time to run into Dad's house and throw on a change of clothes. I think I'll go with a T-shirt and jeans today too. It's going to be a long day of waiting."

Cate poured the coffee and added Meg's usual soy milk to her mug, even though she had only had brunch at Meg's the once to witness Meg preparing her coffee. The simple act of remembering touched Meg's heart. Little things mattered—twenty-eight years and Robert could never remember how she took her coffee. Meg toasted some bread and filled Oscar's bowl, then they sat for a quick bite to eat before departing for the hospital.

Cate was silent for a moment, and then she reached across the table and took Meg's hand. "I know we don't have much time right now, but a lot has happened since dinner last night. We made love for the first time." Cate pulled her in and kissed her hard on the lips before leaning back. "You were perfect. Better than perfect—I was going to take care of you last night, and after Dad, you took care of me. Our night was interrupted…not what I had planned for you. I wanted to show you how much I care, but instead, you took charge when I needed you, and it couldn't have been better."

"I'm glad, Cate. And you know something? I'm good with how it turned out. I thought I did okay for my first time."

Cate raised her eyebrows at Meg. "A virgin."

Meg smirked. "Yeah. A fifty-year-old virgin with three kids." It was a joke, but Meg realized, in a sense, there was some truth in it. She knew it had been a huge step in her life and in their relationship. She was relieved and pleased at Cate's words.

❖

It was a little after half past seven when Meg parked the car in the hospital parking lot and they headed inside. A woman with a name tag reading *Lois* was on duty today, and she had Cate and Meg take a seat in the waiting area. The surgeon would be out to introduce himself before the surgery if he had time, so they needed to wait for him.

They sat quietly, simply biding their time. Meg could tell that Cate had pulled into herself as soon as they'd walked into the hospital, undoubtedly feeling the magnitude of the situation and her dad's peril. Meg had repressed her own feelings last night with Cliff's major crisis, but this morning, as soon as they'd come through the hospital doors the past tried to resurface, and her mind had gone right back to this hospital and her time here with Robert—memories of Robert's illness, the long hours in the waiting room and his hospital room, her emotions at the time—but Meg tamped it down. There was no place for any of that while she was focusing on Cate and Cliff. Meg knew they'd be here most of the day and decided that she'd see if Cate wanted to talk about how she was feeling after they'd met the surgeon.

Lois returned a few minutes later, and to their surprise, the surgeon followed her into the waiting area. "I'm Dr. Pabst, and I'll be operating on your dad in just a little while, Cate. Your dad has been in pre-op for the past few hours, and the anesthesiologist is with him now. He's doing fine." Dr. Pabst turned to head back to the surgery area. "We'll let you know once the surgery is completed," he called back over his shoulder.

"Good bedside manner," Meg noted to Cate. "That's always a bonus."

"And an excellent surgeon," Lois told them. "Now sit down here and relax as best you can, and they'll let you know when there's news. I'm right over there at the reception area if you need anything from me."

"Thanks, Lois." Cate nodded at the receptionist.

Meg took Cate's hand and led her over to two chairs in the corner to wait.

"Do you want to talk? I know how hard this is for you."

Cate shook her head. "Not now. I'd like to get through the surgery first. I need to know that he's going to be okay before I talk about all of this. Okay? I don't want to break down while we're waiting."

Meg touched Cate's hand, and Cate took it and didn't let go.

After they'd sat for about an hour, Cate told Meg she thought she'd give Pete a call. Meg was aware that Pete was Cate's best friend and had known Cate's parents since he and Cate were in law school, and she could understand why Cate wanted to let him know about Cliff. Meg had met Pete and his husband, Matt, at Mullins Investment functions, and she knew that Pete was now the CEO of the company. Meg believed that Pete was good for Cate—that he operated in her professional world, but he'd known her long enough to plow right through that buffer of professional persona. Meg was interested in seeing how she related to him on the phone. She suspected the conversation would be good for Cate while they waited.

❖

Cate took out her phone and called Pete. It took several moments for him to finally answer.

"Hi, Pete. It's Cate."

"How's my favorite lawyer? This must be important if you're calling me early on a Saturday morning. Are you in Trinity Hills with your dad this weekend?"

Cate took a deep breath before she responded. "I hope I didn't wake you. I'm here at the hospital with Meg, waiting while he goes to surgery for an intestinal blockage." Cate looked over at Meg as she spoke her name.

"I was up making coffee. Is there anything I can do? Just say the word." Pete would understand how she was feeling. He knew that her dad had become her entire family.

"I just wanted to let you know because you've been close to Dad over the years. He really likes you…for some reason." Cate heard him chuckle at that last statement.

"Hey, who doesn't like *me*?" Pete was working to cheer her up.

"Everybody likes you, Pete."

"Speaking of liking, how are you and Meg doing? You owe me full disclosure—best-friend insider details. Is there a bounce in your step and a twinkle in your eye because you've made it past kissing?"

Cate remained silent. She wasn't giving Pete intimate details.

"Holy cow, it's no wonder you're telling me your dad actually likes me—you're in a good mood. You and Meg have been shaking the sheets." Pete was laughing now.

"Don't make me sorry I called you," Cate admonished with her best chastising tone.

"Okay, Counselor Sweet Cheeks. So, how long until you know anything more about Cliff?"

"It could be up to four hours, depending on what they find and what they have to do in surgery. The surgeon seems to be good, but I'm nervous. Meg is here holding my hand."

"Of course you're nervous. Will you call me tonight once you have more information?" Pete requested in a serious tone.

"Yeah, I will. And thanks for distracting me. And for caring."

"I'm here for you, Cate. Always have been. Always will be. And I won't even sign off by calling you a bona fide heartless bitch." He was laughing again.

"Damn, Pete. I'd be offended, but you are a good distraction. Thanks for listening."

"Call me tonight."

"I will."

Cate ended the call and looked at Meg. It was obvious Meg hadn't caught everything from Pete's end, but she'd picked up enough of the conversation to comment.

Meg lightly caressed Cate's palm and smiled. "It sounds like Pete's a great friend."

"He is. Like Grace is for you. He gives me a lot of grief over my love life, but to be honest, he's the one who convinced me I needed to give us a chance." Cate pointed between Meg and herself.

"I've always liked Pete on the few occasions I've met him, but now he's moved way up on my favorite people list," Meg said.

"Don't tell him that. It'll go right to his head." Cate hoped her love for Pete came through in her tone.

"I'm glad you've got him, Cate."

"So am I," Cate answered as she settled back to wait.

❖

Three hours had passed before Dr. Pabst came out in his scrubs with a smile on his face. Cate felt herself marginally relax.

"Your dad is still very groggy, but doing great. He probably won't be out of recovery for at least another hour." Dr. Pabst elaborated on Cliff's surgery, prognosis, and long-term aftercare plan.

Cate shook the doctor's hand. "Thank you so much, Dr. Pabst. How long will he need to stay in the hospital?"

"At his age, I'm estimating three to seven days, longer if needed. Then another ten days to two weeks in a skilled nursing facility, depending on his improvement."

Cate nodded her understanding.

"So take a little break. Get some food or a drink, then come back. Someone will get you once he's out of recovery and into a room. At least another hour."

Cate thanked the surgeon again, and he left. She hugged Meg, wiping the back of her hand across her eyes. "I think it's hitting me. I'm so relieved. It was so sudden."

"I know." Meg hugged her back and gave her a kiss. "Shall we go to the cafeteria and get some lunch? We can talk while we eat."

Cate nodded and they headed to the cafeteria.

"Your dad is going to be okay," Meg told her as she took the cover off Cate's yogurt, placing it in front of her and handing her a spoon. "You need to eat."

"I know. But oh God, I could have lost him." Cate closed her eyes and took a deep breath. The reality that she could have lost her dad ached in her chest. Cate knew how she'd felt when she'd lost her mother, and they hadn't even been close anymore. This event crystallized the fact that there would be a time when her dad would not be here. Just imagining that made it hard to breathe. She needed to start processing his mortality. He'd always been so vibrant and full of life. "I know I'll lose him, but not yet." Cate took the napkin that Meg held out and dried her eyes.

"Cliff's okay," Meg reminded her. "The surgery went well." Cate realized Meg's words were soothing her. "He's healthy otherwise, and he's tough. I think he's going to recover and be around for a long while. He knows what he means to you. They offer good medical care here. I know."

Cate realized that Meg was speaking from experience. She took Meg's hand. "This is where Robert was treated, isn't it?"

Meg nodded. "Yes, I have memories of this place. But that was nothing like Cliff. Your dad will be okay. He'll welcome your caring and visits. He's got you to love him. I'll help how ever I can."

Cate took another napkin and wiped her nose before she spoke. "I'm so glad you're here with me now, Meg. I can't imagine dealing with this by myself."

Meg smiled and cleared the table. "Shall we go check on Cliff?"

Cate put an arm around Meg's waist and leaned in to kiss her on the cheek. They walked in tandem back to the waiting area.

It was close to two o'clock before they were led back to Cliff's room. He looked good but was still groggy, so they didn't stay long. Cate was feeling much better.

❖

Meg drove them back to her house because Cate's car was there. Meg was exhausted, and Cate looked like she was feeling the same. She waited for Cate to decide what she wanted to do next. Once they were inside and had greeted Oscar, Meg plopped on the living room couch and pulled Cate down next to her.

Meg puffed out a long breath, then stifled a yawn as she leaned into Cate. "I could certainly use a good night's sleep."

"Didn't get much sleep last night, huh?" Cate shoulder-bumped her. She was obviously remembering the better parts of the past evening.

"I think you already know that I loved every minute of it, except for the news about Cliff, but I'm running on empty," Meg admitted.

"I'm really tired too," Cate admitted. "Again, I didn't mean for you to have to take charge last night."

"Do you see this smile on my face? The one that matches the one in my eyes?" Meg dismissed Cate's apology. "You're human. I like knowing there's that side of you. You'll have time to make it up to me. I'm going to hold you to it when our darn lives don't get in the way. We knew there would be challenges. I just expected it to be me and my kids. Not your dad."

"I'd love to get bossy and have my way with you right now, but I want it to be perfect, Meg—and I don't think that's in the cards tonight." The adrenaline that had kept Cate going all day had likely dissipated with the news that Cliff would be okay, and it was obvious that exhaustion had caught up with Cate too.

"I want to enjoy bossy you when I'm wide awake. I had a sample last night, and I don't want to miss a second of it." Meg took Cate's hand and squeezed it.

"You're right—you're not going to want to miss a second of it. I've got plans for you," Cate warned her and blew a kiss.

"Seriously, Cate. I want you to finish what you started last night, but let's get beyond this crisis with your dad. And you're going to be juggling getting back to your law practice as well because you were here both Thursday and Friday. As I said earlier, I'm happy to help out with Cliff, whatever you need."

"I don't know where you've been hiding, Meg, but I'm so glad I found you." Cate pulled Meg in closer and skimmed her tongue along the sensitive skin just below Meg's ear. "I'll go back to Dad's house tonight so we can both get a good night's sleep—it might be another short night if I stay here." Cate nuzzled Meg's neck as she talked. "I've got to call Pete back too. I owe you a perfect night, but I agree that it won't be perfect right now. We'll have a date night once things settle down. And I want your promise that you'll stay over with me at my place in the city the night of your gallery opening—I want to make it a night you'll never forget." Cate leaned back and looked at Meg.

"That sounds like a proposition I can't turn down," Meg answered with a chuckle. "Okay, I promise."

Cate grinned. "Good. That was an easy negotiation. In the meantime, I'll probably have to do a bit of commuting between Trinity Hills and San Francisco to handle everything I need to take care of."

"I can certainly visit Cliff when you're in San Francisco. Let's get through this with your dad. My gallery opening is the middle of next month, and of course it's on my calendar. I'll just need to add in a reminder about the after-party, just to make sure that I don't forget," Meg said, teasing Cate. "Note to self: dancing in the moonlight."

Cate murmured, "And you call me mushy." She squeezed Meg and then changed the subject. "What if I go see Dad tomorrow morning, then drop by and see how you're doing in the early afternoon before I head to the city so I can start to catch up at work? I'll see what the rest of my week looks like from there."

"That sounds fine. I'll plan to be his Monday visitor, and we can talk logistics after that."

Cate brushed her lips softly across Meg's as she stood up. "Get to bed early, babe." She headed toward the front door. "And you let her sleep late, Oscar," she admonished the cat. "I'll see you for a bit tomorrow afternoon, before I head to the city."

"Good night, Counselor."

"Until next time, Meg." Cate blew Meg a kiss and then whispered, "Thank you."

SLOUCHING TOWARD STARDUST WITH MEG THE UNMUZZLED

"Visit to the Hospital"

    The memory tracked me down as soon as I passed through that door. It must have been nonchalantly standing guard at the entrance. That portal, yawning its welcome to unwary prey before smothering this victim with bruising from the past without regard to opening old wounds that I've struggled to heal—witnessing a body's betrayal, lost in the slow demise of a spouse. A spouse who wanted to pass through this place on self-assigned terms, alone, without assistance from me. Who insisted on cutting the ties that had barely been holding us together in health, severing all bonds as he left me behind, on his way to nirvana. At least, I'm trying my utmost to wish him the best.

    As that memory lunged to ensnare me, I skirted the threshold to yesterday's lesion, stomped it away, and called for its end. Maybe not gentle. Maybe not selfless. But I was not here to remember the history. I was here to silently slip past that prior contusion. To be the strength that somebody else needed today. Somebody else living the role that I had once played, but without any fortification of my own. Somebody willing to reach out and take strength from my handhold. In a hospital meant for mending the wounded, for making new memories to stand sentinel the next time I come.

CHAPTER TWENTY-ONE

At a little after three o'clock on Monday afternoon, Grace knocked on Meg's door and entered to a feline leg rub and a hug from Meg. They headed to the kitchen table.

"Can I get you something to drink?" Meg asked.

"Iced tea, if you have it. I'm anxious to hear what's up in your life. We haven't talked in over a week." Grace waited while Meg retrieved two glasses of iced tea and set them on the table before sitting across from her.

"Where to begin? My lunch with Natalie went about as well as could be expected." Meg decided to skip a retelling of the entire Laurel episode. "But at least I've talked to her now. Told her about Cate."

Grace nodded. "And Cate? How is she? How are you two?"

Meg took a long drink from her glass and considered. She decided that she needed to talk to someone, and she knew Grace was her person for that. "Am I talking to my friendly, iced-tea-sharing best buddy, or to my favorite therapist—the dog fosterer who didn't steer me wrong about being a Cate whisperer?"

"Oh, sweetie. Definitely your favorite therapist to foster dogs. With applications for best-friend advice." Grace made a snorting noise, then grew serious. "I might tease you about installments in the life and times of Meg Mullins, but I love you and will listen and offer my best counsel if you want it."

Appreciation flooded Meg. Grace's support helped ground her. "The easy installments first. Cate's dad had a blockage this weekend and then surgery. I took Cate to the hospital. He's going to be okay, and

I think I was good at supporting her—he's her only family, so while she held it together, she was terrified. And the hospital brought back a lot of feelings about all my time there before—Robert. But being there with Cate…we were good together. Supportive." She knew they had done well together in a crisis. Cate's crisis, but Meg believed their relationship was stronger for it.

Grace sat quietly and waited, sipping from her glass. Then Meg took a deep breath. "I knew I was falling for her a while ago. You should have seen her when I brought that street dog to her office—she canceled our lunch out and bought the poor pooch a sandwich too." The memory still warmed Meg's heart. "I've been attracted to her for a long time. Every recent encounter has reinforced that, but I think that was the moment I felt like I could love the woman, that I was falling in love."

Meg reflected on how each interaction with Cate had expanded those feelings. How hopeful she was that Cate could be a major part of her life. Falling in love made her feel giddy. But she knew there was stress too, vulnerability in opening her heart and her life—her reaction to Laurel had demonstrated that. The logistics she'd had to manage with telling her children and then dealing with their different responses. And there was navigating completely different dynamics than her almost thirty-year relationship with Robert. Those years had affected her. Meg debated what she wanted to say, how to put it all into words.

"It's okay," Grace told her. "I can tell you that fifty isn't the same experience as in our younger years. But it's good for you. How are you feeling about your belated ability to explore who you are?"

Meg's stomach clenched. She'd never talked about this before. She slowly nursed her tea while she organized what she wanted to tell Grace. "Well, there are two pieces for me, but related. One is just about me, my sexual orientation, which I'm realizing I'm at peace with. I know coming out, especially to my kids, is huge. Redefining who I am to them—their reactions were a big worry, but I don't believe I've anguished over my attraction to Cate, or accepting myself for who I am. Every person has their own experience, emotions. I realize I've never acted on it, but I'd still say it's more an acknowledgment, maybe an awakening, than a sudden revelation if you can understand what I'm trying to say. It feels good. The second piece is related to Cate—

making life choices that mean publicly coming out and the reactions, dating and navigating a new relationship, falling in love, hoping for a future with Cate. That's the most challenging piece for me."

"So, let's start with the first," Grace said. "I'm happy for you. So tell me, Meg Mullins, *who* are you?" She added some levity to the discussion with the teasing tone of her delivery, even though Meg knew they both realized the enormity of the question.

Meg felt her throat constrict, then relax. She'd spent so many years making life choices that never required her to address her attraction to women, allowing assumptions by others, but now she was choosing to pursue a relationship with Cate, and it was time to openly acknowledge who she was.

"I'd say that I'm bisexual." Meg paused and looked at Grace. She'd told her kids and Grace about dating Cate, but in fifty years she'd never made this declaration to anyone before. Closing her eyes for a moment, Meg waited for Grace's response to her admission.

"Meg. Sweetie. We've been friends for decades, and I guess I'm surprised that you never shared this with me in all our years. And when I first found out you were attracted to Cate after your trip to San Francisco, attracted to women, maybe even a little hurt because we've been so close." Grace paused before she concluded, "But I can also understand it with the choices you've made…and this isn't about me. And recently, with everything you've already told me over these past weeks, I'd already come to that conclusion."

Meg let out the breath she'd been holding. Grace's response was why they were such good friends. Grace was always there for her. "I've always felt an attraction to some women, and now specifically Cate." She'd never considered that she hadn't felt attraction to the opposite sex. To Robert. She had.

Meg had been doing some reading lately—read that sexual behavior, thoughts, and feelings toward the same or opposite sex weren't always consistent across time. She could accept that her feelings about her ultimate relationship with Robert and the fact that she hadn't felt a strong attraction to any of the men she'd encountered recently were intertwined. Her life had been full of extenuating factors. After all of her introspection, she'd realized that at age fifty what mattered to her was moving forward with her life. Wanting to try for a future with Cate. That was the choice she was making now.

Grace simply smiled, letting Meg continue. Grace's obvious acceptance and willingness to let her finally verbalize what she was thinking and feeling was cathartic.

"The second piece is Cate," Meg said. "I don't know where I'd be in all of this personal acknowledgment without Cate. Finding love in a nursing home when I'm ninety and so old I couldn't do anything but share a bingo card?"

They both laughed.

"I know all serious relationships are complicated. And we both have a lot of life behind us. I couldn't be with someone who didn't accept my kids or my cat." Meg looked down at Oscar, who had wandered into the kitchen. "She's been wonderful with Jessie. And I know she'll be great with Ben. Natalie…I don't doubt that Cate will try, and that's all I can ask."

"If she can win Nat over, you're home free," Grace said.

"Our relationship is advancing," Meg continued. "I don't know if she's falling in love with me because we haven't used that word yet. But we've been there for each other. And she took a huge step. She didn't just hold my hand while Jessie was inking my tattoo—she got a matching one. She isn't the type of person to do that without it meaning something. Something important to our relationship. A commitment."

As she slipped off her shoe and let Grace examine her foot, Meg understood what a huge step the shared tattoo was for Cate. For both of them.

Grace grinned. "Practically engaged."

"That's exactly what Jessie said." Meg couldn't suppress a chuckle. "It makes me realize that Cate wants this to work, like I do."

"Not to be starry-eyed, but it's romantic."

"I know." Meg stopped and looked at Grace. Took a deep breath and then said, "I slept with her."

"Whoa, when did this happen?" Grace asked, her eyebrows rising. "You've been holding out on me."

Meg felt her face warm, and Grace added, "Not the gory details. You'll give me a heart attack."

Meg rolled her eyes. "I wasn't going to give you the gory details. Cate spent Saturday night. All I'm going to say is that Cliff's emergency changed the nature of our encounter, but it was good. Really, really good. And to be honest, as exhausted and worried as we both were because of Cliff, I loved falling asleep next to her. Having her next to me during the night."

Meg had thought a lot about her first experience having sex with a woman. Sex with Cate. It had been different from the night they'd planned. As awful as Cliff's medical emergency had been, Meg wasn't unhappy that their lovemaking had shifted from Cate being in charge. While she loved the bossy Cate and wanted more of that in bed, she also loved that Cate had relinquished control and given it to her. Cate had been willing to be vulnerable, revealed when she was hurting, and trusted Meg as a sexual partner to offer what she needed. Meg knew that the sex hadn't just been about the physical. That emotional connection was part of her make-up and was important to her physical satisfaction. Meg craved that in a partner. Two people meeting each other's needs, caring for each other.

"Again, I'm happy for you, Meg. So, what do you need your favorite dog-fosterer therapist for? And I should add that I'm immeasurably relieved you weren't asking me to be a sex therapist, although I would have done my best." Grace guffawed.

Appreciating Grace's humor, Meg smiled. Then she lifted her drink as she decided how to approach the next topic. "I'm not oblivious to the fact that I carry a lot of baggage from my marriage. I've made my choices in life because of the positives, but there are certainly the negatives of my past too. Where Robert and I ended up and how we got there…it's a part of me and who I am." Meg knew that Grace was not unaware. "And yet, as crazy as it might seem, some of those memories are helping me with Cate. For years, Robert had someone in his office buy my gifts, probably whoever had time. I never believed anyone would do something like get a tattoo for me—a personal and permanent symbol."

"Our histories become integrated into who we are and move forward with each of us—the dogs I foster, the people I know," Grace said. "Putting it in perspective is important. You wouldn't have made the choices you made if they hadn't offered you so much good in your life. And if you can now apply the shortfalls to a positive for you and Cate…"

"I am feeling so good about this. Cate and me. But I have my anxieties too." Meg hadn't forgotten that Cate had spent five years avoiding long-term relationships because she'd been so hurt. Cate seemed to be doing fine, but Meg had considered that Cate could decide she was getting in too deep. Although Meg had to admit that she'd blown the Laurel encounter, and Cate had not.

"You wouldn't be human without anxieties. You're just learning to know and trust each other," Grace said. "And I'm not calling you old, but you're both in a different place than you'd be if you'd started a relationship when you were much younger."

"You're right," Meg agreed. "Past experience matters, and I think we can make our careers work. I know Cate's been nervous about how much she works. She sees it as a huge factor in the fate of her past relationship, but I can live with her dedication to her job, and I think she'd work with me not to let it become an issue. I understand how much it's part of who she is. If we end up together, we can figure out a balance—I know it matters to her because of her history. Plus, I'm launching my own career."

Meg was aware of the insecurities she'd had about what Cate saw in her as a nonprofessional woman who had been devoted to motherhood. This art opportunity certainly helped relieve some of that unease. At the same time, she had an art show opening to make it through, and she prayed it would be successful. The successful launch of her career mattered to her.

"So thrilling," Grace gushed. "I want the details of the opening if you have them."

"She's thrilled for me too. It won't be just a joke—Mona Lisa Meg. I know she'll be supportive, and that matters to me because this is something I've always wanted." It hit Meg how important it was that Cate didn't see her art as a joke or as competition to her own career. "Olivia called and the gallery opening is at five o'clock on the twelfth, a Saturday evening in less than three weeks. I hope to include you and John."

"I wouldn't miss it. John and I will come home after, so count on me to watch Oscar, and you can stay over," Grace offered with a touch of amusement in her eyes. "Don't say I'm not doing my part to advance this romance."

Meg chuckled. "You're a true best friend. Thanks, Grace."

"You're welcome, sweetie. Now I've got to get home to slave over the stove. Nothing exciting in that."

"John's a good guy. There's a lot to be said for solid and

uneventful. Navigating new relationships at our age is exciting, but also new territory."

"I hear you." Grace stood and scooped up Oscar, stroking his chin before setting him down. "I'm happy for you. You deserve this—Cate, your art show, almost engagement tattoos, romance and falling asleep with her, a best friend like me…"

"Get outta here." Meg laughed as she walked Grace to the door.

❖

It was Tuesday after the long weekend, and Pete had insisted Cate join him for lunch. She had so much work to do, but talking to him would be good for her, so she'd agreed. They'd ordered their drinks and lunch entrees, and with Pete's glass of wine, Cate didn't doubt he intended this to be a therapy session. She was sticking to water because she had a busy afternoon scheduled.

"So, Counselor Cuddle Bunny, catch me up on things." Pete sat back and sipped from his glass.

"Cuddle bunny?" Cate shook her head at him, injecting as much incredulity into her tone as she could manage.

"Yeah, that might be a stretch." Pete chuckled before his expression shifted and he became serious. "You called and told me your dad is doing okay, but I want to know about you. How are you doing?"

Thinking about her dad's mortality was painful, but Cate hoped that talking about it might make it easier to accept. "I was just going along like Dad would live forever, until the blockage. It hit me like a train. I know that isn't going to happen—nobody has forever." Cate's chest tightened at the acknowledgment. "It's going to hurt so much when he's gone. But this made me face the fact that he's not immortal."

"I get it. He's such a great father and your only family. But it sounds like he pulled through this okay—otherwise, he's been healthy and likely has a lot of years to go." Then with a touch of levity, Pete added, "As your fantastic, acquired-for-his-brilliance, substitute brother and the epitome of a BFF, I'll always be here for you."

Cate smiled. This was the kind of therapy she needed. "He has had good health, so probably a lot of years left—that's what Meg pointed out too."

"And speaking of Meg, how is she?"

"Smart, funny, kind. Charming. Like we saw at business functions, but our time together has shown me so much more. I realized after the initial shock of Dad that the hospital was hard for her—memories of Robert's illness there. But she focused on me, supported me, and helped me get through it. She's been so willing to accept my workload, and she's willing to help with Dad so I don't get too far behind." Cate drank some water before continuing. "It's obvious she's used to taking care of others."

"From my positions at Mullins Investments over the years, getting to know Robert, my impression was that Meg handled the family stuff, including the drama." Pete chuckled before he added, "Drama— probably a hell of a lot of that with three kids. Robert focused on his business."

Watching Pete shift to an exaggerated leer expression, Cate knew Pete was going to change the subject. She wasn't going to avoid some reference to her sex life, and she hadn't denied the *shaking the sheets* comment he'd teased her about when she'd called him from the hospital.

The waiter brought Cate's salad and Pete's chicken and rice dish, and they each took several bites before Pete said, "So is the sex good? I'll bet way better than your former encounters, the meet, the greet, the sex, the polite good-bye." Pete had such a way with words.

"That twinkle in your eye. Bounce in your step." He grinned at her.

Cate coughed. "Damn, Pete. I don't know why I put up with you."

"Because I get you. And love you." Pete looked across his wineglass at her. "So, deprive me and don't make my day." He offered her his best pout before sobering again. "How are you feeling about things?"

Cate leaned back in her chair before addressing Pete's question. She wasn't going into detail with him, but she thought that Meg had been wonderful. Meg hadn't been with a woman before and it had been their first time together, her dad's emergency with its chaos and fear. Cate had anticipated a night of firsts, but the rest...not at all what she'd planned. She'd been hurting, and Meg had been there for her— what Cate had come to realize was essential in a successful romantic partnership after Laurel. Being there for each other.

"I'm feeling good. Very good. But there's a lot to deal with. Both Meg and the entire situation are so different from anything I've experienced before. I've never been involved with anyone with kids, and there are three adult ones in the mix. She's telling them about us, a huge step for her, and it makes me know she's serious. I've met Jessie and they're great—the tattoo artist." The matching tattoos, grounded in hope for the future—that had been Cate's reason. "It's one kid at a time. She loves her daughter, an evangelical—flying to LA for the face-to-face with Natalie was stressful for her. I still have to meet her youngest, Ben."

"I'm sure this is huge for her," Pete agreed, "and different for you."

"It is. She's had a very different life from mine."

Cate wasn't going to go into the Laurel incident with Pete. While she certainly hadn't forgotten it, she and Meg seemed to have worked through it. They'd talked and that had been critical. Besides Meg's stress of that day with Natalie, she suspected Robert's cheating might have also contributed to Meg's reaction at encountering her with Laurel. They both carried baggage. Cate hoped they were both mature enough to deal with it, that it wasn't enough to sink them.

Continuing her conversation with Pete after they'd both taken several more bites of their food, she told him, "Meg's spent her entire adult life being a mother and wife. She's a widow and her kids are grown. This is an enormous shift—a new relationship with me, an art career. I think Robert convinced her that she'd never be taken seriously as an artist, and she accepted that, boxed into her family role."

"It made it easier for Robert." Pete didn't hesitate with his assessment. "Meg handled the home and was an asset in the role of the CEO's wife at business functions. Like you said, charming, smart…"

Cate knew that Robert's Mona Lisa Meg label had impacted her. "I think professional recognition as an artist will be so good for her. She's talented, even if she doesn't know it. People loving her art should help convince her." Cate took a deep breath, then told Pete, "I want this to work…so much. And I'm terrified if it doesn't, after what happened between Laurel and me, I won't want to take the risk ever again. I'm getting in deep with Meg. I want us to have a future." The thought of this not working out with Meg churned in her stomach.

Pete set down his fork and looked at her. "We both know there's always risk in committing our hearts. But you were miserable before. Is Meg making you happy?"

"She is. It's so much different with all that's going on between our two lives, more than any relationship I ever imagined I'd be in, but we're figuring it out. I think finding out about Robert's apartment helped convince her that she needed to move on with her life." Cate locked eyes with Pete. "And you convinced me that I need to too."

"And you listened to me. I'm glad," Pete said.

"We agreed at our first breakfast together that we're a hell of a pair. To take it slow. But it's working, and I'm hopeful. So thanks for the come-to-Meg talk."

Pete smirked. "I am pretty damn good. Excellent at advice for bona fide heartless bitches."

"And full of yourself." Cate chuckled.

"That's what the hubby says," Pete told her. "But there's one thing I've learned with Matt. And I'll pass on this piece of advice to you, although you've probably figured it out. Relationships take work—that part never ends. So keep figuring this out, Counselor Cuddle Bunny."

Cate configured her face into her best chastising scowl. "I think I prefer the bona fide heartless bitch label."

Pete laughed. "If only you were, but you're not, cupcake."

SLOUCHING TOWARD STARDUST WITH MEG THE UNMUZZLED

"The Best Ways to Fall Asleep"

As the summer sun's faint golden glow glazes the top of the backyard walnut tree, and bushy-tailed squirrels tuck in for the night, and the suffocating heat of afternoon surrenders to the brisker breaths of nightfall's breeze, and the fresh aftermath of cleansing streams of warm shower spray swaddles you in drowsy yawns and soft pale sheets and promising plans for tomorrow...

As rolling credits crawl up the screen in the concluding remnants of a movie whose final hour you fumbled in nods and eyelid droops, with the warm limp body of a sleeping cat tucked into the reclining folds of your embracing form stretched out in the family room recliner carefully positioned to support the napping bodies of two linked souls...

As you stretch out beneath the blankets, propped up against the headboard with fat fluffed pillows, and the soft illumination of a shadow-casting bedside lamp fans across the prose-laden landscape of a good novel with straight lines of words parading across the white paper until they break rank and fall off the page as your eyes no longer focus...

As your sated lover softly snores sweet nothings into the tangle of your hair, and your heart falls into synchrony with her heart, beat for beat, with sunrise not many hours away, but time enough to close your eyes as you lace fingers with her hand in yours and dream the dreams of times to come in this dawning miracle that is the rest of your life.

CHAPTER TWENTY-TWO

It was eight o'clock on Thursday evening when Meg's phone rang. She looked at the caller ID and smiled. She'd visited Cliff in the hospital each morning, and Cate called him each day while continuing to work in San Francisco. This was Cate's nightly catch-up call with her.

"Meg Mullins here. How can I assist you? And have no doubt, I'm here to assist you. The resume of my talents is awe-inspiring," Meg answered in a sultry drawl. She knew her drawl would make Cate wish she could sample those talents right then.

"It's a damn good thing your phone has caller ID or you might embarrass the hell out of one of your kids," Cate responded with laughter. "And yes. My *awe* has been inspired."

"I don't think that was your awe, but I'm not going to argue, Counselor."

Still laughing, Cate said, "Thanks for visiting Dad today. I just talked to him and he enjoyed it. He's on the mend."

"It was no problem. I dropped in and we had a good visit before I went grocery shopping." Meg paused. "And I bought you an official new toothbrush for sleepovers. To replace that flimsy travel one. An official one."

"You know what that means?" Cate cleared her throat.

"Uh. Your dentist will be pleased," Meg nervously joked. Suddenly she wasn't exactly sure how Cate would take it. Meg knew what a toothbrush symbolized for her—another step in their commitment to their relationship. She hoped Cate would agree.

"Yeah, she'll be happy I'm practicing good oral hygiene, but it means a whole lot more to me. It means there are a whole lot more sleepovers in our future." Cate sounded pleased.

"That was my plan." Meg relaxed. "Matching tattoos and all."

"Yeah, babe. Matching tattoos, a toothbrush at your house. You make me happy, Meg."

"Me too, Cate." Meg smiled. "So tell me, how was your day?"

Meg heard Cate sigh. "It's been a long week so far, but the word of the day is *progress*. I'm almost ready for Monday's client, and the hospital called this afternoon and Dad is cleared for the transfer to Vista Care Skilled Nursing Facility sometime tomorrow afternoon. All the arrangements are in place. If I wait and drive to Trinity Hills after the Friday commute traffic, I should be able to finish everything up here and stop in to see him tomorrow night."

"I'm not surprised. He's feisty and ready to leave the hospital. I'll go see him in the morning and then leave it to them to make the transfer."

"It might be fairly late, but I could come by and see you tomorrow night too. I couldn't have managed this without you. I'm hoping I can make it up to you. Saturday night? Use that new toothbrush maybe?" Cate's voice changed into a suggestive purr. "We've got some catching up to do, and I've got plans for you."

Meg felt anxiety compress her chest. "Damn, Cate. You're going to hate me. With that proposition, I hate me. Ben and Sarah are coming in late Friday afternoon and staying until Sunday afternoon. Jessie and Luc are coming for a family dinner on Friday. Ben and Sarah wanted it to be just the four of us on Saturday so they can get to know you. Since I've only recently told Ben about us and he hasn't even met you, I wanted to make his plans work."

"I get it. You know what?"

Meg held her breath. Was Cate mad? Going to make demands? No, that was just her channeling Robert's likely reaction. "What?"

"I'll come to dinner on Saturday and meet Ben and Sarah. I'm sure I'll be exhausted by the time I've made sure Dad's comfortable tomorrow night, so I'll just head over to his house after I see him. I'll need to head back Sunday afternoon due to Monday's meeting." Cate paused as she thought out a plan. "Next week on Tuesday and Wednesday, I'll need to play catch-up at the office, but what if I try to come in Thursday morning and we have a long weekend? I need to break that toothbrush in," Cate said with a chuckle.

"Thanks for being so understanding. We've certainly got our hands full with your dad, my kids, the gallery opening…" Meg was doing her best to fulfill her mother role, her girlfriend role, and her artist role. So much of this was new to her, and she wanted it to work for everyone. She'd told Grace she had no doubts that they could make their two careers work, and she believed that. It was just that she was juggling so many changes right now. So much more than usual.

"We do have our hands full. But I want my hands full of you at the end of next week. Just us," Cate told her.

"Sleepover, my house. It's on my calendar, but put it on the calendar of the gods who are currently keeping life so interesting. I guess we knew going into this that there would be a lot of juggling to do," Meg responded.

"Hey, Meg. We can make this work. We're two smart, mature, grown-ass women. And I want you in my life." Cate's voice was sincere.

Cate's words reassured Meg. This was not just about sex. They were exploring the possibility of a future together, supporting each other, growing closer. Meg knew she was falling in love with this woman. "I want you too. Don't pay any attention to me. Just a lot on my plate. A lot of emotions. It's been over a week now, and I haven't heard anything from Nat since our lunch. It makes me sad."

"I'm sorry. I don't know what to tell you. I know she loves you. Maybe with a little time…I'm happy to do whatever you think might help," Cate offered.

"Thanks. For now, you just get your gorgeous self over here for dinner on Saturday."

"I can do that. I'll sleep in and then go see Dad early Saturday afternoon before heading over to your place if that works for you. Can I bring something?"

"Just your charming self. One kid at a time. Jessie and Luc are sold on you."

"I'm sold on them too. And their mom—I've got the tattoo to prove it."

Meg smiled. "I'm looking forward to seeing you late Saturday afternoon. I'll check on your dad in the morning and can help with any issues related to his transfer to skilled nursing."

"Thanks, Meg. See you Saturday."

"Saturday, Counselor."

❖

Dinner with the kids and their partners on Friday night went well. Meg was hoping that Cliff's transfer had gone well too. She didn't hear from Cate, so she assumed that everything was going according to plan. She spent Saturday morning making breakfast and visiting with Ben and Sarah over coffee. Then she marinated chicken and did some slicing and dicing so she'd have more time to enjoy Cate and the kids later. Cate arrived a little before five o'clock with a beautiful floral bouquet.

"Cate, you know how I love flowers. And the sunflowers—my favorites. Big points for you." The kids were upstairs, so Meg kissed Cate slowly and deliberately before she took the offering and filled a large blue vase that set off the colorful arrangement.

"I'm bringing you flowers more often," Cate declared with a wink.

Meg looked at Cate. She was stunning in a pair of tight black jeans and a fitted cream silk blouse, her hair pulled up loosely into a bun. Meg was going to have to work hard to keep her hands off her with the kids in the house.

"You ready?" Meg smiled at Cate.

"As ready as I'll ever be," Cate replied.

Meg called out to Ben and Sarah that Cate had arrived, and they came downstairs.

"Ben and Sarah"—Meg nodded at the kids—"this is my girlfriend, Cate." Meg had decided she was going to just be straightforward when she introduced Cate to family and friends. She'd never played games with her kids, and she wasn't going to start now.

Ben smiled and held out his hand. Cate took it. "Hi, Cate. I'm glad to meet you."

"You too, Ben," Cate shook his hand. And then she turned to Sarah. "And you must be Sarah. I've heard so much about you two from Meg."

"Hi, Cate. We've been looking forward to meeting you ever since Meg told us that you were dating." Sarah looked over at Meg.

"And we're okay with it," Ben added. "Mom is happy."

"I am," Meg said. "I've made a pitcher of margaritas. Shall I pour them and then we can all go out in the living room while the chicken finishes cooking, and you can all get to know each other better?"

After they were settled in with margaritas, Ben said, "Jessie was here last night and we saw Mom's tattoo. I'd like to see yours too, Cate. If that's okay."

Cate was sitting next to a barefoot Meg on the couch, so she toed off her black canvas slip-on and put her foot next to Meg's. Cate wore a light blue toenail polish that set off the dragonfly's blue shading. Meg didn't wear any polish, but her skin was tanner than Cate's due to swimming, and her dragonfly was equally impressive on the top of her foot.

Ben studied the display of artwork. "Wow. Jessie did a fantastic job. Can I take a photo?" They nodded, and Ben took some pictures of their paired tattoos.

"I think we should get matching tattoos, Ben," Sarah told him. "Once we figure out what we want. I know you have a few tattoos already, but matching tattoos are so romantic." She turned to Meg and Cate on the couch. "Meg surprised us, but seeing you two together—now I get it. Who would have thought Meg would be getting a matching girlfriend tattoo at fifty? All I can say is that it's very cool."

"Hey," Meg said, "I'm young at heart." She shoulder-bumped Cate. "And cool. You just said so."

"She's probably the best mom out there," Ben told Cate, and Cate laughed. It was obvious that she was enjoying Ben and Sarah.

"I think she's very cool too," Cate told them. "And the best. Now I want to hear about how you met and your teaching jobs. I hear you're in your first year of teaching high school math, Ben. And you're teaching third grade, Sarah."

"Well, we met in high school," Ben said. "We've been together for almost seven years now."

"Yes," Sarah said. "He crashed into me in the hallway and knocked all my books on the ground. We bent to pick them up and banged heads. I thought he was a dork, and then he offered to help me with my geometry. A dork *and* a nerd." Sarah laughed and looked fondly at Ben.

Ben laughed too. "And how did you and Mom meet? Jessie said you're a lawyer."

"Well, your mom and I have bumped into each other over the

years at company functions, so I knew who she was—I'm a consulting attorney for Mullins Investments. She came into my office when I had a few questions regarding a matter I was handling for the investment firm, and she realized I had one of your great-grandmother's watercolors on my office wall. We got to talking about art, and I realized I needed to know her better. And the more I knew her, the better I liked her." Cate turned and smiled at Meg.

"And the same happened to me." Meg smiled back. "The more I knew her, the more I liked her. Now, while I finish up dinner, why don't you two tell Cate about your teaching jobs? We should be able to sit down and eat in about ten minutes," Meg advised them.

Ben and Sarah talked about their jobs and their students during dinner, and Cate told them about growing up in Trinity Hills. They were amazed that she had graduated from the same high school they had attended. They discussed Cliff, Meg's gallery opening, Oscar, and several other topics.

It was after ten o'clock when they finished helping Meg load the dishwasher, and then Ben and Sarah told Cate how much they had enjoyed meeting her. They had agreed to brunch in the morning, and then Ben and Sarah headed on upstairs, which left Cate and Meg on the couch. Oscar sauntered in and jumped onto Cate's lap.

"I'm trying to behave myself, Meg, but no promises if this conniving cat does something to thwart that," Cate declared with a chuckle.

"I'll hold your hand, cat or no cat," Meg told her as she reached for Cate's hand and intertwined their fingers.

Cate leaned over and chastely kissed Meg's cheek. Then she burst out laughing.

"What's so funny?" Meg asked.

"Just thinking about how before you, I never would have dreamed that I'd be limited to holding hands with a couple of kid chaperones upstairs, and grateful that a conniving cat even got me to the hand-holding stage."

"Cate, do you know how grateful I am that you're okay with making this work for me and my kids?" Meg asked. She could only imagine how different this was from any relationship Cate had ever had.

"I just spent five years unchaperoned, Meg, and I'll take this any day."

"Mushy," Meg mused.

"Don't push it. I'm already so tempted to show you how much mushier I can be. Chaperones or not," Cate grumbled.

"Your restraint is noted and appreciated. Between the flowers and behaving yourself, you're racking up a lot of points tonight," Meg advised her.

"And I'm just waiting to redeem them."

"Well, walk with me to the porch, and I'll give you a ten-point kiss before you head home."

Cate looked at the cat on her lap and then set him on the floor. "I think that's the best offer we're going to get tonight, Oscar," Cate told him before walking Meg to the porch and collecting her ten-point kiss. "I'm looking forward to the end of the week when I plan on redeeming the other five hundred points I've accumulated this evening," she told Meg.

"Five hundred points," Meg exclaimed. "I can't even imagine what five hundred points will get you."

"Well, you'd better rest up because it's a hell of a lot more than a ten-point kiss," Cate warned her with a sparkle in her eyes.

Meg laughed and affectionately patted Cate on her irresistible jean-clad ass before telling her she'd see her midmorning for waffles.

"Thanks for dinner. Ben and Sarah are lovely."

"Sleep well, Counselor."

"Fat chance of that, Meg Mullins."

Slouching Toward Stardust with Meg the unMuzzled

"A Few Things to Know About Her"

Layered and faceted, so complex that the whole of her may never be revealed in the remainder of time. When we first spoke for an extended period, she wore the armor of the brokenhearted. Until a watercolor on the wall spoke to us both, and we connected. When I cried, she cautiously offered me comfort—someone feeling my pain, but knowing her own. A healing offer of comfort.

A warrior who has fought for independence but willing to surrender some of that self-sufficiency to her love for a parent, to her not-so-secret concealed caring for others. Weakness not in her arsenal, not even a whisper that could be perceived as more. Except for the day she knocked on my door. Risked it all to see if I would take a chance on her. Risked it all to take a chance on me.

Her laugh. Not the simple sound of amusement. Not a giggle, a titter, a tee-hee. A laugh that comes from her essence, deep and sultry—a resonant rumble like rolling thunder. A storm of mirth, of pleasure, of joy, reaching her eyes with a bolt of brilliance. Exhilarating, intoxicating, passionate. A laugh that fills my soul.

Smart, high-class, stunning. A consummate professional, at the top of her game, holding her own in a steamroller setting. Loving my old ochre feline, embracing my independent offspring, dismantling my defenses with sentimental mush and side-eye suggestions. So amazing. So beautiful. So complicated. But to love her—so simple.

CHAPTER TWENTY-THREE

After two weeks out of the pool because of her new tattoo, Meg was happy to get in some lap exercise on Monday morning. Her swimming friends greeted her return and admired the dragonfly. While she swam, Meg reflected on all the changes in her life and the symbolism of the ink on her foot. As she moved through the water, her thoughts were full of introspection about growth and new beginnings—fifty years old and working to find herself, coming out to her kids, building a new life with Cate, becoming a professional artist. She was proud to be close to Jessie, Ben, and their partners, but there were still areas where she had little to no control, including Natalie, and that wore on Meg. She had been good at her mother role, and mostly still was, but her girlfriend role and her artist role with an approaching gallery opening were new and challenging. Meg thought about what Cate had said and repeated it silently to herself—*I am a smart, mature, grown-ass woman. I can handle this.* She certainly hoped so.

After swimming on Monday and Tuesday mornings, Meg consumed her smoothie and a cup of coffee before heading out to visit Cliff. He was happy to see her, and Meg was thrilled to see that he was improving each day.

Tuesday night, just before ten, Meg was reading on the couch in her pj's and robe with Oscar at her side when the doorbell rang. It brought to mind the late night after the Laurel episode when Cate had shown up on her porch.

Meg went to the door, hoping it was Cate, but when she looked out through the peephole, she saw a young woman standing in the yellow porch light. Meg opened the door and, on closer inspection, realized she didn't know this person who was subtly shifting her weight from foot to foot. She was about Natalie's age, maybe thirty, but she wasn't Natalie. Even nervous, she was very attractive with her long, light brown hair and anxious gray eyes. She was nicely dressed in a pale linen blouse, black dress slacks, and black boots.

"May I help you?" Meg asked.

"Maybe," the young woman responded. "I'm Wren." Meg gave her a questioning look. "*W-r-e-n.*" Then she swallowed, looking at her feet as the porch light exaggerated the shadow of her movement. "I had Robert's baby," she blurted.

The name hit Meg first. What the hell kind of name was *Wren*? Then Meg froze. Frowned. She could have sworn that her heart stopped before it started pounding in her chest. She digested what the woman had just told her. For some reason, Meg didn't doubt her. Didn't question the truth of what she said. Would that bastard never die? Meg tried hard to collect herself, collect her thoughts.

"Can I come in?" this Wren woman asked.

Meg contemplated slamming the door, closing it on what she'd just been told, but she couldn't. It was too late. The words had been spoken. This woman had borne Robert's child.

Meg stepped back from the doorway and motioned Wren inside. As Meg led the way into her living room, Oscar jumped off the couch and joined the two of them. Meg pointed to a chair on the far side of the room, then sat back where she'd been reading on the couch. Oscar jumped back up and piled into her lap. Meg embraced him for comfort, and her good ol' boy purred and pushed his head under her chin. Nothing could fix this, but Oscar at least gave Meg a moment to breathe.

Now the reason Robert had kept that apartment was confirmed. Perfectly clear. Way too clear. And much worse than she'd ever imagined. He'd friggin' conceived a child there. A child!

As Meg looked at the young woman sitting across the room, a flashback came to Meg. The flowers at Robert's funeral service, the wreaths, the gorgeous floral arrangements, and the image of a pregnant young woman who she didn't recognize. It had been Wren in front of a display of calla lilies after the church service. It had been Wren wiping her eyes, looking like she'd been weeping for days. Meg had forgotten that image. Until now.

And then Meg's thoughts went to that apartment Robert had secretly kept in San Francisco. The one on Wilton Street—she'd memorized the street name after Cate had told her. After she'd asked Cate. Meg had suffered nightmares about that apartment, although she'd never actually seen it. Nightmares of Robert there with the silhouette of a woman. Intimate. A woman whose face she couldn't make out.

Well, she was seeing it now, and it was a face so much younger than she'd ever imagined. Wren was no older than her oldest child, and Meg couldn't hate her. She was a version of Natalie—unsure, confused, and seeking something. The mother in Meg surfaced, and right now she hated her maternal instincts. She hated that Wren reminded her of her daughter, that Wren reminded Meg that she'd once been a young woman who had also ended up pregnant.

Wren had been sitting and watching Meg pet Oscar while all of these thoughts and images ran through Meg's mind. Meg pulled herself back to the moment and realized a few minutes had passed. She probably needed to find out why this woman was here in her home.

"You had Robert's child almost two years ago, and I'm assuming that now you're here for a reason."

"Look, Meg. Can I call you Meg?"

Meg shrugged.

Wren cleared her throat. "I'm sorry. I know this must be a terrible shock for you."

Meg nodded and held Wren's gaze, waiting to hear why she was here, now that she'd completely upended Meg's world. Bile rose in Meg's throat. Fucking Robert. "Do you want money?" Meg couldn't think of any other reason for her to have come here.

"No, I don't need money. I have a good job and large inheritances from both my parents and my grandmother. I didn't come for money."

"Okay." That information surprised Meg. "You knew he was married? With a family?" Meg asked.

"I knew. Maybe not at first, when he first swept me off my feet. But I wasn't stupid."

Meg cocked an eyebrow and bit the inside of her cheeks.

"Okay, I was stupid. But by then I was in love with him. Or

thought I was. Until he got sick and just closed down into himself. Left me dealing with the pregnancy before he died."

"How old are you?" Meg asked, studying Wren and thinking of Natalie.

"Thirty," Wren answered.

"Did you know that Robert has a thirty-year-old daughter and he married me because he got me pregnant with her?"

"No. I didn't." Wren was looking down at the floor, her embarrassment showing.

"You're here now. I don't mean here in my living room, but here in terms of having a young child by my deceased husband, and that's not going to change. So, what do you want?" Meg asked, not wanting to hear the answer, whatever it was.

"My son is twenty months old. His name is Heath. After my father. My parents are dead. My grandparents are dead. I'm an only child. I want Heath to know his half siblings. He needs to know he has family besides me." Wren looked at Meg with pleading eyes.

Meg's eyes widened. It felt like an avalanche had just rolled over her and buried her ten feet under. She'd been dealing with all the changes in her life, how they were affecting her, and how they would affect her kids because her kids were so important to her. Coming out. Cate. And now after trying to protect them from the fact that Robert had kept a secret apartment that he used for entertaining women, or at least one woman, she was not only supposed to tell them that he was a cheater, but that they had a half brother?

Meg couldn't believe that she was even considering it, but it occurred to her that each of her children had the right to decide if they wanted a relationship with this child—their half brother. But she wanted to think this out. To figure out how to handle this information. To figure out how to handle all the change she'd brought to her life. Meg knew her emotional limits, and she knew that she was surpassing them.

Meg took a deep breath before answering. "This has been a real shock, Wren. And there's a lot going on in our lives right now. I need some time to digest this and figure it out. Not only is this about telling my kids that they have a half brother, this is about shattering their image of their father. Although I pretty much knew Robert was unfaithful because I knew about the apartment, I never let on to them that their father was a cheater."

Wren winced at the word *cheater*. "I'm sorry," she repeated.

"Give me your number. I need to think about this. It's a huge shock," Meg repeated. "I need time. Time to process it. For myself, and my kids."

"Okay." Wren pulled a pen and paper from her purse and wrote down her phone number. "I put Heath to bed tonight and then a friend came over to stay with him. I live in Redwood City, and I have to get back."

Meg nodded.

"I'll wait for a call. I understand about your feelings and protecting your kids. I'm just trying to do what's best for my son too."

Meg nodded again. Then she walked Wren to the door. She managed to say, "Good night, Wren," before she shut the door on another one of those moments that she would remember forever. Before she knew the magnitude of Robert's cheating, and the after, again. Now she just needed to figure out how to deal with the after. And that meant coming to terms with this herself before she ever considered anyone else.

Meg shut the lights and locked up, on autopilot. Then she walked back to her bedroom, stripped off her robe and pajamas, and went into the bathroom. Leaning over the toilet, Meg emptied her stomach. She turned on the shower and climbed in, letting this liquid pain spilling from her eyes mix with the warm water and wash down the drain. Finally turning off the faucet, she dried herself, put her pajamas back on, and brushed her teeth. As she crawled into bed, Oscar jumped up and joined her. Meg took him in her arms and held him. She curled into her old cat for several hours. When she couldn't fall asleep, she finally got up, collected her laptop, and crawled back under the sheets, propped up against the headboard. It was dawn before she finally closed her eyes and slept for a few hours.

SLOUCHING TOWARD STARDUST WITH MEG THE UNMUZZLED

"The Beast of Betrayal"

So, you'd think at age fifty a person wouldn't be naive. Not about love. Would be a hell of a lot better at it than they were at twenty. And I am. I once wrote that it's a wild beast. Sometimes inconvenient. Unpredictable. Nothing a person can coerce. And I've found that to be true—in the best possible way. However, it's that resurrected skeleton of the buried brute that no longer resembles love but is still capable of sneaking up on you, piercing you through the heart, and throwing you on the spit—that's the beast that can kill you.

CHAPTER TWENTY-FOUR

Meg didn't wake up until midmorning on Wednesday. She had a headache and was exhausted, physically and emotionally. She decided that she needed to take a break. She called the nursing facility and asked them to tell Cliff she wouldn't be making it in to see him. She purposefully avoided calling him directly because she didn't think she could keep up a charade of acting normal when she spoke with him, and she didn't want to try. Then she called The Terraces and told them she wouldn't be able to teach the art class for a bit.

After feeding Oscar, Meg crawled back into bed and spent her time on her laptop and dozing. She just let the reality of what she'd learned about Robert marinate. She'd had the inkling last night that she needed to tell the kids, and for that she needed to compose herself. Today, she still believed that they each had the right to know they had a half brother and to decide if they wanted a relationship with Heath. He was just a baby. That meant a relationship with Wren, Robert's mistress. Damn you, Robert! Meg threw a pillow across the room, scaring Oscar. Sorry, ol' boy.

Meg knew she had to give herself time to get control of her shock, her fury, and the added pain of what Robert had done. The news that their father had cheated and that he'd fathered a child with Wren might not hit them in the same way that it had impacted her, but there would be repercussions for them too.

Meg decided to give herself the day's reprieve from life while she pulled herself together. Then she would try to catch up with her kids to talk with them. She could meet with Jessie and Ben in person, but she wasn't willing to fly to LA again, so she'd have to call Natalie. They hadn't spoken since the lunch two weeks ago. Natalie hadn't seemed to come to any terms with Meg's coming out, so finding out that her father had carried on a secret life and had a second family outside of marriage would certainly not go over well. With her heart aching and her head pounding, Meg rolled over and finally fell into a fitful sleep for the rest of the day. It was seven o'clock when she went out to the kitchen, still in her sleepwear, and made herself some toast for dinner. That was all she could stomach. She added food to Oscar's bowl and gave him his pills. Then she steeled herself, took a deep breath, and picked up her phone to call her daughter.

"Hi, Nat. How are you doing?" Meg asked.

"What do you need, Mom?" Natalie's manner was brusque.

Nat was still angry with her. Now she was going to make it worse. "I need to tell you something. It's about your dad." Meg paused, but Natalie remained silent. "I found out a few months ago that your dad had a secret apartment. A young woman came over to the house last night. She has a twenty-month-old son, and your dad is his father. He's your half brother, and I thought you should know." Did Nat have any idea how hard this was for her?

There was another long pause from Natalie.

"I'm sorry, Nat." Meg didn't know what else to say.

Then her daughter responded with a torrent of anger and blame directed at Meg. "Did you ever think maybe you had some responsibility in this? If you had been a better wife…Obviously, there were issues because you've told me that you're dating a woman now. Was Dad an adulterer because of you?"

Meg was shocked into silence. Then she responded in a quiet voice, "Natalie. You know that I devoted everything I had to your dad and this family. For decades. Your father cheated on me because he chose to do so." Meg was fighting tears again. "I just thought you had a right to know that you have a half brother. His mother's name is Wren, and I'll text you her number, as I'll do with Jessie and Ben. You can each choose to have a relationship with him or not."

Meg felt the chasm of hurt between her daughter and herself, and she didn't have a clue how to fix it. She couldn't change who she was, and she'd suppressed it long enough. She'd sacrificed everything for

Robert and the kids. And she sure as hell couldn't change what Robert had done.

When Natalie didn't respond, Meg whispered, "I love you, Nat. Never doubt that." Then she ended the call and cried some more.

When she had control of her emotions, she called Ben and Jessie and made plans to see them over the weekend. It was almost midnight when Meg texted Cate and told her that she wasn't feeling well, that she needed to cancel their plans for a long weekend. Hopefully, Cate was asleep and wouldn't see the message until the morning. Then she turned off her cell phone and crawled back into bed.

❖

Since seeing Meg's text when she woke up, Cate had left voice-mails and texts for Meg all day on Thursday with no success. So, with Meg under the weather and calling off their date night, she decided to work instead of heading to Trinity Hills.

Cate called her dad—he was doing fine, but he told her that the front desk had informed him that Meg had left a message that she wasn't coming in to see him. Cate paced the floor, sat down in her office chair, and turned to face the window looking out toward the panoramic view of San Francisco. A whole day had passed with no word from Meg. So unlike her. What was going on with Meg?

There was no doubt Meg had a lot on her plate. Cate recognized that Meg was juggling her role as a mother and was worried about her relationship with Natalie, that she had the gallery opening in a week, and that their relationship had brought a lot of change to Meg's life. But Cate had thought they could get through anything. Yet again, Meg wasn't answering her phone, as with the Laurel encounter. Cate was worried there was something significantly wrong. Didn't Meg know that Cate would help her through whatever it was? Cate fluctuated between the emotions of worry and anger. What the hell, Meg?

Cate drove to Trinity Hills on Friday morning. She needed to see her dad, and she was worried about Meg. She went to Meg's house first and knocked on the door. There was no answer. She rang the doorbell. There still was no answer. Meg's car was not in the driveway, but Meg often parked in the garage. After several minutes of trying, Cate decided to go see her dad and get that visit out of the way. She knew she'd be distracted with him and that upset her, but she didn't know what else to do. She didn't have Grace's phone number, or Jessie's or Ben's numbers either. She didn't even know Grace's last name. It frustrated the hell out of her. Shit, how did she not know these things? Because she'd never bothered to ask.

After her visit with her dad, Cate drove to his house. After stewing through much of the afternoon, Cate realized that she knew the name of the tattoo shop where Jessie worked. It was Fine Line Ink in Santa Clara. Cate looked up the shop and called.

"Fine Line Ink. How can I help you?"

"Hi, this is Cate Colson. I'm a friend of Jessie Mullins's mother, and she and I both got tattoos at your shop a few weeks ago. I'm trying to reach Jessie."

"They're busy right now working with a client. Can I give Jessie a message?"

"Please. If you could have Jessie call me when they have a chance." Cate left her phone number.

After hanging up, Cate paced while she waited for a return call. She knew she was not a patient person. Finally, a little before seven o'clock, Jessie returned Cate's call.

"Hi, Cate. I'm not sure why you called, but…um…have you talked to Mom lately?"

"That's why I called you, Jessie. She sent me a text at midnight Wednesday saying she didn't feel well and was canceling our long weekend. I haven't been able to reach her since then."

"She called me last night and told me she needed to talk with me. She asked me to come home on Sunday." Jessie sighed. "I don't think she's sick, Cate. But something's really bothering her."

Cate scowled. Crap, what was going on? "I realized that I don't have your phone number, or Ben's, or even know Grace's last name, much less her number. Is it possible to get that information from you? I didn't know how to reach any of you when Meg didn't pick up, and I only had a message she didn't feel well and was canceling our plans."

"Sure, Cate. I can't think she'd mind you having that info, matching tattoos and all." Jessie chuckled before reciting the phone numbers Cate had requested and telling her that Grace's last name was Fuller.

"Thanks, Jessie. Keep in touch. I just want your mom to be okay."

"Sure, I'm a little worried too—it's not like her to ask me to drive in so she can tell me something important."

As Cate hung up, she decided that she'd call Grace, then go over to Meg's again. The call to Grace didn't offer her any additional information because Grace hadn't heard from Meg lately and had only left her a message about getting together with no response. Cate let Grace know that she was headed over to Meg's.

Cate arrived at Meg's place for the second time that day at a little after eight o'clock in the evening. There was still no car in the driveway. Cate went to the front door and knocked. After waiting, she rang the bell. Then knocked again. Finally, as she was heading back to her car on the street, she heard the click of Meg's door opening. Cate turned around and headed back toward the porch. Meg only had the door open about six inches, but from what Cate could see, she looked like she'd been to hell and back. Cate couldn't imagine what was wrong.

"Hey, babe. I was worried about you. What's going on?"

Meg frowned and she blinked several times. "I can't talk about it right now. I need some space, Cate."

Fuck! Was Meg breaking up with her? "I just want to know that you're okay, Meg. I want to help."

"I'm okay." Meg spoke softly and wasn't convincing.

Bullshit. "Are *we* okay, Meg?" Cate asked.

"I've got some things I need to deal with. Things I need to figure out, so I can deal with my kids. I'm sorry." Meg did look sorry. So sorry.

"You need to at least be open with me. Let me help." When Meg didn't answer, Cate told her, "I called the tattoo shop. Jessie said you'd called and asked for a meeting on Sunday." Cate waited.

"I did." Meg divulged nothing else.

"So, this is none of my business, Meg?" What the hell? Where did she fit into Meg's life?

"Cate…" Meg pleaded. "I need some time. Let me handle this. Okay?"

Even though she was terrified, Cate had to ask, "Are you breaking up with me, Meg?"

"I need some time," Meg repeated. "I just don't know what's going to happen," she whispered. "I don't know what to say right now."

Cate's despair was so acute it was a physical pain. She wiped her eyes. Something was wrong. Very wrong. Was this Laurel all over again? Pete had convinced her that Meg was a long-hauler. Cate didn't know what to say either, so she reached in through the door space and brushed her hand gently across Meg's cheek.

"I'm here for you, Meg—*today*. But you've shut me out. Not let me in. Not let me help." Cate backed up and turned around. Her heart ached. She was angry, and growing more upset as Meg didn't respond. Then she swung back to face Meg. "I can't do it this way. It hurts too much." And then she headed to her car, got in, wiped her eyes, and drove away.

❖

As Cate left, Meg closed the door and leaned her head against it. After a while, she decided to just return to her room and crawl back into bed. The cat joined her, and she wrapped him in her arms. She'd thought she'd cried all her tears. But there were more.

Meg had a call and a text from Grace, but she turned off her phone because she wasn't ready to deal with anyone else yet. Friday was another fitful night.

Even though she was exhausted, Meg was up in time to shower and feed Oscar before heading up to Ben's in Sacramento on Saturday morning. She was running on the sheer determination to get through this weekend, to try to put on a face of composure and calm for Jessie and Ben.

"Hi, Mom," Ben said as he let her in and they sat at his kitchen table. "Sarah's gone to a friend's house—we got the sense this was something private, that you'd be more comfortable talking just to me."

"Thanks for making time for me, Ben." Meg offered him a weak smile. She could do this. "Sarah is a wise woman."

"You've got me worried. What's going on?" Ben furrowed his brow in concern.

"I don't know where to start." Meg cleared her throat. "So I'll just dive in."

Ben waited patiently in the chair across from her.

"A few months ago, I got a call from Cate's law office because it turns out that your dad had a secret apartment."

Ben's eyes widened.

"I didn't tell you kids because I thought it was done, and there was no reason to tarnish your memory of your dad."

"Holy crap," Ben exclaimed as he reached across the table and took her hand.

"That's not all." Meg held on to his hand for support. "Tuesday night a young woman Natalie's age, Wren, came to the house and told me that she'd had your dad's baby."

"What the fuck, Mom?"

That at least made Meg smile. "My sentiments exactly."

"What did this Wren woman want?" Ben asked.

"The baby is a boy named Heath. Twenty months old, so just a baby. She has no other family and she wants him to know you kids—his half siblings."

Ben's mouth dropped open. Then he shut it. "So what do you think?"

"I think it's up to each of you kids to decide what you want. This is your half brother. He's innocent in all of this. You'd have to form a relationship with his mom since he's so young, but to be honest, she seems nice enough." Except for sleeping with Robert—Meg kept that thought to herself. "I'll leave you her number so you can call her if you want." Meg swallowed. She was going to let her kids come to their own conclusions about what they wanted to do.

"I don't know what I want. I'm going to have to think about it. I never thought I'd have a baby brother, and you're right. He's innocent. But that doesn't make Dad any less of a total asshole. I'm sorry that he did that to you."

Meg took a napkin off the table and wiped the moisture from her eyes. "I just don't want this to tear our family apart. My dating Cate has already caused huge issues with Nat." Meg did not want to go into what Natalie had said to her. She could see no point in bringing Ben into all the details of her pain regarding Natalie's condemnation and blame.

Ben rolled his eyes. "Cate is wonderful. Nat's going to have to figure it out. Or not. But don't let her ruin your happiness."

"I'm trying not to, but it's hard," Meg said.

"Or Dad. Don't let him ruin things for you either. I love you, Mom."

"I love you too, Ben." Meg stood up and went around the table to hug him.

"So, how about I make you a sandwich?" Ben suggested.

"That sounds good. And you can tell me how your teaching is going."

Meg stayed another hour and chatted with Ben before giving him Wren's cell number and getting in her car to head back home.

❖

Jessie arrived at Meg's house a little after one o'clock on Sunday afternoon. She'd spent the morning drinking coffee and doing a little writing. She made them lunch before they sat down and had basically the same conversation that she'd had with Ben. Jessie's reaction was similar to Ben's, with a few more swear words.

"Have you heard from Nat since you told her that you were dating Cate?" Jessie asked.

"I talked to her on Wednesday evening." Meg frowned.

"Did she realize what a complete scumbag Dad was? Her religion...adultery, and all? Did she finally get off your case about dating Cate?"

"No, not exactly." Meg sighed and thrust her hand through her hair. She knew Jessie could see how distraught she was.

"What did she say, Mom?" they pressed.

"She seemed to blame me for your dad's behavior." Meg's lips quivered. She didn't want to cry in front of Jessie.

"Are you kidding me?" Jessie was irate. "Her beliefs are ripping this family apart. How can that be what Jesus wanted?"

"I don't know, Jessie." Meg had nothing else to offer.

"Okay, Mom. Just know that I think she's being an idiot. It's about time I called her to tell her that I'm nonbinary—I was created this way. And I need to tell her a few other things. It's time she faces reality and decides if she wants to be part of this family or not. I don't know how some people can let religion mess things up so badly."

Meg didn't understand how Natalie could let her religion hurt their relationship so badly either. She was worn out trying to deal with everything. Robert had hurt them all. Natalie had hurt her. And she had upset Natalie in ways she couldn't control without relinquishing who she was. She loved her kids with all her heart, but she knew that she had to love herself too. And then there was the hurt she had caused Cate on Friday. She just didn't have the emotional reserves right now to deal with anything else. And she still had to make it through the gallery opening next Saturday, had to be strong enough to take center stage that evening.

Slouching Toward Stardust with Meg the unMuzzled

"A Mother's Love"

"Whatever else is unsure in this stinking dunghill of a world a mother's love is not."—*James Joyce,* A Portrait of the Artist as a Young Man

When you were five, I remember taking the training wheels off your small blue bicycle, and you happily climbed on and wobbled down the street toward the end of the block, so proud of yourself that you raised your hands into the air to wave at me. You lost your balance. You cried over that skinned knee and that little blue bicycle until I kissed your wound and put a Band-Aid on that hurt, then kissed the bike and put a Band-Aid on the dent. And all was well.

When you were seven, I remember you dancing in the rain in your rubber boots. Dancing with the exuberance of the innocent, not a care in the world. You threw back your head and laughed at the sheer thrill of stomping in a puddle that splashed your joy all over the sidewalk. And I threw back my head and laughed at the sheer thrill of watching you. We laughed together in that shared moment. And all was well.

When you were ten, I remember a downy-feathered bird falling out of its nest. We placed that fledgling in a box, collected a ladder, and then placed it back in the nest. Its frantic mother calmed as if to thank us, then turned back to its baby. You told me that mother bird loved her baby the way I loved you. We shared that moment of love. And all was well.

And when you were grown, I brought you bad news. And all I wanted to do was offer a Band-Aid, laugh together, share a moment of love. So that all would be well.

CHAPTER TWENTY-FIVE

Cate struggled through the rest of the weekend in Trinity Hills because she wanted to visit her dad on Sunday morning before heading back to San Francisco. She was fluctuating between anger and hurt. Meg's actions were the cause of both, while her own lack of control over the situation was certainly contributing to her ill temper.

Cate had just settled onto the living room couch in her apartment in San Francisco on Sunday evening when her phone rang. Was it Meg? Cate looked at the caller ID and realized the call was coming from Jessie.

"Hi, Jessie." Cate hoped for some news.

"Have you talked to Mom?"

"I only saw her for a moment on Friday afternoon, but I don't know much. At first, I thought she was sick, but after Friday…" Cate struggled to keep her voice even. She didn't want to put any of Meg's kids in the middle of whatever was happening between Meg and her.

"It's not her health," Jessie said. "Something happened, but she needs to be the one to tell you what's going on."

"I understand. I've been so worried, just wanted to see if there's anything I can do." Cate knew that Meg would want her to protect Jessie as best she could, and whatever had happened, it was obvious Jessie wasn't comfortable telling her. "She needs to be the one to talk to me." *If she ever will.* The hurt and anger roiled in Cate's stomach.

"Cate." Jessie paused after saying her name. "I can tell you that this is not about you. Mom's not upset with you." Another moment of silence passed, then Jessie repeated, "But she needs to be the one to talk to you."

"That's fine. Thanks for calling me."

"Cate?"

"What?" Cate wondered what else Jessie was going to tell her.

"Cut Mom some slack if you can. You're good for her."

"You're a good kid, Jessie." Cate concluded the conversation before she involved Jessie any further in the issues between Meg and herself.

Once she was off the phone, a new barrage of emotions and questions hit Cate. What could have happened if this didn't involve her directly, if Meg wasn't upset with her? But damn, Meg was not off the hook. If whatever had upset Meg so severely had nothing to do with the two of them, then why the hell wasn't Meg willing to take comfort from her? The questions swirled in Cate's head, and she had no answers. What did Meg really feel for her? Was their relationship even real if Meg was unwilling to tell her what was going on and wouldn't count on her to help?

Cate fought to suppress her insecurities, but she was struggling. She finally texted Pete to see if he could have lunch with her the next day. He responded that he was out of town and could have lunch with her on Tuesday, but for her to call him if she needed to talk with him before then.

❖

Cate was in her office when Piper showed up for work on Monday morning. Cate stayed there while she listened to Piper's loud arrival, followed by her trip down to her paralegal office. Moments later, Piper returned to the reception area, and Cate could hear her singing some song about making love, while she watered the plants. Cate leaned forward and held her head in her hands.

Piper knocked on Cate's partially open door, and Cate immediately sat up straight and looked at Piper.

"Did you have a good long weekend?" Piper asked, a suggestive look on her face.

"Not really," Cate muttered. She didn't want to talk to Piper about Meg.

"Your dad okay?"

"Yeah, he's fine. Can we just get to work?"

Piper was astute, and Cate knew she was studying her. Piper undoubtedly recognized that she was in a mood similar to the one she'd been in before Pete took her to lunch and convinced her to give Meg a chance.

"Anything you need, just let me know." Piper smiled kindly at Cate.

"Thanks. And Piper?"

"Yes?"

"I'm having lunch with Pete tomorrow, so could you make sure my appointments won't conflict?"

"You've got it, Cate."

Piper had just called her Cate. Not boss. That was enough for Cate to confirm that Piper realized that something was going on.

Cate tried to focus on work instead of her pain and anger over the rejection by Meg.

The next morning, Cate was still trying to regain her elusive focus when Piper arrived and burst into her office.

"I hope there's a good reason for the interruption," Cate declared, looking up.

"Yeah, boss. You know my mom?" Piper inquired, exuding enthusiasm.

"I've never had the pleasure of meeting her, but I'm assuming this is the same mother who took the dog." The dog that Meg had found.

"The one and only," Piper told her.

"And?" Cate asked, not feeling like a conversation about Piper's mother.

"Well, she has this friend, Mildred."

"And?" Cate repeated her question.

"A while ago, Mildred got Mom hooked on this blog. I've heard them talking about it, and they love it. It has a ton of followers."

"And?" Cate was losing patience.

"Just hang with me. I took a look at this blog last night, and you're not going to believe it. I'm not going to say anything else, but I'm going to send you the link."

"And I have time for this?" Cate inquired.

"Trust me, Cate. Just have a look," Piper pleaded in earnest.

"Close the door on your way out."

"Sure. Just have a look. Okay?" Piper gently closed the door as she left.

A minute later, her curiosity piqued, Cate clicked the link Piper sent. She started reading. *Slouching Toward Stardust*? What the hell was Piper thinking? Then the rest of the title registered. *Meg the unMuzzled*. Cate took a deep breath. Holy crap, what was going on? And then she started reading.

Cate spent the rest of the morning reading Meg's blog. Working her way through the first entries. Entries made not long after Robert's death when the blog was first launched—well before Cate had first called Meg into her office regarding the audit and the apartment. Cate wiped her eyes, wondering at this additional level of sensitivity and beauty in Meg that she'd glimpsed, but never grasped. She'd seen it in her art, but here it was as words on a page. Cate did not know how to feel. She realized that she loved this woman, but she was feeling angry too. On top of Meg's closing her out, here was a whole world of Meg that she'd had no clue even existed. Damn, she loved a woman she only partially knew. How did she deal with that? How did Meg feel about her? About their relationship?

Even though she hadn't read the last entries, she needed to go join Pete for lunch. She closed up her computer and headed out to join him. As she passed Piper, she let her know that she was going to join Pete for lunch at the Tadich Grill, even though the lunch was on her calendar.

"Did you finish it?"

"No, I ran out of time. I'll finish it when I get back."

"Do that, Cate."

"Thanks, Piper." Cate slipped out the door.

❖

After Cate and Pete had been seated at their table, Pete addressed Cate. "So, are we just having a friendly lunch, or is this a therapy session?" Pete asked.

"Therapy," Cate advised him, hiding behind the menu.

"Then I'm ordering us wine," Pete told her. "I don't do therapy without wine."

Cate had to laugh, even though her emotions were in turmoil. "Just don't let me get drunk. Because I want to." She set down the menu.

"That bad, huh? My guess is it must be Meg."

"You have no idea, Pete."

"Try me."

"Let's order, then I will." After they ordered and their wine arrived, Cate told Pete about her brief porch exchange with Meg on Friday. That Meg had shut her out, and then silence ever since. About the fact that she didn't know if Meg had broken up with her or not. She didn't involve Jessie in the discussion with Pete but did tell him that from what she knew it wasn't related to something she'd done. Then she told him about the blog that Piper had brought to her that morning, and she pulled it up on her phone.

"I didn't finish it, but damn, Pete. It's beautiful, and revealing, and another side of Meg that I didn't know existed. Another thing I'm in the dark about. Her blog—I'm torn between being awed and being totally pissed. She has a lot to answer for because if she can't trust me…" Their meals were delivered, and she handed Pete her phone, and while she sipped her wine and started her meal, he sat there scrolling and reading.

"It looks like she started this about six months after Robert passed away. Well before you let her know about the apartment. How far did you get?"

"Up to the one about the dog that followed Meg into my law office. Where she called our relationship *complicated*." Cate drew out that last word, injecting skepticism into her tone.

Pete laughed. "As if you're not complicated."

Cate couldn't suppress a hint of a smile as she conceded, "Well, maybe just a little bit." Pete always grounded her. That's why she was here.

"I skipped some and read several after that."

"And?" Cate reflected on the fact that she'd had the same question for Piper a few hours ago and ended up with the blog.

"First of all, while Meg has a hell of a lot of followers, my guess is that she hasn't told anyone about this blog. It's her *Meg the unMuzzled* persona. She chose that name because she wanted the freedom to write anonymously. So don't get your knickers all in a twist because she didn't tell you about it. Meg needed this."

Cate digested that observation. She could probably live with the private blog, but not with Meg shutting her out over whatever had upset her.

"A quick look at some of the blogs after the dog blog where you stopped—there's one she called 'The Beast of Betrayal.' It makes me suspect that whatever happened, maybe Robert's involved. Not you."

Cate nodded, feeling relief that what Jessie had told her was probably correct. But Robert? Meg already knew about the apartment. Cate still had so many unanswered questions that continued to upset her. She didn't know if Meg felt she couldn't rely on her, didn't know how she actually fit into Meg's life. She did know that she was grateful for Pete's friendship.

Pete scrolled and read for a while longer, then returned her phone. "Go back to your office and read them. There's one thing that's obvious in those entries after the dog blog." Pete paused and took another bite of his lunch and sip of his wine as he watched her.

"Well, don't hold out on me, Mr. Therapist."

"She loves you, Cate. She writes about her love for you. Go back and read those blogs."

She loves me. Neither of them had spoken that word yet. It offered Cate a glimmer of hope.

"Do you love her?" Pete asked.

"Yes. I do," Cate answered with certainty, suddenly considering all of its implications. For breaking her heart. Or figuring out if they could get past this. To a future together.

Pete rolled his eyes. "So, she loves you. You love her. You two need to fix this, Cate."

On Monday and Tuesday mornings, Meg went swimming and then returned to the solace of her house. She didn't know how to fix things with Cate. Maybe Cate wouldn't want to fix things. Cate had said she'd hurt her too much. She'd told Cate that she didn't know what was going to happen because she didn't know what the fallout from Robert's actions would be for her kids. Jessie and Ben had pleasantly surprised her, but Natalie was another story that she'd need to come to terms with. She hated the thought of losing her daughter.

Meg spent late Tuesday morning trying to distract herself from the turmoil of the last few days. She'd done some writing over coffee, then settled into her art studio with Oscar while she worked on a drawing. Grace texted her that she was coming by after she was off work, so Meg had to decide if she would answer the door. She decided she owed it to Grace to do so. She'd already blown it with Cate.

A little after two o'clock, there was a knock, and Meg went to let Grace in. Of course, Oscar had to get in on the action and raced to the door to greet Grace, which was an act of normalcy that Meg appreciated from her good ol' boy.

"Hey, sweetie." Grace pulled Meg into a big hug. "I talked to Cate on Friday afternoon before she came here, and then I called Jessie last night. They only told me it wasn't Cate who upset you."

Meg nodded. "It wasn't. But I'm afraid she'll never talk to me again." Meg felt so overwhelmed. She'd spent today trying to psych herself into Saturday's huge event, crucial to her art career. She'd wanted it for so long. Meg wished she was sharing it with Cate, but she knew she deserved Cate's rebuff. She also realized that she wasn't ready to call Cate only to find out that Cate was too angry to get back together. She couldn't handle that right now. She wouldn't make it through her professional launch.

"Cate seemed frantic on Friday," Grace said. "She cares about you."

"Yeah, but that was before I shut her out. Sent her away. Told her I didn't know what would happen. She told me that I'd hurt her, and it sounded like she was breaking up with me."

Grace nodded.

Meg's eyes flooded, but she didn't cry. "I just didn't have the reserves to hold it all together with Cate. I had to deal with the kids. I talked with Ben and Jessie. And Nat." Meg wasn't ready to talk about Natalie's condemnation, and she wasn't going to discuss Robert with Grace today. Cate was on her mind. She knew Cate was who mattered to her. "I was a weak-assed jerk, and I wouldn't be surprised if she's done with me. I'd be done with me. I just can't take on any more right now. And I still have to get through my gallery opening on Saturday." Meg gulped.

"I know you do, sweetie. An art career has been something you've wanted since way before I met you. I'm not going to ask what triggered all this because Cate deserves to hear about this first, so I'll wait on that."

That made Meg shed the tears she'd been holding back. "Yes, she does. And she said she was willing to try that Friday when she came to my door. But because of how I hurt her, how I wouldn't share—it sounded like she was done, and I can't make it through Saturday if she confirms that right now."

Grace nodded again. "So, how can I help you?" she asked.

"If you're going to my opening, can you and John take me?"

"You've got it, sweetie. We'll get you there. And we'll be heading home after."

"Thanks. You don't know how much I appreciate you." She gave Grace a tearful smile.

"Anytime. Now let me go home and cook up some dinner—then I'm going to drop you off a plate. You look like you haven't eaten much in a week."

Meg laughed through her sniffles. "Damn, Grace. If nothing else, we both have a mother mode."

SLOUCHING TOWARD STARDUST WITH MEG THE UNMUZZLED

"Blog: A Shortened Version of Weblog"

My blog: A means of playing my opus in keystrokes. Irrelevant that a reader is only one click from rejecting me, because I only write for myself. A digital diary. Writing that world trapped inside my mind. Divulging a description of my heartbreak, byte by byte. Laptop proclamations of love. Sanity on a screen. So much cheaper than a therapist. And I can write damn *as many times as I want, and there's no one to stop me.*

Here I am, writing the damn remarkable narrative of my damn thrilling life. Taking one damn choice word and placing it adjacent to the next damn choice word until I've got a damn compelling sentence that with the next damn compelling sentence and the next damn compelling sentence creates a damn captivating paragraph and then a damn mesmerizing blog, and pretty soon I'm passing myself off as a damn tolerably adept writer.

CHAPTER TWENTY-SIX

Cate headed back to her office after lunch with Pete on Tuesday. She'd ordered a serving of Belgian chocolate cake to take with her before she left the restaurant. As she walked into the office reception area, she set the box on the desk in front of Piper as she passed. Piper looked at her in surprise.

"Whoa. What's this?"

"Your next pay raise," Cate advised her as she kept moving.

Piper peeked inside and smacked her lips, then followed Cate into her office.

"Hey, boss?"

"What, Piper?"

"I don't know what's going on with you and Meg, and it's probably not any of my business…" Piper trailed off.

Cate pretended to scowl at Piper. "It's probably not, but that's never stopped you before."

Piper grinned. "Hey, you need me. I know something's going on. You don't hide it very well."

Cate had to agree that something was going on, but she'd never admit that to Piper.

"And?" Damn, she was saying that a lot lately.

"And…" Piper paused. "I found you Meg's blog. And she loves you, Cate. Really loves you."

Cate felt her face flush. "I haven't gotten that far in my reading."

"Well, go finish. Then make things right."

"Now you're sounding like Pete."

"That's a compliment." Piper smiled at Cate.

"Dubious," Cate muttered.

"You need her."

If she could just get past being furious with Meg. Upset by how Meg had handled this. "Well, I'm not going to get any reading done standing here with you advising me on my love life."

"Just don't blow it." Piper turned to leave.

"Hey, Piper."

"Yeah, boss?"

"Thanks."

"Thank me by inviting me to the wedding." Piper flashed her another grin.

Cate shook her head and fixed a frown on her face as she pointed Piper out of her office door. Piper threw back that head of short curly red hair and laughed.

As upset as she was, Cate bit her cheeks to keep from laughing too. It was lucky Piper was such a damn good paralegal. And Cate could certainly use her levity. She walked over and closed her office door so she could finish reading Meg's blog in privacy. Cate needed to read that Meg had admitted to loving her.

❖

Cate tried to distract herself with legal work and her dad's recovery, planning for his return to The Terraces the next week. She wasn't sure if she was trying to avoid her emotions where Meg was concerned, or if she was just trying to work through them. What if she went to Meg's gallery opening and Meg wanted nothing to do with her? Cate even entertained the reasons she'd had one-night stands after Laurel. Good sex, sometimes. No damn inner turmoil—she'd never felt this angry and confused after one of those encounters. Who the hell was she fooling? There hadn't been much sex with Meg yet, certainly not under the best of circumstances with her dad's medical interruption, but it had been off the charts. Knowing that she loved the woman whose neck she wanted to wring. And Meg loved her—she'd told the whole damn blogosphere—just not Cate. But trust—that was a big one. Meg had been there when Cate needed her—coming out to her kids for Cate, letting Cate into her home, helping with her dad, understanding her work schedule. But Meg hadn't let Cate be there when Meg needed her.

And that was a problem they'd have to resolve. If they ever got back together.

Oh, hell. She hated being in love right now. But it was the most important thing in her life. She wanted to fix this, like Pete and Piper had advised her. The problem was, she wasn't quite sure how. And that left her frustrated because she hated uncertainty, things that were out of her control. Was she really any good at relationships?

❖

Meg spent more time in her studio on Wednesday trying to focus on an art project. After swimming Thursday morning to relieve some stress, she worked in her garden in an effort to calm the nervous energy she was feeling about the scrutiny she and her art would be under on Saturday evening at the gallery opening. She finished the drawing she'd been working on and slipped it into a frame with a mat, then packaged it for transport. But the opening was only a fraction of her anxiety. Would Cate be there? If so, how hurt or angry would she be with Meg? Or were they finished? Meg didn't know how her decisions and actions regarding this past week would play out with Cate. She'd pushed Cate away. Shut her out. Because dealing with Robert and his actions had left her with no reserves. Dealing with her own anger and pain, telling her kids, and Natalie's accusations and judgment had drained her. *Fucking Robert.* But he was gone. And she'd let the fallout from his actions overwhelm her, been afraid to trust that Cate would be there to support her through this. Now Cate was gone too.

Meg's phone rang early Thursday afternoon and she saw it was Olivia.

"Hi, Olivia. Is the opening still on?"

"Not only is it still on, but it's going to be terrific. The invitations are out, the caterer is scheduled, the art is matted and framed—I'm just calling to make sure the artist is ready."

Was she ready? She'd wanted this for so long. "I guess I'm as ready as I'll ever be. It's been an exhausting week, but I'll be there." Meg exhaled, a long slow breath.

"Sorry to hear it's been a tough week. Anything I can do to help?" Olivia offered.

"No. I'm telling myself that this is probably what I need right now. It certainly has been a dream of mine for most of my life. I know it would have made my grandmother happy, especially that her old gallery is representing me. So, I want to say thank you again."

"You're welcome. Opportunities and events like this are what make this job enjoyable. Now for the nitty-gritty. I called to let you know we are expecting over a hundred people, besides your family and friends. Plus some press members. There's a lot of interest in your work."

Meg gave a nervous chuckle. "No pressure, huh? That's a lot of people."

"Relax, Meg. They'll come in spread out over the four hours we've planned for the event. Now, I'd like you here by four o'clock on Saturday—an hour early if that works for you. We'll hang the art tomorrow, and I want you to see it in case you have any issues. The framer did a fantastic job, so I think you're going to be thrilled," Olivia gushed.

"I'm riding in with friends, and I don't think four o'clock will be any problem. I know two of my kids are coming, so that should be fun. I don't know that they've ever taken my art all that seriously, probably because I never let myself do that. But I'm pleased that maybe this will make them pause and consider what their great-grandmother accomplished back in her day," Meg told her.

"I've got two kids," Olivia said. "I get it. I'm looking forward to meeting yours. You're going to make them proud."

"I hope so. I'll see you then at four o'clock on Saturday."

"I'm looking forward to it," Olivia assured her.

As they signed off, Oscar wandered into the kitchen. Meg picked him up and held him.

"Wish me luck, Oscar. Saturday is going to be a hell of a day. I just hope I survive—all of it." Meg's mind went to Cate. If Cate was there, what would she say? If Cate wasn't there, what would she do? Meg sighed into Oscar's head.

Oscar purred.

❖

As Meg prepared for John and Grace to collect her on Saturday afternoon, she worried—that her art wouldn't be good enough, just

Mona Lisa Meg's silly housewife hobby, that she wouldn't represent her grandmother's legacy, and about her deteriorating relationship with her daughter. But most of all she worried about Cate. When she was ready, she looked around. This was likely going to be another one of those times with a clearly demarcated before and after. Where would things stand with Cate the next time she walked into her house? She was so damn tired of dealing with stress.

John came to the front door and escorted her to the car. He carried the small wrapped rectangular package for her that she'd had waiting in the foyer. As she rounded the car with John and entered the back seat, Grace looked at her with appreciation. "You look absolutely gorgeous, sweetie."

"Thanks. I'm anxious as hell. It's a huge night." In so many ways. John handed Meg the package, and she set it onto the seat next to her.

"That it is. But relax. You'll be a smashing success." Grace did not bring up Cate, and Meg was grateful.

"Thank you so much for agreeing to drive me in. I know you're having to leave much earlier than you would otherwise."

"We're going to get you delivered, and then we'll go get a bite to eat." John locked eyes with Meg in the rearview mirror.

"That makes sense. You might want to take your time because I don't think you're going to want to hang out for the entire time in the gallery," Meg said.

"Hey, I've read that these openings are catered with drinks and finger food, so by the time we view your work and celebrate with the catering, I bet time will fly by," Grace responded with a chuckle.

"Are you ladies all buckled in and ready to hit the road?" John asked, looking again at Meg in the rearview mirror.

Meg and Grace answered in unison that they were, so John backed out of the driveway, and they were on their way to the official launch of Meg's professional art career.

Slouching Toward Stardust with Meg the unMuzzled

"Across the Generations"

Art Show Opening—sixty years ago: My grandmother
Art Show Opening—my turn, finally: Meg the unMuzzled

I have a sheet of watercolor paper, a palette, some paints and brushes, a container of water in front of me. I take a deep breath and reach for a paintbrush. As I pick it up, I'm once again six years old, sitting in the kitchen on a chair next to my grandmother. Perched on a chair with the worn family Bible and a handsewn pillow my grandmother had made, stacked to boost me up to a height that paralleled Nana's.

"Well, my girl. Let me show you how to hold that brush. Grasp it in your hand like this." She held my small hand in hers as she gently positioned the brush. "Do you see?"

"Yes, Nana."

"Do you think this is just a stick of wood with a tuft of squirrel hair on the end?"

I studied her. I studied the bristles.

"You need to know this is not just a simple paintbrush. It's filled with magic and beauty. It will take you places you could never get to from here, but only if you learn its secrets."

I nodded, eager to learn its secrets. And she showed me how to use that brush. How to wet it. How to dip it in the palette of paints brought from Europe years ago. How to stroke it across the page of paper before me. And how to create those images floating through my head. But best of all, she showed me how an older woman shared her passion for painting with a little girl because she loved me. And I loved her in return.

CHAPTER TWENTY-SEVEN

Although the traffic was heavy and came to a full stop in several locations, the drive into the city was fairly uneventful. John and Grace fell into discussing some medical issues that John's mother was having, so Meg took the opportunity to write and post a blog from her phone while they were stalled in traffic on the bridge. She was nervous, and it was calming. After they left the car in a parking garage a few minutes before four o'clock, John and Grace walked Meg to Legends Art Gallery and promised they'd return in about an hour, and then Grace hugged Meg as John held the door for her.

Meg exhaled. "Thanks for being good friends. I'll see you in a bit," Meg told them as she walked past John into the gallery. She carried a gold sequined clutch and the flat wrapped package that she'd brought from home. Once she'd stepped inside, Meg stopped and looked around, remembering the times she'd been here with her grandmother and the last time she'd come in to meet with Olivia and been offered the opportunity for this showing. She admired the updated interior again—the large space, the high ceilings, the warm oak flooring, the professional lighting set at the perfect angle to reduce glare on each piece of well-spaced artwork on the walls. She appreciated the openness that the white walls offered, not only the structural walls, but also the several freestanding ones. And then there were the scattered tables and pedestals displaying metal, ceramic, and glass sculptures.

After her cursory scan, Meg was contemplating moving farther into the interior and focusing on the detailed images of the framed artwork when Olivia came out of her office to greet her. Olivia wore a pale smoke-gray pencil skirt with a matching blazer over a white silk blouse, an outfit that painted her as the image of the professional gallery owner that she was.

"Here you are, Meg. I'm so excited for you. You look exquisite tonight. Would you like to leave your purse and package in my office before I show you the setup?"

Meg nodded and followed Olivia into her office, and Olivia had her set her belongings on a side table near her desk. Then she led Meg back out into the gallery and walked her over to display walls with several paintings—paintings that Meg recognized as her own artwork, but matted and framed into the professional pieces she'd always dreamed of.

"What do you think, Meg? The framer did a great job, didn't she?" Olivia was clearly pleased as well.

Meg's words caught in her throat. She cleared it. "It makes me feel like a professional. Thank you."

"You are a professional. After tonight, you're going to be a known professional. I hope you're ready."

"I guess I'll find out," Meg said softly, again realizing that tonight was truly going to be a landmark night in so many ways.

Meg wandered the studio while Olivia oversaw the final preparations for the opening. By five o'clock, people had started to trickle in. Many just wanted to look, while others wanted to talk with the artist. Meg smiled and greeted art enthusiasts as they engaged her. Olivia had additional staff present, and they were busy with the viewers as well. Meg kept an eye out for the family and friends she had invited, and she nervously watched for Cate.

At almost six o'clock, Grace and John returned, and behind them Meg watched Ben and Sarah pass through the door. She waved at them, and as they waved back, she saw Luc and Jessie come in. And then to her astonishment, following Jessie, Natalie entered. *Natalie.* Meg worked hard not to change her demeanor but finished her conversation with a patron and headed over to her children. They were all dressed up for her show. She hugged Ben, Jessie, and their partners while making eye contact with Natalie.

"Thanks for coming, Nat. You don't know what this means to me." Meg sniffed as she embraced her. Damn, if she wasn't careful, she'd ruin her makeup.

Nat spoke softly into her ear as Meg held her. "Jessie called me—

convinced me I only had one shot at your one-and-only first opening night. I'm still upset with you. And confused."

"Fair enough," Meg told her. "I just don't want to lose you." Meg stepped back from Natalie and smiled. "I love you, Nat."

"I'm staying with Jessie. And Luc." Meg wondered how that was working out for Natalie, but she certainly wasn't going to ask. "I'm going to go look around with Ben and Jessie, if that's okay, Mom."

"You go do that. And thanks again for coming. Having you here is important to me."

Meg continued to visit with people and watch the door. At almost half past seven, Pete and Piper showed up. The dark-haired Pete was as handsome as ever in a charcoal-gray business suit, and the mop-haired Piper looked cheerful in a burnt orange shirt adorned with a bright turquoise tie, pleated black slacks, and black dress boots. No Cate, though. Meg's heart hurt, but she was glad to see Pete and Piper.

"Thanks for coming, you two. I'm so happy to see you," Meg said, welcoming them.

"We wouldn't miss it." Pete hugged her. "You look gorgeous, as usual."

After Meg thanked him, Piper greeted her. "I'm so excited for you. I can hardly wait to see your work."

"Let me take you over and introduce you to my kids," Meg suggested, guiding the two of them to where Nat, Jessie, and Ben were looking at her art with their partners. She introduced everybody before she headed back into the crowd of people Olivia had invited.

"Your mom's an artistic genius," Piper told Meg's kids, while she was still in earshot. "I'm so happy for her. Now you've just got to help her get her girl."

Meg continued to mix with the art crowd as she paid attention to the people entering and leaving. It was half past eight, and while she tried not to show it, her spirits were plummeting. She'd hoped so much that Cate would show up. But as late as it was, she was pretty sure she wasn't going to do so. Meg had avoided the alcohol tonight because she wanted to be fully in control if Cate came, and she didn't want to be tempted to overindulge if Cate did not come.

She was just reconsidering her decision not to touch a drop when she looked toward the door and saw Cate walk in. Her heart went straight to her throat. So beautiful. Cate was wearing a garnet dress and heels, her mahogany-hued hair down tonight instead of up in a loose bun or ponytail. She surreptitiously kept an eye on Cate as Cate ignored her, or at least didn't seek her out. Cate studied Meg's paintings on the walls as she made her way over to where Pete and Piper were visiting with her kids. Meg stayed where she was. Maybe she wasn't welcome, and it would be hard to act like everything was normal. Meg observed Cate give Pete a hug and offer Piper a smile. She continued to watch as Jessie introduced Cate to Natalie, as Natalie's eyes widened in appraisal of Cate, as Cate took Natalie's hand and smiled at her. Then Cate chatted with Jessie and Ben before turning and spending more time in a serious conversation with Natalie.

❖

Cate stared across the art gallery at Meg. She tried to look away. Then she gave her another glance. God, Meg was mesmerizing. And she was wearing the formfitting dusty-rose dress with the above-the-knee hem and a hint of cleavage. The one that Grace had labeled the Cate acquisition dress. Cate's mind wandered—was she wearing those black silk high-leg briefs underneath? That black lace bra that curved perfectly over Meg's beautiful breasts? Cate's mind wandered even farther to that night she had kissed those breasts. Maybe there was nothing but Meg under that dusty-rose covering.

Cate shook her head, bit the inside of her cheeks to bring herself back to reality. She was angry at Meg. Furious at Meg. They had to have a talk. A serious talk. That was why she was here. The only reason she was here. Or at least that was what she told herself.

It was after nine o'clock, and the gallery was emptying out. Cate went over to the food table and selected an egg roll. She'd skipped dinner. She avoided the alcohol because she wanted to be stone-cold sober for whatever followed. She watched Meg hug her kids before they left. Then she headed over to introduce herself to the one person—well, besides Meg—she didn't want to miss meeting tonight.

"Hi. I'm Cate, and I think you must be Grace. Thanks for calling me and letting me know you were driving Meg in tonight."

"It's nice to finally meet you in person, Cate. I can't believe we haven't actually met until tonight. I'm glad you came. For Meg's sake."

"I need to speak to Meg. Can you wait a bit?" Cate asked.

"John wants some coffee. We'll go around the corner to a diner I saw and get some. You have my cell number. We'll wait." Grace smiled.

"Thanks." Cate returned her smile. Then she introduced herself to the gallery owner. She explained that she was a good friend and needed to speak to Meg alone if she could. Olivia pointed Cate to her office and told her that while the opening was officially ending, she had at least an hour of closing out clients and paperwork to do.

Cate took a deep breath. She was going to convince Meg to come into Olivia's office and talk to her. She was absolutely not going to kiss the fuck out of her.

"Hi, Meg." Cate was working hard to control her voice as the heat of both arousal and anger rose in her.

"Cate." Meg spoke her name, her striking blue eyes looking directly at Cate.

"Can we talk for a moment? Olivia said we could use her office." Cate managed to keep her tone neutral.

Meg looked nervous, but she nodded before she followed Cate. After they'd entered Olivia's office, Cate turned around and reached past Meg, closing the wooden door. She dropped her purse to the floor. Then she put her hands on Meg's shoulders and pushed her up against the inside of that door before moving her hands onto the wood on either side of Meg, fencing her in, but relinquishing all physical contact with her.

Meg's eyes darkened and she closed them. She bit the corner of her lower lip.

Cate leaned in, almost close enough to capture Meg's mouth with her own. *Remember how pissed you are*, she lectured herself.

"We need to talk," Cate told the beautiful woman in front of her whom she desperately wanted to kiss. Hell, she wanted to kiss her in places she'd probably never been kissed. "In private because I've got a lot to say."

Meg opened her eyes and nodded. "We do," she agreed. Cate could hear the husk in her voice.

"Will you come to my place like you promised you would, not so long ago? I have a spare room, or I can even drive you home tonight if that's what you want. I promise. After we talk." Cate struggled to keep the desire out of her voice. This was not about sex. This was about their future. "I think you owe me that," she added, putting the steel in her voice that she'd used on the occasions she'd needed to represent a client in the courtroom.

Meg swallowed. Cate stared at her throat as she did so, then looked away. She still had Meg fenced up against the door, so she stepped back, giving Meg some room.

❖

Emotions roared through Meg. As Cate fenced her against the door, she could only think about how much she loved the bossy Cate. But besides the hunger in Cate's eyes, she could also see other emotions, anger and hurt, looking back at her.

"I keep my promises, Cate. And I know you'll keep yours. So okay. But I need to talk to Grace and John. They're waiting for me. And Oscar is home, so if Grace can't take him, I'll need to get home."

Cate picked up her purse from the floor where she'd dropped it and pulled out her phone. She was texting. Then her phone dinged.

Meg wondered who Cate was communicating with.

"Jessie gave me Grace's cell number. She and John are getting coffee. Grace says they can go by and collect Oscar on their way back into town."

This was take-charge Cate. So damn sexy. But she was really upset. They had to settle this or there was no chance of a future. "Okay. Let's give Olivia back her office and go to your place." If Cate could project steel, then she would too. "To talk. Just to talk."

Cate stepped back farther to give Meg space to move so the door could be opened. Then Cate turned the handle and stepped out around her. Meg reached over to the side table and collected her gold clutch and the package, then followed. Cate waited while she went over to talk to Olivia.

"It was a great opening. I've got to close out a few things yet tonight, but why don't you head out? It's getting late. I'll call you once we have a handle on just what we sold tonight. We'll keep all of your remaining work up until the end of your show the middle of next month, and we can decide which ones to keep up longer," Olivia advised her. "If there's anything left," she added with a chuckle. "And I believe you still have some in your studio we can add. You've hit the big time, Meg. Congratulations."

SLOUCHING TOWARD STARDUST WITH MEG THE UNMUZZLED

"Spanning Two Worlds"

I am sitting on a bridge that spans two worlds. On one side is my old life where I have dwelled for decades. The other side holds the dreams I have hungered for—and I am hopeful.

I am approaching a night that spans two worlds. On one side is my old life where I have dwelled for decades. The other side holds the dreams I have hungered for—and I am hopeful.

How many other people have crossed this bridge? Had such a night? Never to be able to return, never wanting to return to who they were on the other side. Leaving the past for the future.

Breathe deep and offer a prayer. For love. For validation. For the future you have hungered for. Amen.

CHAPTER TWENTY-EIGHT

The taxi that Cate had hailed arrived as Meg finished with Olivia. Cate gave the driver her address, and they headed to Cate's condo, sharing the back seat in silence. Cate's demeanor conveyed to Meg that she wasn't going to make this easy. When they arrived, Cate unlocked the door to the foyer common area, and they rode the elevator up to her unit. Meg had her package and clutch, but she wished she had brought a change of clothes so she could get out of the dress she'd been wearing for so many hours.

After they entered the condo, Cate pointed to a couch and told Meg she was going to go change. She asked Meg if she'd like to borrow some sweatpants and a T-shirt, and Meg nodded. Meg set the flat wrapped package on Cate's dining table and held on to her small purse. Cate returned in faded jeans and a white T-shirt. She tossed Meg a change of clothes—a blue T-shirt and tan sweatpants. Then Cate pointed down the hallway.

"It's well after ten o'clock, and I haven't had much to eat today. I bet you haven't either. I'm going to go fix us a little food, so no need to rush because it's going to take me a little while," Cate told her.

Meg took the outfit and her clutch to the primary bedroom to change. She passed a spare room with a twin bed, a desk, and a treadmill on her way down the hall. Since Cate was going to be in the kitchen for a while, Meg took a moment to boost herself up onto the edge of Cate's king-sized bed after she'd changed into Cate's clothes. Once she was sitting, she pulled her phone from the small purse and wrote a very short blog. She was so damn nervous. She draped her dress over an ivory armchair in the corner and pushed her shoes under before returning to the living room. She was now barefoot.

As Meg just stood there admiring the contemporary furnishings of the living area, Cate came from the kitchen with a carefully arranged plate of sliced cheese and crackers, a bowl of grapes, and two glasses of water. Cate set the food on the table in front of the couch and sat.

"In case I have to drive tonight," Cate said in explanation of only offering water.

Meg sat on the couch too, a few feet from Cate so she could reach the food. She sipped the water and looked over the top of her glass at Cate.

"Where do we start?" Meg asked.

"How about trust? With you not letting me be there when you needed me? You were there for me—coming out to your kids, inviting me into your home, Dad, understanding my work schedule. But you couldn't let me be there for you, Meg?" Cate was obviously hurt. And there was anger in her voice too.

"I'm sorry, Cate. I don't know exactly what you know."

"I only know that you shut me out."

Meg took a deep breath. "I did, and I'm so sorry. I know I'm the one who blew it. I want to tell you."

When Cate nodded, Meg began. "A young woman, Natalie's age, came to my door. She'd had an affair with Robert—at the apartment." Meg felt her chest tighten as she prepared to tell Cate the next part. "She'd had his child." Meg paused and collected herself as Cate's mouth dropped open before she shut it. "I thought she wanted money, but she didn't. She wanted him to know his half siblings." Meg had told this story to each of her children, but it didn't get easier in the telling. Cate arched her eyebrows at Meg's last disclosure.

Continuing, Meg explained, "I'd never mentioned the apartment to the kids because I didn't want them to have to deal with learning those things about their father. But I decided they each had the right to decide about a relationship with a half brother, so I had to tell them everything. Jessie and Ben were mad at Robert, but Natalie blamed me for Robert's actions because I'd not only come out, but I'd told her that I'm in a relationship with you. And that hurt. I never backed down with Nat about you, Cate. But my own kid telling me I'm going to hell and then blaming me for Robert's adultery was the final straw. And I was losing her. I shut down. It's wrong, and I know it."

Meg paused and wiped her eyes. She looked at Cate and took a deep breath, then continued. "That's what Robert wanted from me. For me to handle any issues on my own. He ran Mullins Investments. I ran the rest because he didn't want to deal with it. They were all my problems to cope with, and I learned to just pull into myself, shut up, and manage."

Cate took a moment, clearly digesting what Meg had just told her. "And that's what you did when you saw Laurel in my office. You didn't give me a chance. You left and went home to deal with it alone. And now with all of this bad news..." Cate wiped her eyes too. "I need you to count on me, Meg. And I don't just want your mother mode— you taking care of me. I want partner mode." Cate repeated it. "Partner mode."

Meg closed her eyes as she processed this. She wasn't happy with her reaction and knew it didn't work in a healthy relationship. "I hear that you want a partnership. I know I'm a better mother than a partner." Meg looked down. "After my marriage"—she looked back up at Cate—"I'm going to have to learn. I should have told you, so we could have handled it together. I focused on everyone but me and you."

"You did," Cate said. "I need you to talk to me when you're upset. So we can figure out how to be there for each other. I didn't do that with Laurel, and we both know how that turned out. I learned my lesson, Meg."

"Don't take no from me, Cate. I need to change. To trust that you aren't Robert. That you'll be there for me. I promise I'll give you a chance to help."

"That emotional component that you once mentioned was necessary—it includes trust, communication, giving and taking support. In good times, day to day"—Cate's dark umber eyes didn't blink—"and during personal crises. What we're doing right now, talking about this, it's essential."

Meg nodded. "I love my children, but they're grown. I knew it was time to put myself first, and pursuing a chance to be with you was part of that. But I put the kids, and even Wren, first, trying to solve things for them. Falling back into handling a crisis all by myself, not trusting you'd be there for me, is not putting either of us first. I want an art career and I have the opportunity for that. I want you in my future, as a priority in my life. I want a partnership. A healthy one." Meg felt the truth of her admission as she waited for Cate's response.

"Me too. And the best thing is I'm believing we can make this work," Cate responded.

Meg felt a flood of relief. Optimism that they were both willing to learn from mistakes of the past. A swell of deep love for Cate. She nodded, then asked, "What else? We need it all on the table."

Cate pursed her lips, paused as she studied Meg, then said, "Meg the unMuzzled."

Meg's eyes widened and she shoved her hand through her hair. Oh crap. "No secrets, huh? You read it?"

"I did, Meg. Maybe it took Pete explaining it to me, but I get it. You needed a place where you could be free to write what you felt, where you wouldn't be judged by people who know you. Cheaper than a therapist." Cate chuckled. "But after you'd already closed me out and refused to let me help, finding out that you had a secret blog…"

"I can't apologize for it, Cate. I needed it. And I'd been writing it for a long time before I met you. It was not only liberating—the ability to express myself anonymously—it was another source of sanity for me after Robert." Meg waited for Cate's reaction.

"There are so many beautiful entries, Meg. And revealing ones. I guess I was upset because it was an entire aspect of you that I'd only barely glimpsed, and I want to know you. But I get it." Cate offered her a hint of a smile. "I won't tell you that I'm not going to read them." And then she grew serious. "Do you really love me, Meg?" It was a question. Maybe a plea. The most vulnerable Cate had presented all evening.

"If you read it, you know that I love you," Meg told Cate with certainty.

"I love you too, Meg," Cate told her. "I've liked you for a long time. Way before you ever came to my office and we talked. And I've known it's love for a while now. Is this the night I get to show you how much? Without some crisis to interrupt us?"

Meg smiled and held up her hand, palm out. "Hold up. Anything else? I want everything on the table."

Cate grinned and her eyes twinkled. "The table, huh? I was thinking the bed, but if the table makes you happy…"

Meg faked a huff. "I'm fifty years old. I want a bed. A comfortable bed. But a shower first, it's been a long day." A little levity felt good.

"It has been. I thought eight thirty would never come—for me to walk into that gallery. Timing is everything." Cate's lips twitched.

"I'll have you know I missed enjoying most of my gallery opening because I was watching that damn door for you," Meg grumbled.

Cate grew serious. "I needed to convince you to come talk to me. I had to time it so we could head out after you agreed."

"And you knew I'd agree, Counselor?"

"I could say yes, ma'am, because I know that you're easy. But I won't," Cate said, teasing her.

"Well, that's good because if you said that, you might just be driving me home to spend the rest of the night with my cat instead of showing me where your shower is," Meg responded. It felt so good to flirt with Cate again.

"Before we do that, I want to tell you how talented you are." Cate's voice was so sincere. "Your art is amazing, and I know that people recognized that tonight. They loved it. Your grandmother would be so proud."

Meg felt a flash of modesty, still not used to such praise for her art efforts. And that it was coming from Cate meant so much to her. "Thanks. I appreciate that you like my art, but even more, I like that you think my grandmother would be pleased."

Cate moved closer, leaned in, and kissed Meg. A slow and passionate kiss, full of longing. Meg responded with her own longing before she leaned back. "I have one more question."

"You better make it fast. I'm not a patient person," Cate replied.

Meg chuckled. "As if I didn't know that about you, Cate Colson." Then she became serious. "I'd like to know what you were talking to Natalie about, if it isn't confidential. She's still upset with me, but after Jessie told her she'd never get another chance to come to my first gallery opening, she decided to come." Meg's eyes moistened. "We're not okay, but we're still talking, and we love each other."

Cate leaned back and sighed. "I told her that I once had a mother too. A religious mother who rejected me because of who I am. That she destroyed our relationship because I'm a lesbian." Cate frowned. "I told her that we lost years of time together. Years of sharing our lives.

Years of loving each other. And my mother is dead now, and there will never be a chance to change things. I asked Natalie if she thought that's what her religion wanted. If she thought Jesus would have wanted that burden." There was the profound sadness in Cate's eyes of a woman who had lost her mother for no good reason.

"Thanks for trying. I don't know where Nat and I will end up. But maybe she'll think hard about our relationship. Not want to destroy it. Tonight gives me hope." Meg pulled Cate up from the couch and embraced her. Kissed her again, gently on the neck, up her jawline, her ear, and then her closed eyes and sighed. "I'm so sorry about your mom."

"It's done—too late. But Natalie still has a chance with you. I wanted her to realize that. I want it to end differently for you two. Differently than what happened with my mom and me." Cate took Meg's face in her hands and softly kissed her before taking her hand and interlacing their fingers to lead Meg down the hallway.

Meg stood still and didn't move. She looked down at their hands. Cate turned to look at her, then down at their interwoven fingers too. Meg released Cate and walked over to the dining room table to collect the package she'd been hauling around all day. She carried it back to Cate and handed it to her.

"For you, Cate."

Cate gave her a quizzical look and then began to unwrap the package. As she took off the paper, the side of a cherrywood frame emerged. As she continued to remove the wrapping, it became clear that there was a black lip with a thin gold inner border to the frame, and a light off-white linen mat—an elegant presentation. As she pulled off the last of the paper, the entire picture was revealed. It was a graphite sketch of two hands, with wrists and lower forearms. They were slightly different and angled to show they belonged to two different people. Two people holding hands. Rather feminine hands. And the fingers were intertwined.

Meg cleared her throat. "I've been studying the anatomy of hands—if you remember from that first visit to my studio. I wanted this to represent us."

"It's perfect. Perfect. My own Meg Mullins original." Cate gave Meg a tender smile.

"It's signed *Margaret*. Just Margaret. Because that's what my grandmother called me. If you noticed at the gallery, that's how I'm signing my work. And this one represents us, if you'll take it."

"I'm honored, Meg. And if you didn't hear it earlier, I love you."

"Well, are you going to get around to showing me?" Meg winked.

"I suggested the table, but you turned me down." Cate took Meg's hand again. "To the bedroom. To my comfortable bed, you fifty-year-old woman. And I'm in charge tonight." Cate winked back at Meg.

"If you insist," Meg drawled as Cate led her toward the bedroom. Cate's dark eyes communicated that she loved that drawl. And the woman to whom it belonged.

SLOUCHING TOWARD STARDUST WITH MEG THE UNMUZZLED

"Happily Ever After"

Advice from my cat: Don't fuck it up. You only have nine lives. Were you ever your own worst enemy for that HEA? Well, analyze the shit out of yourself. Fess up. Tell her you love her. Get the girl!

CHAPTER TWENTY-NINE

Cate's slate-blue bedroom carpet caressed Meg's bare feet as they left the hardwood flooring of the hallway and entered the well-lit room with the king-sized bed as center attraction. Meg's gallery wear was draped over the ivory armchair in the corner, and the spike heels that had gone so well with her Cate acquisition dress peeked out from underneath, exactly where she had kicked them off in exchange for bare feet earlier. Meg watched Cate glance at her formal attire. Then Cate turned and looked her up and down, studied her wearing the blue T-shirt and tan sweatpants that had come from Cate's own wardrobe.

"You're irresistible, no matter what you're wearing."

Meg could hear the desire in Cate's deep, throaty voice. Cate raised their interlocked hands and rotated them, touching her lips to Meg's knuckles, then let go and faced Meg.

"I've noticed that you find bossy me a turn-on, and there will be plenty of opportunity for that bossiness here in the bedroom in the future." Cate paused and Meg loved how her eyes danced with amusement before she continued in a more serious tone. "And there will probably be other times when my bossiness is just an irritation. What I want is to make love to you tonight—show you how much I care. I know we started this the night Dad became ill, but"—Cate gently skimmed a finger across Meg's lower lip, causing Meg to suck in a deep breath—"now I want to finish what I started. Show you how much I love you." Cate lightly drew that finger across Meg's cheek and then down her neck to where skin met cloth.

Meg wanted Cate. Needed Cate so desperately that she didn't trust herself to speak, so she nodded as she communicated to Cate with her eyes, begging for more.

"Back to me worshipping every square inch of you." Cate moved her finger and thumb to lightly compress the peak of each of Meg's breasts through the thin fabric of the T-shirt. "I'm going to make you forget everything except you and me making love. If there's anything that you don't like, I want to know. I want this to be perfect."

"*Cate.*" Meg spoke her lover's name as a plea. That's all she could manage. Not just because of the exquisite physical assault, but an emotional assault beyond anything she'd experienced. God, she loved this woman. And she wasn't going to last long under these combined assaults.

Cate fondled the hem of the T-shirt that Meg wore. Cate's shirt. She lifted it up past Meg's breasts and over Meg's head. Meg watched Cate smile at the realization that Meg had removed her bra along with the dusty-rose dress earlier in the evening—there was nothing underneath that shirt except skin. Cate dropped the top on the floor. Then she caught her fingers in the elastic waistband of the sweatpants and lowered them until Meg could step out of them. All that remained were her black silk briefs. As Cate bent forward and worked her lips down Meg's abdomen, Cate's hands slid that scant piece of silk past Meg's hips and all the way to the carpet where it joined the other clothing that had covered Meg a few minutes ago. Meg closed her eyes as she listened to the unevenness of Cate's breath. To the unevenness of her own breath.

❖

Cate remained standing in her white T-shirt and faded jeans directly in front of Meg, her inspection taking in the scenic view of smooth skin. She noted the meeting of pale against golden, where Meg's swimsuit had shielded her from the sun. This was Meg in all her glory.

Cate wanted to make love to Meg in the slow, seductive manner that she had envisioned. She wanted to explore Meg, create a maelstrom of sensation that Meg would never forget. Before embarking on any survey of Meg's body, Cate wanted a shower—but not a shared shower.

She knew how fast that could escalate into pure lust. She wanted this encounter to translate into what she felt for Meg. So, she led Meg to the shower stall, warmed the water, and gently placed a hand on Meg's back to guide her in.

"You get rinsed off, babe, and I'll take a quick shower after you." Cate went out and adjusted the bedroom to her liking before stripping down. She wrapped a towel around Meg's shoulders as she departed the warm stream, then jumped in to rinse off too. Meg was still drying off as Cate exited the shower, grabbing a towel for herself. Cate wrapped it around her own nude body and reached over to complete drying Meg.

Then Cate led them out into the bedroom where she had dimmed the light to a minimal warm glow and already pulled back the off-white spread and top sheet. She removed Meg's towel and dropped the one she was wearing. Cate gently bent Meg forward at the waist over a stack of pillows she'd placed at the edge of the bed, Meg's feet just touching the floor, Meg's face flush against the mauve sheet, the firm swell of her raised lily-white ass laid bare to Cate's reverence. Meg groaned her surrender into the mattress.

"Are you okay?" Cate asked.

"Um-hmm." Meg's breathless affirmation followed without hesitation, muffled by the bedding.

"And you'll let me know if there is anything you don't like?" Cate continued to clarify as she stood behind Meg.

"Um-hmm. Please, Cate." Meg's hips rose and fell, proclaiming Meg's passion for Cate, and then Meg turned and looked over her shoulder. Cate read Meg's visual plea, silently beseeching relief.

"Please, what?" Cate inquired with a hint of a chuckle, wanting to hear Meg's response, pleased that Meg wanted her so much.

"Fuck." Meg groaned an expletive, then buried her face back into the mauve cloth. "I need you."

"I know you do, babe. Now who would have thought I'd be the adult in the room with the patience to give you all the pleasure that I can, to make love to you? You must be a good influence on me." Cate stepped forward to insert her legs between Meg's, widening Meg's stance and revealing the landscape of her scorching desire. She applied pressure with her fingertips along the vertebral ridge running down Meg's back, tactilely conveying that Meg was exactly where she needed to be. Then Cate kneeled down, her torso now splaying Meg's limbs before planting kisses across Meg's gorgeous gluteals. Cate carefully nipped each rounded cheek as Meg pressed back into Cate's teeth and lips.

Meg whimpered as she swore her frustration again. "Fuck, Cate…" Meg rode the pillows, searching for satisfaction.

"Yes, ma'am," Cate purred.

"Now," Meg growled. "And I'll take the *ma'am* out on you later."

"I'm holding you to it." Cate's hands played up and down Meg's inner thighs, stopping short of strumming her saturated center. Meg's body clenched as she beseeched Cate for more, breathing heavily as Cate danced her fingers up and down Meg's legs, blowing warm air on her exposed core.

"*Please.*" The repeated request came out as a tortured prayer.

"We'll get there, babe, but I want you to feel me worshipping you. Take our time—you won't be sorry." Cate used her tongue to follow the same topography her fingers had mapped, eliciting a thrust of Meg's pelvis toward the gratification that was stopping well short of the ultimate summit her body was clearly craving. Then Cate moved to linger back and forth at the juncture where buttocks became legs, traveling the terrain, but skirting the destination where her culminating touch was so desperately desired.

Meg was moaning for more when Cate finally relented with an intimate sweep that passed through Meg's sensitive folds, and then Cate stood up. She assisted Meg in standing, removed the pillows, and returned Meg to the bed. Meg sucked in a ragged breath as she stretched out on her back, her hungry, imploring look an invitation for Cate to join her, for Cate to love her completely, and Cate accepted the silent invitation.

"I want to see you." Cate met Meg's eyes—naked heat in Meg's gaze. She leaned close to Meg's mouth, skimming it with her lips before shifting so that she warmed Meg's ear as she spoke. "Are you ready for this?"

Meg nodded.

"Because I've got plans for you tonight, Meg Mullins. Just don't scream too loud." Cate continued her pilgrimage across the body of this woman she felt bound to, her mouth sucking at the firm peaks of Meg's breasts, followed by a tonguing that brought her nipples to full alert, then marked a course down Meg's abdomen, moving slowly lower.

Meg rasped, "You're killing me, Cate. After what you've already done to me, I might be waking your neighbors in a very short time."

"You know what? That's okay. I want the whole world to know how much I love you," Cate murmured, tasting the flesh of Meg's ribcage, her hips, her navel as she continued to share this connection with the woman she was trusting with her heart.

"God, Cate. You're driving me crazy. I'm begging…"

"Every square inch, Meg. And I've got miles to go."

Cate traveled those miles with her gaze, her lips, her tongue, her teeth, her fingers. Up and down Meg's body, turning her from front to back to front again, mapping every area except the one she knew that Meg wanted most.

"I plan to make love to you for the rest of my life." Finally, with Meg panting and rocking her body into Cate's relentless torment, Cate concluded a final trail of gentle nips across the toned, smooth swell of Meg's alluring ass before flipping her back over and falling into the ocean-blue depths of Meg's entreating eyes. Finally, decisively, Cate walked her wandering fingers down to where they needed to go, skimming and caressing until she eventually reached her destination.

As Cate claimed that last square inch she hadn't yet explored, Meg's breathing accelerated and then came out in a series of gasps. She thumbed and stroked Meg to a world of pure sensation before she placed her mouth into the escalating tsunami. Feeling Meg stiffen before throwing her head back, Cate knew Meg had caught the rising wave of fulfillment that would course from her center out to her entire body. She let Meg ride that peak of ecstasy to the place where it was just Meg's heartbeat pounding against the beauty that was Cate sharing her love.

❖

When Meg had taken charge and intimately idolized and indulged the woman who owned her heart, when Meg's respiration was no longer raging, when she had held Cate in her arms until the dark turned to dawn, when that dawn brought the knowledge that she and Cate were truly okay, that nothing had ever felt this right, Meg whispered, "Thank you, Cate. For everything."

Cate turned her head and tenderly captured Meg's lips. Then they lay on their backs, side by side with intertwined fingers. Shoulder to shoulder, hip to hip, foot to foot—with matching dragonflies.

Meg finally broke their comfortable silence. "I know who I am and where I belong. For the first time in my fifty-year-old life. For the rest of my life. I love you."

"I love you too," Cate said softly into Meg's ear.

Meg chuckled. "And in finding that love, we've certainly weathered some storms. Life has not been boring."

"I know," Cate agreed. "Your life. My life." Cate paused, waiting for Meg's response.

"*Our* life," Meg said. "Dancing toward stardust, Cate Colson."

"Dancing toward stardust, Meg Mullins. Together."

SLOUCHING TOWARD STARDUST WITH MEG THE UNMUZZLED

"Dancing Toward Stardust"

It was not an epiphany. It was a slow dawning, that the breaths in a life, the beats of a heart, the opportunities for love are finite—stacking one moment upon the next in the passage of time. That the world was simply on loan to the ancient microbes of warm seas, to prehistoric fish, to Tyrannosaurus rex, to Neanderthal man, to my grandmother. And now to me.

The loss of loved ones. Early widowhood. The reality of sprinkled silver hairs and permanent laugh lines. Not even close to finished, but growing older. All the price for the unequivocal joy of watching the handoff as the next generation steps into their own lives. Their own loves. And for finally reaching the moment in time for finding myself. The compulsory cosmic balance...

And the price for dancing toward stardust with someone I passionately love.

About the Author

Julia Underwood (https://juliaunderwood.net) grew up loving animals and pursued a degree in veterinary medicine. She's been blessed to have wonderful family members, friends, and a parade of pets to enrich her life. She's an avid writer and reader. The joy of discovering the journey to novel writing cannot be overstated. She hopes her admiration for the love, dedication, and competence women bring to the multitude of roles they fill in this complicated world comes through in her writing.

Books Available From Bold Strokes Books

All This Time by Sage Donnell. Erin and Jodi share a complicated past, but a very different present. Will they ever be able to make a future together work? (978-1-63679-622-2)

Crossing Bridges by Chelsey Lynford. When a one-night stand between a snowboard instructor and a business executive becomes more, one has to overcome her past, while the other must let go of her planned future. (978-1-63679-646-8)

Dancing Toward Stardust by Julia Underwood. Age has nothing to do with becoming the person you were meant to be, taking a chance, and finding love. (978-1-63679-588-1)

Evacuation to Love by CA Popovich. As a hurricane rips through Florida, so too are Joanne and Shanna's lives upended. It'll take a force of nature to show them the love it takes to rebuild. (978-1-63679-493-8)

Lean in to Love by Catherine Lane. Will badly behaving celebrities, erotic sex tapes, and steamy scandals prevent Rory and Ellis from leaning in to love? (978-1-63679-582-9)

The Romance Lovers Book Club by MA Binfield and Toni Logan. After their book club reads a romance about an American tourist falling in love with an English princess, Harper and her best friend, Alice, book an impulsive trip to London hoping they'll both fall for the women of their dreams. (978-1-63679-501-0)

Searching for Someday by Renee Roman. For loner Rayne Thomas, her only goal for working out is to build her confidence, but Maggie Flanders has another idea, and neither is prepared for the outcome. (978-1-63679-568-3)

Truly Home by J.J. Hale. Ruth and Olivia discover home is more than a four-letter word. (978-1-63679-579-9)

View from the Top by Morgan Adams. When it comes to love, sometimes the higher you climb, the harder you fall. (978-1-63679-604-8)

Blood Rage by Illeandra Young. A stolen artifact, a family in the dark, an entire city on edge. Can SPEAR agent Danika Karson juggle all three over a weekend with the "in-laws" while an unknown, malevolent entity lies in wait upon her very skin? (978-1-63679-539-3)

Ghost Town by R.E. Ward. Blair Wyndon and Leif Henderson are set to prove ghosts exist when the mystery suddenly turns deadly. Someone or something else is in Masonville, and if they don't find a way to escape, they might never leave. (978-1-63679-523-2)

Good Christian Girls by Elizabeth Bradshaw. In this heartfelt coming of age lesbian romance, Lacey and Jo help each other untangle who they are from who everyone says they're supposed to be. (978-1-63679-555-3)

Guide Us Home by CF Frizzell and Jesse J. Thoma. When acquisition of an abandoned lighthouse pits ambitious competitors Nancy and Sam against each other, it takes a WWII tale of two brave women to make them see the light. (978-1-63679-533-1)

Lost Harbor by Kimberly Cooper Griffin. For Alice and Bridget's love to survive, they must find a way to reconcile the most important passions in their lives—devotion to the church and each other. (978-1-63679-463-1)

Never a Bridesmaid by Spencer Greene. As her sister's wedding gets closer, Jessica finds that her hatred for the maid of honor is a bit more complicated than she thought. Could it be something more than hatred? (978-1-63679-559-1)

The Rewind by Nicole Stiling. For police detective Cami Lyons and crime reporter Alicia Flynn, some choices break hearts. Others leave a body count. (978-1-63679-572-0)

Turning Point by Cathy Dunnell. When Asha and her former high school bully Jody struggle to deny their growing attraction, can they move forward without going back? (978-1-63679-549-2)

When Tomorrow Comes by D. Jackson Leigh. Teague Maxwell, convinced she will die before she turns 41, hires animal rescue owner Baye Cobb to rehome her extensive menagerie. (978-1-63679-557-7)

You Had Me at Merlot by Melissa Brayden. Leighton and Jamie have all the ingredients to turn their attraction into love, but it's a recipe for disaster.(978-1-63679-543-0)

Appalachian Awakening by Nance Sparks. The more Amber's and Leslie's paths cross, the more this hike of a lifetime begins to look like a love of a lifetime. (978-1-63679-527-0)

Dreamer by Kris Bryant. When life seems to be too good to be true and love is within reach, Sawyer and Macey discover the truth about the town of Ladybug Junction, and the cold light of reality tests the hearts of these dreamers. (978-1-63679-378-8)

Eyes on Her by Eden Darry. When increasingly violent acts of sabotage threaten to derail the opening of her glamping business, Callie Pope is sure her ex, Jules, has something to do with it. But Jules is dead…isn't she? (978-1-63679-214-9)

Letters from Sarah by Joy Argento. A simple mistake brought them together, but Sarah must release past love to create a future with Lindsey she never dreamed possible. (978-1-63679-509-6)

Lost in the Wild by Kadyan. When their plane crash-lands, Allison and Mike face hunger, cold, a terrifying encounter with a bear, and feelings for each other neither expects. (978-1-63679-545-4)

Not Just Friends by Jordan Meadows. A tragedy leaves Jen struggling to figure out who she is and what is important to her. (978-1-63679-517-1)

Of Auras and Shadows by Jennifer Karter. Eryn and Rina's unexpected love may be exactly what the Community needs to heal the rot that comes not from the fetid Dark Lands that surround the Community but from within. (978-1-63679-541-6)

The Secret Duchess by Jane Walsh. A determined widow defies a duke and falls in love with a fashionable spinster in a fight for her rightful home. (978-1-63679-519-5)

Winter's Spell by Ursula Klein. When former college roommates reunite at a wedding in Provincetown, sparks fly, but can they find true love when evil sirens and trickster mermaids get in the way? (978-1-63679-503-4)

Coasting and Crashing by Ana Hartnett. Life comes easy to Emma Wilson until Lake Palmer shows up at Alder University and derails her every plan. (978-1-63679-511-9)

Every Beat of Her Heart by KC Richardson. Piper and Gillian have their own fears about falling in love, but will they be able to overcome those feelings once they learn each other's secrets? (978-1-63679-515-7)

Fire in the Sky by Radclyffe and Julie Cannon. Two women from different worlds have nothing in common and every reason to wish they'd never met—except for the attraction neither can deny. (978-1-63679-561-4)

Grave Consequences by Sandra Barret. A decade after necromancy became licensed and legalized, can Tamar and Maddy overcome the lingering prejudice against their kind and their growing attraction to each other to uncover a plot that threatens both their lives? (978-1-63679-467-9)

Haunted by Myth by Barbara Ann Wright. When ghost-hunter Chloe seeks an answer to the current spectral epidemic, all clues point to one very famous face: Helen of Troy, whose motives are more complicated than history suggests and whose charms few can resist. (978-1-63679-461-7)

Invisible by Anna Larner. When medical school dropout Phoebe Frink falls for the shy costume shop assistant Violet Unwin, everything about their love feels certain, but can the same be said about their future? (978-1-63679-469-3)

Like They Do in the Movies by Nan Campbell. Celebrity gossip writer Fran Underhill becomes Chelsea Cartwright's personal assistant with the aim of taking the popular actress down, but neither of them anticipates the clash of their attraction. (978-1-63679-525-6)

Limelight by Gun Brooke. Liberty Bell and Palmer Elliston loathe each other. They clash every week on the hottest new TV show, until Liberty starts to sing and the impossible happens. (978-1-63679-192-0)

Playing with Matches by Georgia Beers. To help save Cori's store and help Liz survive her ex's wedding, they strike a deal: a fake relationship, but just for one week. There's no way this will turn into the real deal. (978-1-63679-507-2)